PRAI…

G…

No Forwarding

AND

JOE GORES

"Everything about these [DKA] novels—the backgrounds, the tight and unsentimental writing style, the plotting—goes back to Hammett and Chandler. . . . Mr. Gores, as always, writes beautifully, with never a wasted word and with a fine feeling for characterization."

—Newgate Callendar, ***New York Times***

"[A] taut, irresistibly readable novel. . . . A heart-stopping ride through six major cities and a gallery of characters at every social level, all observed with Hammett-like precision."

—St. Louis Globe-Democrat

more. . .

"Kearny's crew functions as a group here, in the manner of Ed McBain's 87th Precinct. With nitty-gritty realism, Gores sends the sleuths down dozens of what Raymond Chandler called 'mean streets.'"

—*Cincinnati Post*

❑

"Fans of Hammett and Chandler will enjoy this fast-paced thriller which... leads through three violent ghettos into a taut courtroom scene. The author's sharp ear for dialogue and keen eye for character make this action-packed mystery entertaining and suspenseful."

—*Publishers Weekly*

❑

"This ex-shamus author knows the unglamorous grit and street tricks of real private-eyeing, and his operatives manage to be hard enough to brawl through their jobs and soft enough to make us care about them."

—*Kirkus Reviews*

❑

"A first-rate puzzler.... Tough and suspenseful."

—*Milwaukee Journal*

❑

"One of the very few authentic private eyes to enter the field of fiction since Dashiell Hammett."

—**Anthony Boucher**

❑

"Gores employs lean and direct prose, jump-cuts from scene to scene and does it all expertly."

—*USA Today*

❑

"Dan Kearny detectives are Lew Archer in concert."

—*Saturday Review*

❑

"The private-eye procedural basis is Gores' specialty, maybe his invention."

—*San Francisco Chronicle*

❑

"Gores has established himself securely as one of the best and most versatile authors of crime novels."

—*Twentieth-Century Crime and Mystery Writers*

THE DKA FILE NOVELS

23 Cadillacs
Final Notice
Dead Skip

Joe Gores

Gone, No Forwarding

THE MYSTERIOUS PRESS

Published by Warner Books

A Time Warner Company

MYSTERIOUS PRESS EDITION

Cover illustration and design by John Mattos

This Mysterious Press Edition is published by arrangement with the author.

Mysterious Press Books are published by
Warner Books, Inc.
1271 Avenue of the Americas
New York, NY 10020

A Time Warner Company

Printed in the United States of America

First Mysterious Press Printing: January, 1993
10 9 8 7 6 5 4 3 2

For my beloved wife, Dori
A small fire to warm
her hands at

On the way from Harlem, Bart Heslip switched cabs three times, and then caught a plane from Newark because he was afraid they might be watching Kennedy and La Guardia. Six hours until the plane landed at San Jose, fifty miles south of San Francisco. He hadn't called ahead to tell Dan Kearny he was coming, because of the phone taps.

Sleep began to wash over him. He knew who'd hired them. He even knew what they were trying to do. But why?

It had to go back to that rainy Friday in November, almost a year ago which he now knew had been

The First Day

The premature rains had dumped 3.6 inches of water on the Bay Area before easing off to allow a patch of honest-to-God blue sky to appear around noon on Friday, November 5. Finally you could wait at the curb for a light to change without getting a wet lap from passing autos. You could drive across the Bay Bridge without being bounced into the next lane by gusting winds. Down at San Francisco International, in fact, Western's 1:50 P.M. flight from Mexico City touched the rain-slick runway only ten minutes behind schedule.

Adán Espinosa, who had chosen a Friday flight because of California's late bank-closing hour, was well pleased as he slapped his credit card and Mexican driver's license down on the Avis counter near the lower-level luggage carousels.

"You are to be holding a late-model Fairlane for me," he said in heavily accented English.

"Your reservation is right here, Mr. Espinosa."

She ran his contract through the BankAmericard franking machine, checked the deductible insurance as directed and gave him the keys. "It will be right outside at—"

"I know, *señorita*." Espinosa winked at her. He was a lean, swarthy mid-thirties, with a bad complexion and a drooping *bandido* mustache. "I am in this country often."

"Thank you for driving Avis."

"We try harder." He winked again. "*¿no es verdad?*"

He turned to the exquisitely shaped woman standing beside the four matched Samsonites. "Elena," he said. She turned hot black eyes on his flat gunmetal ones and touched a hand to her gleaming black hair. Espinosa hooked the arm of a passing porter. "You. The Samsonites."

Kasimir Pivarski looked like a Polish joke. Plaster dust outlined the seams and lines of his flat, broad middle-European face. He had a thick trunk, arms, legs, hands. An A's baseball cap was backward on his thick brown hair. He slapped clouds of plaster off his pants and resolutely opened the door of his stake-body truck.

"Listen, dammit," said the job foreman, "we need another two dozen sacks of plaster here this afternoon so Monday we can—"

"I tole you, I'm knocking off early. I gotta check in with my lawyer an' then see some bastards at a collection agency in Oakland before six o'clock."

"That still leaves you time to—"

Pivarski spat a glob of plaster-thickened saliva on the bare subfloor boards at the foreman's feet, then heaved himself up into the cab of the truck unbothered by the foreman's enraged glare.

Kathy Onoda, office manager of the collection-agency bastards at the Daniel Kearny Associates Oakland office, looked at the clock and sighed. Four o'clock. Two hours yet. She was an ice-slim Japanese woman with an ice-pick mind, classical features and straight black hair maned down over her shoulders. She stood up and went to the door of the office.

"Jeff." A nondescript brown-haired man, doing phone collecting at a desk midway down the main office, looked up. "I thought I told you an hour ago to bring me the tabbed legal file on Kasimir Pivarski."

She returned to the desk wondering why so many closet gays made good inside collectors. Maybe because they got a chance to be bitchy without personal exposure. Not, she realized, as bitchy as she was being. It was being stuck over here in the East Bay for a month trying to pull this Oakland operation together, when her work as general office manager for DKA's statewide operation piled up on her desk over in San Francisco.

Jeff Simson came into the officer with the Pivarski file. "You could be a little *nicer*," he said petulantly.

"Yes, I could be." Kathy sighed. "Sorry, Jeff." Then, as he left, she opened the file of the truck driver with the 5:30 appointment.

Espinosa checked Elena into a Fisherman's Wharf motel, then drove the rented Fairlane across San Francisco's roller-coaster hills to park in the Alhambra Theater white zone on Polk Street. Almost ten blocks from the bank, but why be stupid, right?

He turned in at Golden Gate Trust, thinking that Wen . . . Elena probably had been in a cab for the Union Square shops before he was out of the motel lot. Let her. Nine months of waiting with nobody else for company besides the enchilada-eaters had gotten to him, too. But now the papers had been approved in Buenos Aires. Argentina. A country to stay alive in.

The girl behind the safe-deposit window said, "Do you wish a private booth, sir?"

He signed the entry slip. "Please."

In the closed booth he began transferring the banded bundles from the dark-green metal box to the leather satchel he had carried from the Fairlane. Outside, the girl was dialing the internal number of Arthur P. Nucci, Vice-President for Personal Loans.

"Mr. Nucci, you wanted to be notified when box 6237 was signed out."

Nucci was a pudgy, fussy man in his late forties who fostered a conservative-banker image at odds with his life style. *Stall him*, they'd said. "I see that tab is a year out of date." *Call us, and stall him*. "Apparently some estate tax question that has been settled." *We'll do the rest*. "Bring that card up right now, Darlene, so I can void that notation."

"Yes, sir. As soon as—"

"I said *now*," snapped Nucci. "Use the elevator."

His heart thundering in his chest, he clattered down the interior stairs as Darlene started up in the elevator. He pushed the pebbled-glass stairwell door ajar. Espinosa, looking about for the missing girl, was a profound shock: he was the *wrong man!* Then Nucci realized, of course—he would have altered his appearance. On the stairwell pay phone Nucci dialed the number memorized months before.

"There in five minutes," said the unknown voice. "Can you stall him that long, Mr. Nucci?"

"I already have arranged it."

"What does he look like?"

"A Mexican." He described Espinosa's clothes. "And carrying a leather satchel." He hung up, sweating profusely. It was 5:22 P.M.

At 5:22 Verna Rounds, the pretty-faced black file clerk, showed up in the doorway. Kathy Onoda looked up at her. Why was it she could never sleep at night, but get her into the tag end of a rotten day in the rotten Oakland office, and—

"That dude phone up, Pee-somethin', he's in the outer office."

Kathy had kept Verna late to work the switchboard because the PBX girl, Rose Kelly, would be late back from her doctor's appointment.

"Kasimir Pivarski?"

Verna was chewing bubble gum. "That's the dude."

"Send him in."

Verna slopped splay-footed away. Poor Verna. Giselle Marc had hired her on that job-training thing she'd doped out with the welfare people, and now, when Verna had just about learned that it was the sharp end of the pencil that made those marks on the paper, she'd given notice because she was tired of working for what she referred to as chump change.

Verna reappeared, trailed by a mobile Polish joke. Kathy gestured the big truck driver to a chair. Verna leaned in the doorway with her arms folded, blowing a bubble.

"Lissen," said Pivarski belligerently, "you shit-heels took my goddam car two years ago, you got no call come around now. . ."

"You ignored repeated calls and letters concerning this delinquency, sir." Then Kathy explained what a deficiency judgment was. "Even though your car was repossessed and resold, the resale price was $789.35 less than the contract you signed with General Motors Acceptance Corporation. When you didn't appear at the court hearing, we were awarded a Judgment by Default. To get you into our office we placed a Writ of Attachment on your wages—"

"Yeah, well, I'm here now." Pivarski grubbed in the breast pocket of his faded blue workshirt with cold-chisel fingers. The chisels brought out folding money. "Two hundred bucks."

Kathy counted it and read aloud as she wrote the receipt: " 'Two hundred dollars received on account from K. Pivarski, November fifth, 5:46 P.M.' " She looked up to break Verna's *Bubble-Yum* catatonia. "Ask Jeff to come in, will you, please?"

Five minutes later the Polish joke had departed with a payment schedule worked out for the remainder of his delinquency, and Jeff Simson was waiting beside Kathy's desk as she made out the bank-deposit slip for the trust account.

"This is on your Pivarski file. Run it down the street to the bank before the six o'clock close, will you?"

It was 5:56 P.M.

* * *

At 5:56 P.M. Elena gently kicked the bottom of the motel-room door. Espinosa, lying on the bed in his shorts with a drink balanced on his bare chest and the TV turned to the Channel 4 news, yelled at her without turning his head, "Use your goddam key!"

More gentle kicks. Jesus. Women. She could have had the cab driver carry her packages to the door for her. He swung his bare feet to the rug and set his drink on top of the bureau.

He swung the door open, saying, "Wendy, why in the hell—"

"Goodbye, Phil."

The bulky, swarthy man in the heavy topcoat pulled both triggers at once from three feet away. Assorted bits of Espinosa were blown against the side of the dresser by the sawed-off 12-gauge shotgun.

The killer stepped unhurriedly across the threshold to roll the eviscerated corpse over onto its face. He jerked down the boxer-style shorts and shoved a shiny new penny up between the buttocks with a quick jabbing motion. The body had voided in death, so he wiped his middle finger on the shorts before crossing the room to pick up the leather satchel.

Screams started behind him as he walked across the blacktop to his stolen car, but he ignored them. His tires yelped his escape against the damp blacktop. A linen-truck driver, just about to deliver fresh towels to the motel, exclaimed aloud, "Holy Christ! I know that guy!"

Then he looked around quickly: a screaming woman, eyes tight shut, and a snot-nose kid eating a slice of pizza. He jumped back into his truck and accelerated away without bothering to leave the towels, turning in the opposite direction from that taken by the murderer.

One

Kathy Onoda was twenty-nine years old when she died of a massive blood clot on Saturday, October 15. The funeral was on Monday; because she had been a Buddhist, it was at night. On his way there, Dan Kearny picked up Giselle Marc at her apartment just off the MacArthur Freeway in Oakland. Giselle was a tall, lithe blonde whose high cheekbones and sensuous mouth often made men overlook the intelligence which animated her clear blue eyes.

Usually clear. Tonight they were red with crying. She settled back against the seat and sighed, and then snuffled. "Why Kathy? She was so alive and so . . . so vital . . ."

"What can I tell you? Her number was up? We worked her too hard? She worried about her kids too much because after nine years of college her old man's idea of going to work was filing for food stamps?" Kearny was a compact, hard-driving fifty, with a jaw to batter down doors and gray eyes hard enough to strike sparks. "Twenty-nine goddam years old."

He cut across the Oakland flatlands to the Nimitz Freeway. Giselle was snuffling again but had forgotten her handkerchief. Probably cogitating upon some poem about death she'd read in college, Kearney thought. He hadn't had time for college; he'd been knocking off hot cars for Walter's Auto Detectives down in L.A. at an age most kids, then, still wore knickers.

"You're the new office manager," he said gruffly.

Giselle asked wearily, "Does a raise go with it?" then wailed, "Oh! Dan, why did she have to die?"

The Alameda tube was clad in gleaming pale tiles crusted with engine dirt. Yellow emergency phones studded the right wall at regular intervals. Giselle looked over at Kearny curiously. What was he thinking? Feeling? Kathy had been with DKA since the start.

Weep not for the silent dead, their pains are past, their sorrows o'er.

What was she feeling so smug about? Her M.A. in history, her six years of university? As of a few moments before, she was office manager for a very hard-nosed detective agency specializing in skip-tracing, repossessions and embezzlement investigations. None of which suggested sensibilities that Dan Kearny didn't have.

Kearny turned on Buena Vista and started looking for a place to park. Alameda, which lived off the Naval Air station, had somnolent mid-thirties streets once you cleared the industrial clutter along Webster Street. Streaming up the walk to the white frame building which housed the Jodo Shinshu Universal Church were dozens, hundreds of Japanese, with a sprinkling of non-Orientals. Kearny caught a flash of O'Bannon's red hair, the ebony gleam of Bart Heslip's tough impassive face as they drove by. He had to go three more blocks to find a parking place.

"Popular girl, Kathy."

Giselle merely nodded. Her eyes were leaking again. Lucky she was here to step into Kathy's shoes at the agency, Kearny thought. Then he felt a stab of guilt. Kathy'd really hated the Oakland office, but that's where the troubles were and he'd kept her there, month after month. And now she was gone, like your fist when you open your hand.

One DKA hand who wasn't mourning Kathy was Larry Ballard. Letting himself into his stuffy two room apartment after a long weekend of skin-diving, he didn't know she was dead. He dropped wet suit, crowbar, flippers, mask and snorkel on the floor, put the twelve cleaned abalones in the fridge and tore the tab off a cold beer. The phone was balanced on the arm of his big saggy living-room easy chair. Ballard dialed.

"Hi, beautiful. Larry."

"Oh, Larree!" Maria Navarro's voice was oddly tense, almost frightened. "I . . . tried to call you Saturday."

"Up the coast after abs, baby. I'll bring you over half a dozen in an hour."

"Oh, Larree, No! I—"

"One hour *exactisimo*."

He went, whistling, through to the bedroom to undress, sipping his beer on the way. He was just under six feet tall, conditioned like an athlete, with a thatch of sun-whitened hair and even features saved from male beauty by hard, watchful eyes and a slightly hawk nose.

The phone started to ring. Ballard ignored it. Maria, to say don't come—she'd refused to see him since That Night, three weeks before, when he'd finally gotten her into bed after two years of trying. And her with two kids from a busted marriage.

The phone stopped ringing, then started again.

Ballard whistled his way down the hall, nude, to the bathroom he shared with the Japanese couple in the rear apartment. He dropped a five-flavor Cert with that sparkling drop of retsin, then stepped into the shower. What was he complaining about? A woman so hard to get into bed probably would be a pretty good long-haul sort of woman, *¿no es verdad?*

Their seats were in a crowded anteroom set up to handle the overflow from the church proper where the coffin, banked by hundreds of flowers mingling their scents with the heavy drugged odor of as many joss sticks, was located. A saffron-robed, shaven-headed monk spoke in Japanese, the next eulogist in English. There were many eulogists. Giselle let her mind wander through her memories of Kathy. The infectious laugh. The high-pitched voice switching from perfect English to regional accent to Japanese sing-song without missing a syllable.

Ah, so sorry prees, me poor rittre Japonee girr trying to make riving in new countree . . .

And they'd fall all over themselves on the phone, giving her what she wanted to know. She could be anyone on that instrument, from a lady minister to a Southern slut.

Aftah one nahght with li'l ol' me, shugah, youah goin' to want it every nahght . . .

And inevitably she'd turn the dead skip everyone else had thought was gone for good. And she'd clap her hands with that joyous laugh, and sometimes kick one foot high into the air from behind her desk, showing a careless length of nyloned thigh as she exclaimed ritually, "*Got* that son of a bitch!"

Giselle realized that Kearny had thrust a handkerchief into her hand. She had begun crying again, silently but uncontrollably. She used the handkerchief.

Kearny stood up. "Let's get it over with," he muttered.

The bad part. With the eulogies finished, the mourners were to queue past the open casket. Ahead of them she saw O'Bannon's flaming hair. O'B and Kathy had been the two original DKA Associates. And there was a glum-faced Bart Heslip. For him, no more Kathy to giggle extravagantly at the filthy jokes he'd picked up out on the street.

But where was Ballard . . . Larry Ballard? After all the time Kathy had taken to turn him into a top investigator! The least that bastard could do was show up for her funeral.

Ballard, in his ignorance, had showed up at Maria Navarro's second-floor flat in a shabby white Mission District stucco with varicolored Algerian ivy twining up over the front. From the street-level door he called up the stairwell, "Only thirty seconds late!"

"Larree, no . . ."

Maria was petite, five-two perhaps, wearing a short skirt and tight blouse. Ballard balanced his package of abalone on the newel post at the head of the stairs. She avoided his kiss with incipient panic in her huge Latin eyes.

"Hey, baby, I made certain with Certs—"

He was ripped away, slammed headfirst into the wall, spun about to see a hard brown fist coming at him.

"*¡Hijo de la flauta!*"

Ballard slipped the punch and drove the heel of his hand at the enraged brown face. He missed.

"Federico! No! *¡Está un amigo!*"

". . .'way from *esposa mía*, man!"

Ballard gaped. "Your *wife*?"

Unfortunately, when he gaped he quit moving. Federico didn't. Ballard tried to roll with it, but this carried him up against the newel post and then down the stairwell after his dislodged abalone.

"Hey! Ouch! Ugh! Uh! Oh!"

In a Western, the stunt man would have stood up and brushed himself off after the director had yelled "Cut!" But when Ballard finally moved it was like a half-squashed bug. He had realized with horror that his back had burst open and spilled part of him out on the stairs. At each movement he could feel himself squishing around under him. Oh, God! A cripple in his twenties!

"Larree?"

Hot dam, how about that? Just the abalone. Maybe not even broken bones. Maybe bring that leg over there and . . . ah! Now. This arm will go down . . .

"Larr-*eee*?"

He paused in his unsnarling. "Yeah?"

"You are oh-kay?"

He opened some more, like a carpenter's rule unfolding. He got a hand on the stair rail. "I'm dandy."

She said, aggrieved. "Larr-eee, I was *sola*, you took advantage. *Mías hijas* need father, you no marry me, and Federico . . ."

Ballard was on his feet. He had a goose egg on one side of his head. His nose leaked blood. His jaw creaked when he opened his mouth. He needed a drink. "Yeah, swell," he croaked. "Congratulations."

He limped out into the night, tenderized abalone in hand, thinking. This is it, this is the end. Never again. He was never going to mess around with another Catholic as long as he lived.

Giselle was shocked to see Kathy's two Japanese-doll daughters alone in the front pew, watching the proceedings with fathomless shoebutton eyes. "Dan," she hissed, "where in God's name is their father?"

"Probably out shopping for a new missus."

Then she was at the casket. Directly above it was a full color life-size portrait of Kathy. She was laughing and alive and vibrant. She didn't have a care in the world.

Three feet below was the waxen dead face of the real girl. What made it worse was that the laughing Kathy and the still-faced corpse both wore the same dress, the yellow brocade number with the scoop collar that Kathy had bought to be sexy at last December's DKA Christmas party.

Giselle turned away, abruptly nauseated. The memories, the overwhelming heaviness of flowers and incense . . . Then she realized that Kearny had brought her outside, where she could gulp in great breaths of fresh air.

"Little close in there," he said conversationally.

"That was . . . the worst experience . . . of my life. That color photo . . . those little girls sitting there all alone . . ."

He shrugged. "They better get used to it. Poppa isn't going to be around much, not without Mommy's paycheck to keep him there. Probably the only deadbeat Jap in the history of the world, and Kathy had to marry him."

Terrific. Trust Kearny to give Kathy the worst possible epitaph. Could anyone, ever, get any more gross than he?

Two

Sure. It happened the next night, as she and Kearny were leaving the Berkeley flatlands home of the grandmother who was going to end up taking care of Kathy's kids. Kearny had delivered a check to the bereft woman from a nonexistent DKA retirement fund. As they stepped out into the surprisingly mild late-fall evening, a voice hailed them. ''Hey, Dan! Dan Kearny!''

The man coming across the narrow strip of lawn wore a topcoat and a broad smile on his face. Kearny, his mind still with Kathy's kids, didn't catch on until the newcomer's left hand slapped a thin sheaf of folded papers into Kearny's outstretched right, announcing, ''You have been legally served in the matter of the Accusation brought against Daniel Kearny Associates by Thomas V. Greenly, Supervising Auditor for the Private Investigation Agency Licensing Bureau of the State of California.''

Kearny thrust the papers into a pocket without opening them. His face was the stormiest Giselle had ever seen it. ''I have an office for this sort of thing.''

The man snickered. ''Fat chance I'd have of serving you there. But I figured those orphaned kids would get you out in the open.''

Kearny let out a deep breath and turned away. But Giselle, in passing the process server, stepped on his foot, hard, before she even knew she was going to do it. He started hopping on the other foot, yelling, “Filthy . . . filthy bitch . . .”

Kearny’s thick hand closed around his collar and spun him around. The hand began shaking him like someone emptying a trash bucket. *What was that?”*

“I said I’m a member . . . of the staff of the Attorney General . . . for the State of California. If you assault—”

“I see,” said Kearny.

As he turned away, his left foot happened to pass through the space occupied by the foot the process server had on the ground, a maneuver sometimes known as a judo foot-sweep in martial-arts parlance. This left the process server, who was still holding the foot Giselle had stepped on, without any feet on the ground. His head bounced against the sidewalk with a sound like a wet dishrag slapping a drainboard.

Looking down at him, Kearny said, “You know, Giselle, you can always recognize a civil servant.”

In his own way, he had said a final goodbye to Kathy Onoda.

But death terminates only the person, not the complexities of the person’s life. Thus, Dan Kearny’s face was somber when he parked on Wednesday morning where the tow-away had ended sixty seconds earlier. He crossed Golden Gate Avenue to the narrow old charcoal-gray Victorian that had been a specialty cathouse in its gaudy youth, entered his bleak little cubbyhole office in the DKA basement, jabbed Giselle’s intercom button and lit a cigarette.

“You know what those bastards in Sacramento are up to?” he demanded as soon as she came on. “Listen to this: ‘WHEREFORE, it is prayed that the director’— that’s the Director of Professional and Vocational Standards—‘hold a hearing to suspend or revoke the license of the respondent’—that’s us—‘or take such other action as may be deemed proper.’ I wonder what they have in mind—castration?”

Giselle was horrified. “ ‘Suspend’? ‘Revoke’? My God, Dan, which case are they—”

“Something Kathy was handling out at Oakland—” He was leafing through the Complaint. “A General Motors

Acceptance Corporation deficiency judgment against a guy named Kasimir Pivarski. That ring any bells with you?''

''I vaguely remember something, Dan'l, but—''

''Dig a copy of the file out of Legal and bring it down here. And I want this under your hat, Giselle. I think the State's just shooting marbles, but until I know for sure I don't want word of any possible disciplinary action leaking to our clients.''

Kearny saw her twenty minutes later through his one-way glass door, a steaming cup of coffee in each hand and a manila folder clipped under one arm. She looked as if she should have dropped a couple of Dalmane the night before. Kathy had hit her hard, all right.

''Your stuff moved into the front office yet? I want you in there today.''

''All right, Dan'l,'' she said in a subdued voice.

One cup she retained, the other she reached across his massive blondewood desk to set beside the ashtray in which his day's seventh cigarette smoldered. She knew she had to move, but God, how she hated it! Even more than the wax figure in the coffin, violating Kathy's private domain meant she was gone, dead and gone forever.

She made herself sit down and sip her coffee and open the not particularly fat folder. ''On March 21, 1975, GMAC assigned a deficiency collection in the amount of $789.35. Usual split . . .''

''What was it on?''

''1974 Olds Toronado V-8 Custom Hardtop.''

''We repo it for them originally?''

''No. Their own fieldmen. This was part of the paper we bought from the Zippy Finance bankruptcy over in Oakland.''

''What I don't understand,'' Kearny began, then stopped and drew on his cigarette. ''No. Go ahead.''

''We queried GMAC for a current status of the account a year ago June. No payments had been made. Two months later, in August, we got a reassignment of the case to us. On October first we filed a complaint for money against Pivarski in Oakland Municipal Court in the amount of $789.35 plus interest and attorney's fees. Pivarski didn't show up, so immediately afterward we got a writ of attachment on his wages from Padilla Drayage Company.''

Kearny came bolt upright in his padded swivel chair. ''*Padilla* Drayage?''

Giselle's face went slack with surprise. ''Oh, wow, Dan, it went right by me.''

Padilla Drayage was an East Bay Mafia-connected concern with which DKA'd had a brush a couple of years before. Kearny leaned back. ''Maybe just coincidence. But why in hell Kathy didn't alert me when that name came up in the file . . .''

''It wouldn't have meant anything to her, Dan. You kept her out of that whole mess because you were afraid her kids made her too vulnerable.''

Kearny lit a cigarette and shut his eyes momentarily. Who was running Padilla Drayage now that Padilla was dead and ''Flip'' Fazzino, who'd arranged his murder, had fled the country? Only he, Kearny, knew about a certain rainy night at the big quiet mansion in Pacific Heights, when he'd made the phone call that blew the whistle on Fazzino to his erstwhile organized-crime associates.

He nodded to Giselle. ''Go on.''

''On October eight the sheriff of Contra Costa County collected $26.32 of Pivarski's wages from his employer on the writ of attachment. On the eighteenth, through his attorney, Pivarski filed a demurrer to our complaint of the first. He stated—''

''Who's his attorney?''

''Um . . . a . . . Norbert Franks.''

''Good old Norbert.'' He jabbed a finger at Giselle. ''An associate in the law firm of Wayne E. Hawkley at 1942 Colfax Street in Concord. Right?''

''Dan, how did you know?''

''Franks is Hawkley's sister's kid . . .''

Wayne Hawkley. An attorney who did favors for the mob. Not that Kearny could see, at the moment, why Hawkley should be involved in the State's move against his license. It was Hawkley he'd called when he'd blown the whistle on Flip Fazzino.

"Hawkley himself didn't show on this? Just Franks?"

"Just Franks."

He drummed puzzled fingers on the desktop. "Go on."

"On November fifth Pivarski showed up at the Oakland office." She read from Kathy's carbon receipt. " 'Two hundred dollars, received on account from K. Pivarski.' Kathy's signature, the date, the time-stamped at five forty-six P.M."

"Okay. Check the trust-account deposit for that day."

"I don't understand."

"Item Four of the Accusation: 'On November fifth, Pivarski and respondent'—us again—'entered into an oral contract where Pivarski made a voluntary payment of two hundred dollars to respondent which' "—Kearny paused to emphasize the words—" '*was to be held by respondent in trust* awaiting the outcome of said lawsuit. Said payment was to show good will and'—"

Giselle burst out, "Kathy would *never* take a payment that way! Why, under state licensing laws, anything she collected would *have* to go into the trust account with half of it paid over to GMAC."

"Exactly. And the receipt shows that's what happened. But the State is alleging that"—he found his place again—"that 'said payment was to show good will and prevent further attachment of Pivarski's wages. Said oral contract contemplated that the payment was to be returned to Pivarski if he prevailed.' "

On November 12 the court which was hearing Pivarski's demurrer entered judgment in his favor. Two weeks later he filed suit against DKA for $226.30—the $26.30 which they had recovered by attachment, plus the $200 Pivarski had paid Kathy on November 5. On February 18, judgment was entered in favor of Pivarski for $226.30 principal, $4.48 interest and $15 costs.

"A grand total of 245.78 lousy bucks," Kearny stormed, "and what does Kathy do about it? She *sits* on it! She doesn't tell me anything about it. She doesn't repay the money as directed by the court. She must have been a hell of a lot sicker—"

"Dan."

"—for a hell of a lot longer—"

"*Dan.*"

"—than any of us realized, to pull a bonehead—"

"DAN!"

He fell abruptly silent.

"If Kathy *had* come to you with it," Giselle asked, "would you have given Pivarski his money back?"

After a moment Kearny gave a sheepish laugh. He smeared out his half-smoked cigarette and shook a fresh one from the pack. "Not one goddam dime," he said, then scaled the Summons and Complaint across the desk at her.

She found the summary paragraph. " 'The conduct by respondent alleged in Paragraphs III through VII above is grounds for disciplinary action against respondent under the provisions of sections 6930 and 6947(k) of the Business and Professions Code in conjunction with section 6863 of the Business and Professions Code.' " She looked at Kearny. "So what do we do about it?"

"First, we call Hec Tranquillini and ask him to hustle his bustle down here. Maybe we can just pay Pivarski the money and the State'll back off." He gulped coffee he'd let get cold and lit the cigarette he'd taken from the pack earlier. "But I doubt it. So we'd better find out who was working in the Oakland office on November fifth who might have witnessed the transaction."

"It'd be so easy if Kathy were still . . . still . . ."

"But she isn't. And, short of a séance, she isn't going to be." He gestured at the Summons and Complaint. "One break we got, the deputy attorney general who'll serve as prosecutor at the hearings is Johnny Delaney. The sweet deal I gave him on that Kawasaki for his kid last year . . ."

"Dan, leave the wheeling and dealing on this to Hec."

Kearny shrugged. "Sure. Now, you get started on those Oakland-office employment records. I want 'em all—inside men, outside men, skip-tracers, collectors, file clerks . . ."

"What do I do with the names once I've got 'em?"

"Which investigator should we bring in on this? Of O'B, Ballard and Heslip, which one has the lightest workload?"

After a long pause Giselle said unwillingly, "Larry. He was up the coast after abalone over the weekend and called in sick yesterday. Bart handled his hot ones while he was gone."

"Why the hesitation?"

"He didn't . . ." She paused, unwilling to impeach Ballard's character, but then the image of Kathy dead in her coffin rose up within her. "Dan, he didn't even show up for Kathy's funeral."

"Maybe he doesn't know she's dead."

Giselle was silent again for a long moment, then felt a great weight lift from her mind. Of course, that had to be it! She said eagerly, "Okay, I'll get on the radio and bring him in."

Three

Now, as taught long ago to Ballard by the master, Patrick Michael O'Bannon, ducking a radio summons was child's play. One merely monitored without responding. But Ballard's problem was ducking the phone, with its hypnotic ringing, while he was still at home. This had entailed taking the top off the baseplate and wrapping electrician's tape around the clapper. Thus, when the phone was turned to LOUD, the clapper struck only one bell and rang as if SOFT. On SOFT, it didn't make a sound.

But that system worked not at all when one passed out beside the phone after forgetting to turn it to SOFT.

The scream crashed into Larry Ballard's ears. He sprang from the easy chair in a shambling run to ram headfirst into a wall. He fell down. The scream crashed again. He crawled upright against the wall, staggered back across the room to turn down the phone. Bending over made him want to vomit. Panting shallowly, he leaned his forearms against the mantel of the fake fireplace. Something horrible and bright was worming through the frayed lace curtains.

Sunlight. Ballard peered at himself in the speckled mirror above the mantel. His eyes were too bloodshot to tell whether one pupil was dilated or not, but even without that he knew it was a brain tumor. What else could make a head hurt like that? Unless . . .

He squinted at the front bay window again, which looked across Lincoln Way to the fog-haunted reaches of Golden Gate Park. He could *see*! Could it just be . . . a *hangover*?

He staggered back to the chair and collapsed into it, to sit with the now dead phone in his lap as he tried to piece together the previous day and night.

Maria had married someone else. Oh God, the agony, the betrayal! So he'd gotten drunk Monday night. Yesterday . . . yes, he'd called in sick to nurse *that* hangover. Last night, out and around. Drinks. A whole lot of drinks. Oh pain. Oh woe. Oh agony. Oh . . .

Giselle looked out of Kathy's city-grimed bay window at the grade school across Golden Gate Avenue. Not Kathy's window anymore. *Her* window. Oh damn, damn. Three weeks ago the fall term had begun. Maybe she ought to go back, get her teacher's credentials . . .

Kearny buzzed on the intercom. "How's the list coming?"

She regarded the masses of paper strewn across the desk. Personnel folders. Payroll records. Old collection and field-investigation reports. "I think I've isolated everyone who could possibly have been working out of Oakland that day. But I can't raise Larry."

"Dammit, let's get off the ground on this thing."

Why is he so uptight? she wondered. So Kathy was gone, all they needed was someone else who'd been there that day to substantiate their version of events. Right? Then she had to smile to herself a little as she reached for the phone again. In just about every tough private-eye novel she'd ever read, some cop ended up threatening to take away the detective's license.

Now the State was doing it to them. In real life.

Ballard sat up abruptly in the big saggy chair. He'd just peed in his pants. Then he realized it was the vibrations from the silenced phone in his lap as it tried to ring. He yawned. Man, that was the end of boozing for a while. Say, six or seven years. How did O'Bannon manage it a couple of nights a week? That must be one tough Irishman. He picked up the phone.

"Can you come in right away?" asked Giselle's voice flatly.

"Ohh-h-h," he groaned. "I am not a well man."

"There's a big flap on. Dan wants you on special assignment for a couple of days."

As if by magic, his brain tumor was receding. "Flap about what?"

"He'll want to tell you himself."

Better and better his head felt. "On my way." Then, trying to ungrump her, he asked, "By the way—who died?"

She told him, in a sudden hysterical burst of words. Which made it the unfunniest remark of his life.

Hector Tranquillini—Ettore in front of Italian judges because, *insomma*, it couldn't hurt—had the sort of thick-lipped joviality Al Capone supposedly possessed. He stood, however, only five-four in his high-heeled boots and weighed only one hundred and forty-five pounds after a heaping plate of Mama's pasta. He had thinning black hair and black marble eyes, which could snap like a hard frost. They were snapping now. "Just because you government boys have been busting it off in people ever since California joined the Union, don't think you're going to keep on doing it."

Jack Delaney beamed across the plain wooden table. He was a very big Irishman with freckles and gray-shot red hair who out-weighed Tranquillini by a hundred pounds but was bright enough to be afraid of him in a law court. He hoped it wouldn't come to that.

"Look, Hec, Kearny got caught trying to steal second and got tagged out. It's simple as that. If DKA'll plead guilty—"

"Now my client is a thief? Before the hearing?"

"Hector, Hector, that was just a figure of speech."

But Tranquillini had bounced to his feet. Before hanging out his shingle in the heart of the Tenderloin because he could afford only Tenderloin rents, he'd been a tax attorney for the IRS. For his first two years of private practice he'd not had a client, not one, who wasn't a hooker. He still had a lot of hookers, but now he had DKA, too. And he knew all there was to know about being legally nasty.

"Figure of speech?" He was at the corner where he knew the concealed pickup was. To the wall he thundered, in case the tape was turning, "I HOPE YOU'RE GETTING THIS ALL DOWN!"

Delaney was also on his feet, visibly shocked. "Hec! Hey, cool down! What's got into you? You know—"

"But remember," Tranquillini bellowed at the corner, "I'm subpoenaeing the goddam tapes!"

"Hec, for God's sake, man! You know this is just a routine accusation and hearing. No deep dark motives, no—"

Tranquillini hurled his copy of the Accusation on the table. "You call that *routine*?" he cried dramatically. "Over a couple of hundred lousy bucks Kearny didn't pay on a point of law?"

"Which point of law is that?"

"Which one do you want? Was DKA to return *all* of the money? Or half of it? Because in accordance with state law, they'd remitted half the collected sum to their client. So is GMAC their co-defendant? Or is GMAC excluded from the suit because they're big and powerful?"

"Hec, that money was never supposed to have been paid into the collection trust account. It was supposed to be held separate until the judge's decision in the Pivarski countersuit."

"And then the State would be after Dan's license for being out of trust because he held the money out of the trust account."

Delaney contrived a dazed look. "All we're saying is that—"

"—that Kathy was stupid enough to take money under those circumstances. Do you really believe that?"

"That's what's alleged."

"That isn't what I asked."

"Don't cross-examine *me*, for Chrissake. I just work here."

"Just a good German," sneered Tranquillini. "It's damn convenient for the State that Kathy isn't around to testify as to what happened that day, isn't it?"

"Aw, c'mon, Hec, you think Pivarski snuck into her bedroom and gave her a blood clot when nobody was looking? He and his attorney have stated under oath that she verbally agreed to hold the money until the judge's decision came down. She didn't."

"They're going to have to state it again under oath. To me."

He stuffed his Accusation in his suitcoat pocket, meanwhile maneuvering Delaney out into the hall where no recorders could reach them. It was for this thirty seconds he had come. "Okay, Johnny, tell you what," he said as if it had just occurred to him, "how about Dan pays the man back his money, plus costs and interest, and picks up his attorney's tab? If Pivarski is satisfied with that, would the State butt out and drop charges?"

"I hadn't thought of that, Hec. Have Dan give me a call after I talk with Greenly at the licensing agency. Maybe it's a way around it for all of us."

The two attorneys shook hands and parted. Tranquillini was due in court on behalf of a raven-tressed whore whose civil rights, he was claiming, had been violated after a routine soliciting bust by a prison matron's discovery of an ounce of heroin in one of her body cavities. Delaney got on the horn with Tom Greenly, supervising auditor for the Private Investigation Agency Licensing Bureau, who had brought the charge against DKA.

"I think we should go with their offer, Tom," said Delaney into the phone. "Any violation was inadvertent and in good faith. And if Tranquillini gets Pivarski on the stand, there's no telling how it'll come out. Pivarski is sort of a dim bulb, and Hec is—"

The phone squawked back. He listened. And listened. And finally hung up and stared out of his window down at

Golden Gate Avenue's busy traffic. He'd worked long and hard, and honorably, for his own office with its own view.

After a while he stood up and put on his topcoat and departed for Rocca's bar. Screw Tranquillini and his bullshit about good Germans. He just worked there, right? Did what he was told, right? What the job demanded, right? He was on the side of the angels.

But maybe he needed a couple of double Bushmills to keep on thinking that way.

Four

Ballard had never really liked the East Bay. No *there* there, as Giselle had once told him some lesbo writer back in the twenties had put it. Like going to L.A. or drinking a low-cal beer or eating chow mein: when you thought about it afterward, you realized that nothing very much had happened.

Before riding the creaking single elevator to the top floor of the narrow three-story building a block off Oakland's Broadway, he stopped to look at the list of names Giselle had given him. Giselle. Wow. He'd apologized to her for that stupid mark, but he still wasn't sure she was over being sore at him. And Kathy. He couldn't think about Kathy. Not yet. Him out getting drunk while she was being buried. Talk about stupidity. No. The names. Concentrate on the names and on keeping the investigation quiet.

Norman Ponts	field agent	(currently employed)
Simon Costa	field agent	(currently employed)
Irene Jordon	secretary collections	(currently employed)
Rose Kelly	secretary/PBX, field agents	(quit 12/31 last yr)
Jeffrey L. Simson	inside collector	(fired 2/13)
Donna Payne	inside collector	(fired 8/5)

Verna Rounds	file clerk	(quit 11/12 last year)

Ballard pushed open the glass-paneled door with DANIEL KEARNY ASSOCIATES on it in black letters. Slightly offset below this was the name of the defunct outfit from whom DKA had picked up a lot of quasi-worthless finance papers, including the Pivarski headache. ZIPPY COLLECTIONS. No wonder they'd gone bust.

"May I help you, sir?"

Ballard had passed the field agents' narrow office, afternoon-deserted, and had started for the closed hardwood door beyond. The field-agent secretary who doubled as PBX girl—Rose Kelly's job until she'd quit the previous December—came to her feet when she saw he wasn't going to stop. She was a big slow tranquil brunette obviously too nice for the job.

"Ballard." He shook hands with her. "San Francisco. To see Irene Jordon back in Collections. I know the way."

It was a long narrow room with half a dozen waist-to-ceiling windows in the left-hand wall which let in enough October sunshine to make Ballard squint his hangover-sensitive eyes. At the far end was the plush private office, empty now, where Kathy would have relieved Pivarski of his two hundred bucks. Irene Jordon was machine-gunning out a letter at the first desk with dazzling speed. She was a fat girl with a bad complexion and two uncles who had gone into local politics. The connections made her doubly valuable to DKA.

She looked up at him and grinned. "Hi, beautiful."

Ballard winced. "I said that to a girl the other night, and her husband threw me down the stairs."

"That's what husbands are for. What brings you slumming?"

"You."

They went down the block to a cafeteria that sold, at that time of day, mostly coffee and pie while setting up for supper. Ballard had tea; he trusted few people's coffee but his own.

He ran the scam on her which he and Giselle had dreamed up to explain the investigation. "Pivarski is claiming that he slipped on a loose rug in our office and injured himself. An attorney has talked him into suing and we need any eyeball of him entering and leaving the office."

"How much of a stink is he making?"

"Enough so they sent me over here."

"November fifth, huh?" mused Irene. Her acne-blotched moon face was thoughtful. She was having a hot-fudge sundae. "What time'd he come in?"

"Between five-thirty and six, by the time-stamp on the payment receipt Kathy gave him. If you can remember whether—"

"Kathy. My God, wasn't that terrible about her?"

Ballard, more keenly aware than she of just how terrible it was, agreed shortly and steered her back to November 5. "We're also interested in anyone who heard him and Kathy talking while he was making the payment."

"What use would that be to DKA in an insurance hassle?"

Yeah, a very sharp chick. If her uncles had her brains, they'd be fighting over which one should run for governor rather than grafting retirement incomes out of local government.

"We want to know if he said anything about slipping on the way in. If he didn't, and didn't slip on the way out, we can tell him to go pound salt."

She sighed. "I don't remember him at all, but I wouldn't. All the Legals are typed over in San Francisco." She wiped the last trace of her sundae from her lips, and studied her wallet calendar. "I left at five that night, so I was gone before he got there."

"You *sure*? The office was open until six . . ."

She poked a stubby finger at the calendar for the previous year. "Rose and I alternated late Fridays, and it was her week. She would have been there until about six-fifteen. I imagine Jeff Simson or Donna Payne would have been in the office, too. Kathy liked to keep one collector late on Fridays."

On the way back to the office Ballard asked whether she

and Rose had kept up, but they hadn't. Nothing in common except work. And when he went back upstairs with her he found the two outside investigators, Norm Ponts and Simon Costa, in the field agents' room one-fingering reports of their day's activities. Neither one had ever heard of Pivarski, or had the slightest recollection of whether he had been in the office on that Friday nearly a year before. Ballard thanked them and went off to look for Donna Payne.

It was a new experience, looking for someone who wasn't trying to avoid him. New, and frustrating. Because Mr. or Ms. Honest John was just as hard to find, in our mobile society, as Mr. or Ms. Deadbeat. People seemed to get lost just sort of by accident. Like Donna Payne, with whom he had started because she had been fired on August 5, only about ten weeks before, and because her given residence address was just a couple of miles from the Oakland office.

Mather Street featured old frame houses set against the hills off Oakland's Broadway. The street curved around the face of the hill; the house Ballard wanted had a steep lawn and concrete stairs leading up from the street.

When he rang the bell a woman wearing slacks and a sweatshirt opened the door. "The apartment's been rented. I meant to take down the sign, but what with one thing and another . . ."

"I'm looking for Donna Payne."

"Moved."

Ballard leaned against the door without seeming to, so she could not shut it. She had the bloated face and pasty color of a gin drinker.

"No forwarding?"

Her eyes looked slightly unfocused but her breath was innocent of gin. Vodka, maybe? "Maybe she went back to Nevada."

"Where in Nevada?" Nothing in the file on Nevada.

"Her car had a Nevada license."

Very cautiously, like a fisherman with a nibble, he asked, "You wouldn't remember the license, would you? Or the kind of car she drove?"

"The license, no. The car . . . You wait right here."

He waited. You never knew. Across the street, a black-and-white alley cat was on the hood of his DKA Cutlass, washing its face as if using the windshield as a make-up mirror.

The vodka drinker returned with a twelve-year-old boy. "Tell him."

"Austin Marina GT two-door coupé. Red. Pin stripes painted outside. Tach. Walnut-finish instrument panel. White-walls. Heated rear window."

He turned away to go back into the house. Ballard said to his back, "What do you do? Sell used cars for a living?" But he was alone on the porch.

In the car he called KFS 499, Oakland Control, and told them to relay to Giselle he needed a "previous res and work add" on Payne. Then he consulted his list. Rose Kelly, the PBX operator had been living at 15321 Redwood Highway when her W-2 was mailed to her in January. Santa Rosa, fifty miles north. He'd save that for last, if he missed on Payne and Simson.

Oh, and on the file clerk. Verna Rounds. No file clerk would stay around for an extra hour of work on a Friday, but on the other hand, she lived just a couple of miles away, off MacArthur Boulevard in North Oakland. Get her off the list before heading back to the city and Jeff Simson's listed residence address on Twenty-fourth Street in the Mission District.

Five

When Interstate 580 went through Oakland a few years before, it had reduced MacArthur Boulevard to a freeway-feeder street. The motels which once had catered to through-travelers slid—at the same time that girls from nearby recently black residential areas were growing up hungry for the good life.

Ballard drove north along MacArthur past quite a few who had found it. Maybe. On every street corner, in front of almost every motel, all he could see was legs. Long legs, short legs, thin legs, heavy legs—under short, scruffy, artificial fur jackets, or red blazers with brass buttons, or no jackets at all, just T-shirts and blouses. Many of the legs were covered only by body stockings and black boots, or outdated hotpants. He was glad to turn off and drive over a few blocks to the 3000 block of Thirty-fourth street, where Verna Rounds was supposed to live.

It was a run-down frame house with an old-fashioned front porch, its roof supported by squat, square pillars. One of the street numbers was missing from beside the open doorway, but the paint where the metal numeral had been was a different color from the house's current hue. The front walk had broken into three separate sections tilted in three different directions. There was a three-inch gap between the top of the sunken concrete front steps and the porch. He knocked on the doorframe, unheard over the voices raised within.

"*Whut* you sayin' to you mother?"

"Sayin I put thutty dollar in de pinball machine down to de rib joint."

"Samuel, where you get dat sorta money?"

In a momentary silence, Ballard knocked again. A huge fat black lady came up the straight hallway from the kitchen, talking as she came. Her remarks seemed addressed more to herself than to the husky teen-age boy behind her. ". . . de baddest boy I ever *did* hear of . . ."

"Hey, Ma, I was kiddin' you. Spent a dollar."

This stopped her just short of the door. "Dat God's truth?"

"Ask Ophelia."

The fat woman shook her head, starting to grin. "I swear you bad to de very minnit, Samuel, fool you poor dumb mammy dat way." She turned the grin on Ballard. "Yassuh?"

Ballard returned it. "I'm looking for Verna Rounds. Is she—"

"Ain't no Verna Rounds here." The face had closed like a fist.

He took a chance and said softly, "You're her mother, aren't you?"

"And if I is? Verna ain't here."

"It's very important that I get in touch—"

"Look, caint you leave that poor girl alone?"

Ballard held up a placating hand. "She's not in trouble—"

"Lot you know 'bout trouble."

He stood without moving for a few moments, staring at the door just slammed six inches from his nose. "Terrific," he finally said and went back to his car.

He had to try three pay phones to find one that was working. With it he called Giselle. "Oh, Larry, good, I didn't want to put this out on the radio." So she was over her mad, anyway. "Donna Payne worked for six weeks in the credit office of Royal Foods on Valley Drive in that industrial park down in Brisbane. She lists a Mary McCarthy there as a personal reference."

"You got anything on her in Nevada? She might be there."

"Nevada?" There was a rustling of papers. "No. Cincinnati, Ohio. And I remember her saying that's where she was from."

"Okay, I'll hit the McCarthy reference tomorrow. Tonight I'll check on the Jeffrey Simson residence address. And I'm going to ask Bart to work the file clerk. I'm the wrong color."

By the time Ballard had gotten a hamburger and driven back to San Francisco, dusk had fallen and the fog had rolled in. He parked on Valencia around the corner from Simson's Twenty-fourth Street address. A narrow foot passage led to the small court on which the apartment opened. There were potted plants and a strong catbox smell, but no lights in the apartment and no answer at the door. He left one of his business cards in the slot of the mailbox, which his flashlight showed bore the names BETTE and MILFORD DENNISON.

On his original employment application, Simson had listed a father living in the 1300 block of Stevenson Street. Ballard drove in on Valencia, contemplating once more his insight that straight arrows were as hard to track down as flakes and deadbeats. On the way he passed Eighteenth Street; half a block over on Linda Street lived Maria Navarro and her new husband. He didn't even know her married name. And was surprised to realize he hadn't even thought of her since hearing of Kathy's death.

The father lived in a detached bungalow. He was a benign-countenanced, round-faced man with a fringe of white hair and a limp. He balanced himself on his good leg while admitting he was Ellis Simson and waving away Ballard's apologies with his cane. "No, no, glad of the company. It beats television."

"I'm trying to get in touch with your son Jeff."

In the act of turning away, Ellis Simson stopped abruptly. He put the rubber tip of his cane against Ballard's stomach and smiled tightly. "You a fag?" he demanded in a challenging voice.

"Huh?"

The cane was lowered. "Come on in."

"Gotta blame myself, I guess." Ellis Simson and Ballard were each having a can of beer. "Moved out on his ma nearly twenty years ago."

"She never remarried?"

"Too ornery. Good-looking girl then. I was a merchant sailor, met her during the war..."

The three-room apartment was that of a man who'd grown used to small living quarters which had to be kept neat. Handmade hardwood bookshelves held a sailor's reading: The Bible and Shakespeare, Stevenson and Kipling and Conrad, Matthiessen's *Far Tortuga*; books to be read and reread during the long still watches far at sea.

"So she raised him alone?" prompted Ballard. All he needed was Jeff Simson's address, but the old man was lonely and his beer was good.

"From six years old on. When we were docked in San Pedro I had to deliver the alimony payments in person. She liked that. Wouldn't remarry because that would let me off the hook. A good hater, that woman. After I got this"—he slapped the bad leg—"I used the settlement to buy this place. At least it's four hundred miles away from her."

Ballard drained his beer. Out into the foggy foggy night.

"You said you have a recent address on your son..."

"Son!" he snorted. "Didn't lay eyes on him for eight years, despite the support payments, then he showed up two years ago."

He limped over to the old-fashioned rolltop desk which had been restored and hand-oiled to a soft glow like distant fires. As he rummaged in the center drawer he kept up his rapid-fire talk. "Jeff came to me with a lot of talk about his roots, authority figure, father figure—what really happened was his mother got wise to him and threw him out. Not that it stopped the alimony payments. They'll go on until the day she dies. Or I do."

"So Jeff got the apartment nearby?" asked Ballard.

Ellis Simson nodded. "So he could live near me, he said. Had a roommate called Ferdie. Should have known." He came back with a sheet of scratch paper. "Here's the address."

Ballard copied it down. Way out in the avenues, almost to the beach.

"Dropped by his place one afternoon, got no answer from the bell and the door was open so I went in. Him and Ferdie were in bed together. I was sick on the bedroom rug." His eyes suddenly brimmed with tears. "Maybe, if I'd stuck with Eleanor..."

"And maybe not," said Ballard.

At the address on Forty-third Avenue just off Balboa, Jeffrey L. Simson was listed for Apartment One, but Ballard's flashlight through the uncurtained window showed there was no furniture and the place was being repainted. Ballard went home and dreamed he was being attacked by a water buffalo in the paddock at Golden Gate Park off Chain of Lakes Drive.

Six

Bart Heslip was a plum-black man with such an exaggerated breadth of shoulder that he looked like a light-heavy instead of his middle-weight hundred and fifty-eight pounds. As he typed reports in his field agent's cubicle along the left wall of the DKA basement, his hard bony face and deep-set eyes gave away few secrets. Not that he was trying to keep any just then. He was pissed off with Larry Ballard and didn't care if the whole world knew it. In fact, he stepped to the door of his cubicle and cupped his hands around his mouth. "I'm pissed off!" he yelled.

O'Bannon's flame-topped head appeared in the doorway of the end cubicle. "Ah ha!" he exclaimed. "The primal scream." His head disappeared and his typewriter began rattling again.

Which made Heslip look over at his own, an old IBM bought by Kearny at a bankrupt stock auction yea-many years back. The "E" key stuck, so his reports always began: Follow d to th giv n addr ss, cruis d th ar a, could not spot assign d v hicl .

Which made Heslip even madder. He strode resolutely back to Kearny's private office and threw wide the sliding door with its one-way glass. Kearny was behind his massive blondewood desk.

"Dan, I want—"

"Shut up! Get the hell out of here!"

"Oh," Heslip agreed quickly, his head already jerking back like a turtle's into its shell. He slid the door shut whisper-soft and tiptoed across the concrete to O'Bannon's cubicle. The red-headed Irishman paused in his work.

"Oh," Heslip told him.

"Yeah." O'B's freckle-massed features were ruddy with incipient alcoholism and his eyes were wise with a quarter-century of investigating every conceivable foible, weakness and perversion of human nature. "Ever since Kathy died."

The door at the far end of the basement opened, and Ballard came through washed by sunlight so fierce he looked like an over-exposed black-and-white print of himself.

"You!" Heslip yelped. *"I'm pissed off with you!"*

Ballard came down the basement with his attaché case and turned in at his cubicle. "It's going to be a scorcher," he said.

Heslip went in and plopped down in Ballard's spare chair. Like Heslip's, the cubicle held a desk, a typewriter, a phone and a set of trays with the various forms demanded by their profession.

"You hear me talking to you, man?"

"I had a bitch of a dream last night, Bart."

"You hear me telling you I'm pissed off with you?"

"I was out in the buffalo paddock at the park, and this huge goddam water buffalo charged me. An African *water* buffalo, they don't even have any of them out there. I started running—"

"You dumped so much work on me, man, that Corinne is—"

"Then, you know the way it is in dreams, I was somewhere else. In a farmyard. Still running. With this water buffalo chasing me. I ran into the farmhouse and up the stairs and up the ladder to the attic room under the eaves."

"How much time you need to get over a weekend of skin-diving?"

"And that buffalo right after me. So I went out the window to the roof. Here comes the buffalo."

"Corinne is really on my case, man."

"You know what that buffalo did when it caught me?"

Heslip was intrigued despite himself. "What?"

"He *queered* me!"

"*Queered* you? You mean . . ."

"Right there on that farmhouse roof. And the whole time I was yelling, 'Not a *buffalo*! Not a *water* buffalo!' "

"You better come to Corinne's to supper tonight, man, get your head on straight."

"I think I woke up yelling it, Bart. I really do. 'Not a *water* buffalo.' " Still worried of face, he said abruptly, "The State's going after Dan's license."

Heslip's mouth dropped open. "Whatever in heaven for?"

"It's complicated. Something Kathy worked on over in Oakland. That's why you still have my caseload. And why"—he was grubbing in his attaché case for a manila folder—"you're going to have to take another one for me, too."

"This have to do with the State trying to punch Dan's ticket?"

"Yeah."

"Gimme."

Giselle, having read Ballard's reports of the previous day's investigations, had been busy with the cross-directories. She got on the radio. "KDM 366 Control calling SF-6. Come in, Larry."

"This is SF-6. Over," came Ballard's voice.

"I have a res add on Simson for you from the new criss-cross. Just confirmed with Information. Jeffrey L. Simson, 1950 El Camino Real, San Bruno. Over."

"Ten-four," said Ballard. "I'll hit it on my way back in. I'm down by the Cow Palace now en route to Brisbane to talk with Mary McCarthy."

A few years before it had been a grassy, deserted fold in the hills a mile short of the tough old village of Brisbane nestled up against the base of the San Bruno Mountains. Then an industrial park had been staked out, and over the years had been filled up by industry fleeing San Francisco's rising crime and tax rates.

Ballard turned in off old Bayshore Boulevard and went down the rows of anonymously modern glass-and-synthetic buildings along Valley Drive until he found Royal Foods. It was indeed the scorcher he had predicted, so his shirt was sticking to his back as he got out of his car.

A uniformed security guard was waiting at a table inside the double glass doors. "'Nye help ya?"

"Mary McCarthy, please."

"Which department?"

Ballard took a guess. "Credit."

It was down the hall, third door on the left; there were only three people in the room and only one of them a woman.

"Ms. McCarthy?"

She was about Ballard's age and wore a plain gold wedding band on her right hand. She had premature crow's-feet around her quizzical, pale eyes, and brown hair cut in a soft bob; in truth, a somewhat pudgier woman of body than her thin face would suggest. Ballard gave her his name and whom he was looking for.

"Donna's not in any trouble, is she?"

Ballard chuckled to show how little trouble Donna Payne was in. "We just need a statement from her about an insurance matter."

After listening to his scam, Mary McCarthy reached under the desk for her purse. "I've been meaning to get in touch with her, but one thing and another..." Like the landlady and her FOR RENT sign the previous day, Ballard thought, except this one wasn't a boozer. She was thumbing through a small black address book. "Yes. It is 573 Ashley Avenue in San Carlos."

Except that when Ballard called Information from a pay phone near the security guard's table, he was told there was no listing for Donna Payne in San Carlos. Or anywhere else on the Peninsula south of the city. Another dead end? Getting into the Cutlass, he remembered he had not asked Mary McCarthy about the Nevada lead the boozing landlady had given him. Must be getting old.

* * *

His ma had named him Samuel after some dude in the Bible, and always insisted on the full name. Samuel Rounds. Showed respect, she said, because the original Samuel had been a prophet of the Lord's. But out of the house he liked Sammy. He was only fourteen, but looked seventeen easy. The counterman at Fisher's Ribs and Chicken, on Friday nights sometimes he'd let Sammy watch the crap game in the storeroom. He wouldn't do that with no little kid, because that was one high-stakes game.

Sammy pulled back the plunger, delicately released it. The ball shot forward. Arced around. Began to bounce from bumper to bumper, clanging and lighting them up and clicking up points.

"You're pretty good at that, blood." The man was very black and very wide-shouldered, with cool eyes and a hard face, and under his short-sleeved flowering *aloha* shirt, forearms which were ridged with muscle.

"Bes dere is," said Sammy, expanding under his attention.

"You must be Sammy Rounds."

Sammy was instantly guarded. "Where you hear 'bout me?"

The stranger lifted a shoulder fractionally, and an eyebrow fractionally. He was bad, Sammy could see that. Bad clear through.

"I'm a' old friend of your sister Verna's."

Sammy was now downright suspicious. "You jivin' me, man?"

The stranger shook a couple of cigarettes from his pack, offered one to Sammy. "Been away," he said.

Sammy returned to his game so he could lay the cigarette on the edge of the pinball machine once it was lighted. He didn't want to start coughing in front of the stranger.

"Whut you want with Verna?"

"Now whut you suppose I want with a foxy lady like that?"

Then the stranger bought a pint of sneaky pete and he and Sammy went to sit in his short and drink it and jive a little.

* * *

Nineteen-fifty El Camino Real in San Bruno turned out to be the Cable Car Motel. A *motel*? Ballard parked in front of the office and went in. A bell jangled when he opened the door. He could hear a TV in the apartment behind the office. A mid-fifties man with a springy stride and ill-fitting dentures and old-fashioned suspenders came out. The dentures made his smile sharklike.

"Does a Jeff Simson live here?" asked Ballard.

"Certainly."

Weird old duck. "Which unit?"

"Here. This one."

"He's the manager?" The phone listing suddenly made sense. The old guy was still looking at Ballard expectantly, as if waiting for him to dance a jig or throw a fit or walk a tightrope. "May I speak with him, please?"

"You are."

Oh no, including the middle initial? "Jeffrey *L.* Simson?" demanded Ballard, just to be sure.

"Oh." The old man chuckled wisely. He had the breath to go with the dentures.

"This has happened before?"

"Last week, was a policeman with a warrant for unpaid parking tickets. A month ago, some feller from the State of California."

"What did *he* want?" asked Ballard quickly.

Too quickly. The wrong Jeffrey L. Simson drew himself up and clicked his porcelain teeth over a curt good day. Almost, Ballard thought as he drove away, as if the feller from the State of California had elicited his patriotism about keeping quiet concerning the State's interest in the *other* Jeffrey L. Simson.

Which didn't make a whole lot of sense. Unless . . .

Seven

"It doesn't make a whole lot of sense," said Kearny, as he hung up the phone. "Unless . . ."

Giselle hung up the extension. Kearny began pacing the postage stamp of space behind his desk, carrying the cup of hot coffee she had just brought down from upstairs. Ballard's call had caught them still at the office even though it was long past closing time.

". . . unless they were checking whether they had a case before they made their move. Which means they need somebody to back up Pivarski's version of what went on that day between him and Kathy."

"That would be perjury, Dan."

"By both Pivarski and our man, yeah." He added absently, "Or woman. And maybe Pivarski's attorney as well. Franks." He quit pacing. "Leave Ballard a note to find out whether the state investigator talked with Donna Payne, too. Tomorrow, stop at the Oakland office on your way in. Ask Irene Jordon if anyone was around bothering her. We want to find out if they were trying to reach anyone *except* Simson."

Giselle was writing. "You aren't coming in tomorrow?"

"After I talk with old man Hawkley. You take a cab to the Oakland office, I'll pick you up there." Giselle didn't drive. "If this is a *deliberate* move by someone to jerk my ticket, Hawkley's going to be in it somewhere."

He went back to his desk, sat down and drew on a cigarette which had been smoldering on the edge of the ashtray. His eyes were watchful and alert, almost cruel in their concentration. "It *could* just be the State. I've stepped on a few toes in the Licensing Bureau over the years."

"Tom Greenly's toes?"

"Greenly might have corns, at that." He stood up abruptly. "They've been pushing us; it's time we pushed back. Ready to go?"

"Should I leave a note for Bart, too? He's trying to get a line on this Verna Rounds."

"Let's see if he comes up with anything, first."

The Bide-A-Wee Motel was a block down MacArthur from a gun store that had been hit enough times to bristle with the sort of security devices it would take an antitank gun to breach. The Bide-A-Wee wasn't quite so tough to get into. All it took was money—or a scam. Heslip, parking his DKA Ford with the whippet aerial in the motel lot, was running a scam. His *aloha* shirt was on a hanger in the back seat; he now wore a suit and tie and carried an attaché case. He looked very straight indeed.

The man behind the counter was white and sufficiently mugged by life to be mean when he had the edge. "Room for the night, sir?" he asked in a bright I-hate-niggers voice.

Heslip swung the attaché case up on the countertop with a solid thump, took out his wallet and gave the manager just a glimpse of his private investigator's registration card.

"I'm an investigator registered with the State of California," he said coldly. All he had allowed the clerk to see was STATE OF CALIFORNIA across the top of the card, with Department of Professionals and Vocational Standards and the state seal below that. His voice had stroked the word "registered" as lightly as a snowflake hitting the ground. The clerk missed the word, as intended.

"Ah . . . yes, sir."

"Complaints," Heslip said sternly. A Buick Electra hardtop coupé had just pulled into the parking lot. "We've been getting complaints about this motel. We know certain members of the Oakland police force . . ." The manager shifted nervously from one foot to the other. A white man and a black girl in a skirt which barely covered her pudenda were coming toward the office from the Buick. "But *we*'re involved in the investigation now."

The door opened, the bell jangling merrily and the odd couple entered. The man was juiced enough to be high, wide and handsome.

The girl winked at Heslip. "Hi, Charlie," she said to the motel clerk.

"Ah . . . we're filled up," said Charlie. He was sweating.

The john's face had gotten ugly. "Whadda ya mean, filled up? You got out a sign says 'Vacancy.' An' she told me—"

Charlie reached down under the counter. He flipped a switch. The VACANCY sign outside went off.

"Quit yo' jivin'." The girl reached over the counter and scooped a key off the nearly full rack. With her other hand she was expertly honking her john. "*Pay* the man, honey," she said in a breathy little-girl voice. "I can't hardly wait."

The john's face was excited from having his crotch massaged. "How much?"

"Twelve dollars, but you have to sign the register and—"

The john dropped a five and a ten on the counter, and pulled along by the girl avid to score and get back out on the street again, went out the door. Charlie looked up at Heslip from the $15 with a sickly grin on his face.

"I can close this dump down in twenty minutes," said Heslip. He whirled to point at his car with its suddenly menacing CB antenna. "I go out there and get on the air and I have three carloads of state *and federal* investigators in here. And you're out of business, my friend."

"Look, mister, I don't know what you think—"

"I said out of business. And not only that. In the custody of federal marshals. You know why?"

When Charlie didn't answer, Heslip thrust his nose across the counter to within six inches of the other man's face. He had gotten a beautiful break with the unregistered couple.

"You know why?"

Charlie shook his head numbly. Heslip started to wing it, making it up as he went along. He had to admit it *sounded* real, if he did say so himself.

"You're going to the slam for fifteen, my friend, because a little black hooker named Verna was working a badger game with her mack in this motel."

"Shakedowns? None of that goes on here, Officer."

"You go up to their rooms with them?" he sneered.

"Well, no, but—"

"Then I'm *telling* you what went on here. She had her mack in the closet taking pictures, and she sent prints to one of the johns she was with, a construction contractor from Decatur, Illinois. When he got the pictures he died of a heart attack. His wife found them *and* the extortion note. She went to the fed, they came to us."

"Jesus Christ," breathed Charlie.

"So now you're going to tell me every single thing you know about Verna Rounds, and the pimp who was running her, or—"

Charlie started to talk. He told Heslip things not even his accountant knew. He would have told Heslip about his childhood if Heslip had asked. Most of it was dross, but there was a crumb or two.

Ballard, down on the Peninsula south of San Francisco, wasn't getting even a crumb. He couldn't find Ashley Avenue, let alone number 573. The closest he came was an Ashley in East Palo Alto, but the numbers there ran, for some obscure reason, from 1700 to 2300.

Back in San Carlos he checked two gas-station maps against his own. Still no Ashley Avenue. So he went to a fire house. The bored strapping youngster behind the night desk was delighted to abandon his *Penthouse* for the big board map posted beside the communications desk. "Sure, here it is. Ashley Avenue. South of the San Carlos airport and just west of the Bayshore. New street within the past year."

Ten minutes later Ballard discovered that 573 was half of a new duplex. What would a single girl like Donna Payne be doing out here in the sticks in tract housing? He wasn't going to get a chance to ask her, because the name on the mailbox was Childers and the house was dark. Lights out at eleven-forty at night? Didn't she even watch Johnny Carson, for Chrissake? Everybody watched Johnny Carson. Johnny Carson made three mil a year and had a great program to repossess cars during.

Ballard went next door, where lights *were* on. He found a woman who believed in haircurlers and cold cream and to hell with what her husband might prefer to get into bed with. Yes, a young couple named Childers had moved in next door three weeks earlier. The landlord? That was Mr. Haynes.

"Just bought the duplex to live in that side, 573, and rent out this half, when he got a job in electronics in Los Angeles and moved down there. If you want his address . . ."

"No. Thank you very much, ma'am." Ballard turned away.

"The Childers, guess they must have moved down here from Nevada and wanted to rent until they could find—"

"Nevada?"

She was mildly surprised at his reaction. "He drives a car with Nevada plates, anyway."

"An Austin Marina coupé?"

"No. One of those little foreign things. Red. They sleep *very* late in the mornings, I guess he works nights and she goes to wait for him. Two-thirty, three every morning . . ."

How many night jobs were there where your wife could go to watch you work? Ballard started on San Carlos Avenue, and just a couple of blocks off El Camino, found a red Austin Marina GT hard-top with Nevada plates parked in front of The Haven.

It was a neighborhood place with an outdated shuffleboard and a husky, tight-eyed bartender with sleek black hair and sideburns three inches below his ears. He was at the far end of the stick hovering over a good-looking blond who was a bit too blond to be true. When Ballard slid onto thc stool next to her, the blond looked over at him and did a double-take. "Larry Ballard! How are things at good old DK and A?" He told her, using the insurance scam and ending up with his pitch. "And we were hoping you could remember whether you were in the office on the day Pivarski showed up."

She could. She wasn't. Hell. Scratch Donna Payne.

Eight

It was a big rambling ranch-style house set back against the elegantly barbered brow of a hill off exclusive Glen Alpine in Oakland's Piedmont district. Kearny parked his station wagon and pressed the button on the talk box set twenty feet back from the wrought-iron gates electrically operated from inside the house. On the side of the spacious graveled area outside the gates was a modernistic white light box with the word HAWKLEY down the front in black letters which could be illuminated at night.

"What is it?" asked a speaker-distorted voice.

"Dan Kearny to see Counselor Hawkley."

"Just a moment."

The morning sky was overcast; yesterday's heat had broken. A tatterdemalion burst of bush tits, like scraps of blown paper, landed in the pyrocantha bushes flanking the drive to chatter in soft excitement for a few moments before tumbling out and away again.

One of the twelve-foot gates began to swing open majestically, as the talk box said, "Don't worry, the dogs are in."

Kearny, who put dogs pretty far down the list of things he worried about, walked up the gravel drive to the house. The door of the enclosed veranda which ran the length of the house opened before he got to it.

"Dan Kearny!"

Hawkley was standing just inside the door, beaming,

six-three and a hundred and sixty pounds, tops, seventy-five years old if he was a day. He wore a brown three-piece suit with a gold watch chain looped across his narrow gut. What was a man like Hawkley doing still involved with the mob? Or maybe this $300,000 house in the Oakland hills answered the question.

"Counselor." Kearny nodded. They shook hands.

"Little early in the day for Wild Turkey, but how about some coffee in the breakfast room? It's Venezuelan, I buy it whole-bean and grind it fresh."

Kearny followed the tall stooped figure down a carpeted hall to a huge bright kitchen in yellow set off by the soft tones of hardwood cabinets. A black maid was scouring the stainless-steel sink.

"Savannah Lee," said Hawkley. "Coffee."

The breakfast nook was done in blondewood furniture with green cushions. Floor-to-ceiling glass on three sides, sliding panels which opened on the rear patio. A red hummingbird feeder hung from one limb of an ornamental red Japanese maple, a regular bird feeder on the branch of a flowering cherry.

Hawkley waved a hand at them. "Don't get much except spinnies and jays this time of year. When they're nesting in the spring, house finches and once in a while a rufous-sided towhee. And of course robins and catbirds."

"Well, you've answered one question," said Kearny as they sat down. "You're talking too much about too little not to know why I'm here. Spinnies?"

"Sparrows. That's what we called 'em in the Midwest when I was a kid." He chuckled reminiscently and took a long cigar from his vest pocket. Savannah Lee came in with a bone-china coffee service on a silver tray. As she poured, Hawkley admitted, "Can't say as I'm totally unfamiliar with the State's suit."

"What's the big idea? Somebody had to whisper in their ear."

"Norbert." Hawkley bit the end from his cigar.

Kearny lit a cigarette, saying, "Norbert could set off a

bomb on the front lawn of the state legislature and nobody would hear it."

Hawkley chuckled again in his cultivated folksy manner, which disarmed juries and, at times, judges. "He's awful, ain't he? Still, my sister's boy and all. Try to tell her that . . ." He puffed clouds of aromatic cigar smoke. "You ever met this Pivarski feller?"

"Nope."

"A big dumb Polack truck driver. Came to Norbert when you got the attachment on his wages. Norbert dreamed up this idea of two hundred dollars to be held in trust until a court decided whether the deficiency judgment would stand up. Then damned if your girl, what's-her-name, didn't accept the money and—"

"Kathy Onoda."

"Right you are. When she went ahead and took it, *and* signed Norbert's letter." He shook his age-frosted head. "Well . . ."

"Convenient, isn't it?" Kearny had let calculated disbelief seep into his tone.

"Convenient?"

"We buried Kathy Onoda on Monday."

Hawkley's eyes narrowed in the tanned, leathery face. He said, as if to himself, "That explains why the State's so all-fired sure they'll get your license over this."

"You're saying the whole thing originated in Sacramento?"

Hawkley refilled their cups from the silver urn. "Don't twist my words, young feller. When Norbert saw you were going to treat that $200 as a payment, why, of *course* he filed a formal complaint with the state licensing agency."

"And I thought you people owed me one after Phil Fazzino," said Kearny with deliberate bitterness.

"We do. That's why I ain't done anything more than advise Norbert on this, *when* he asked me."

Kearny stubbed out his half-smoked cigarette. He said casually, "But I suppose you'll just happen to come along to the hearing before the licensing commission next week, and Norbert will just happen to testify on behalf of—"

"Hell, I won't be there," exclaimed Hawkley. "Neither

will Norbert, come to that. Or Pivarski. I grant you it started with Norbert's complaint, but the State of California is the one bringing the charges.'' He was on his feet, following Kearny's lead, and asked, concerned, ''No hard feelings?''

''Your man has to represent his client.'' Then, in apparent afterthought, Kearny added, ''So I guess you wouldn't have any objection to accepting Pivarski's money, plus reasonable costs, interest and attorney's fees, to get the file closed.''

''Not an objection in the world,'' said Hawkley. ''I can't speak on behalf of Norbert, but I wouldn't see him objecting either.''

On his way in, Kearny called Oakland Control, so Giselle was waiting when he got there. As he had instructed on the radio, she had Heslip and Ballard on tap in the San Francisco office, and Hec Tranquillini had juggled his court schedule so he could get there for a strategy session also. After he arrived, the five of them moved out on the little porch opening off the back office used by the inside collectors. The fog had lifted and the freeway traffic, booming by a hundred feet away on the raised skyway, ensured absolute privacy.

''What a place for a mad sniper!'' Tranquillini exclaimed. He raised an imaginary rifle to squeeze off a series of imaginary rounds at the zipping autos.

''The world lost a great mass murderer when you passed the bar,'' said Giselle.

''Gimme time, sister,'' he said breathily in his best Al Capone manner. ''I might make it yet.''

''Only with your bills for service,'' said Kearny. He turned to Ballard. ''So Donna Payne wasn't working that Friday afternoon?''

''Not after five o'clock. Simson might have been, but—''

''How can she pin it down so exactly?''

''She and Simson split late Fridays by the month. But Kathy didn't always keep the collector on duty after five-thirty.''

''Giselle told me no state investigators had been around to the Oakland office asking questions, but I want you to get hold of Payne again and ask her if the State Licensing Bureau has—''

''It hasn't.''

''You asked?'' Kearny was surprised.

''It bothered me that they had talked with the wrong Jeffrey L. Simson out there at the motel in San Bruno.''

''You think she's straight?'' asked Tranquillini.

''Sure. She's shacking up with a bartender out of Reno who's working down here now. They're going back to Nevada next month.''

Kearny said, ''Bart?''

Heslip told them about his talk with Verna's brother Sammy.

''You gave a fourteen-year-old kid cigarettes? And drank wine with him?'' demanded Giselle, a bit outraged.

''His mammy lost him long ago,'' said Heslip indifferently, ''she just doesn't know it yet. Big sis showed him the way last November when she quit DKA. A pimp calling himself Johnny Mack Brown turned her out just three days later. A week after she left DKA she was hustling commuters out of a MacArthur Boulevard motel called the Bide-A-Wee. But sometime in December something happened and she dropped out of sight. Sammy didn't know what, but—''

''You got all this from the kid?''

''Him, and from the manager of the Bide-A-Wee. The pimp disappeared around then too.''

''How'd you get the manager to open up?'' asked Tranquillini.

''You don't want to know.'' Heslip turned to Kearny. ''You want me to keep after her, or. . .''

Kearny looked at Tranquillini. ''Hec?''

''Couldn't hurt. We need an eyewitness, bad.''

''Okay,'' said Kearny. ''Stay with it. Larry, Simson is starting to look damn important. And we want to hear Rose Kelly's version of things too.''

Nine

When Heslip and Ballard had departed, Kearny said, ''I had a session with Wayne Hawkley this morning.''

Tranquillini made a disapproving face. ''That's one very slippery dude, Dan.''

''I wanted to see whether he was behind the State's move.''

''Is he?''

''He says not.''

Kearny related his conversation with Hawkley, omitting all reference to blowing the whistle on Flip Fazzino to the attorney—and thus to the organized-crime people for whom he fronted. He did tell of the letter Hawkley had mentioned. This bothered Tranquillini.

''If the state produces that letter at the hearing on Monday, with Kathy's signature on it, and the letter states that she took the money on trust rather than as payment, we're in big trouble,'' said the attorney. ''Their position then will be that Pivarski gave Kathy a copy of the letter, and she destroyed it. Or you did.'' He slammed a fisted hand against the open palm of his other hand. ''Dammit, we need whoever else was in the office that day.'' He fixed snapping black eyes on Kearny. ''You're sure Hawkley doesn't plan to be there Monday? Or Franks or Pivarski?''

''That's what the man says.''

Tranquillini, scowling, started to pace the porch as if it

were his office, his head lowered and thrust slightly forward, his hands clasped behind his back. Like Napoleon on St. Helena, thought Giselle. She wondered if it was a pose common to short men.

Tranquillini stopped abruptly. "It's damn risky, but I want you to call Johnny Delaney and ask him what Greenly said up at the Licensing Bureau about DKA paying off Pivarski and Franks, his attorney."

"Dangerous?" asked Giselle.

"Delaney tried to feed me a ration of crap about it being a routine disciplinary procedure, but he's the best trial lawyer the state attorney general's office has. What we have going for us is that Johnny is pretty straight, and he knows I can get damn mean." He was stating a fact, not boasting. "If they've got that letter with Kathy's signature on it, they're going to crucify us at the hearing. If Delaney says go, pay Pivarski off before they get us in front of that referee on Monday."

"That sounds like the solution to everything!" Giselle exclaimed.

"Then why ain't I laughing?" Tranquillini demanded morosely.

"Delaney," said the big Irishman into the phone.

"How's tricks, Johnny?"

"Hey, Dan!" Sunshine was in Delaney's voice. "I'm glad you called." He shook three Tums onto his blotter from his desk-drawer bottle. He and his wife had eaten Italian the night before—that was it, of course. "I had a chat with Tom Greenly."

"And?" Kearny's voice was tense.

Delaney crunched Tums silently between his teeth. "He says off the record that restitution before the hearing would make a material difference in the State's pursuit of the revocation action."

"Hey, that sounds great! Many thanks, Johnny."

"Part of the job." Delaney smothered a belch.

"How's the boy's Kawasaki running?"

"Like a dream." He turned his head from the phone

ve a forwarding on him?'' asked Ballard.
him an address in the 3900 block of Twenty-
et. Again, just a few block away. Right on the
thought. It was in that area Simson's car had
up the parking tickets. Looked like Ferdie and
a lover's spat, had busted up their act, but now
back in together again.

se was an old Victorian, a Queen Anne which
nverted into rental units. This part of Noe Valley
ntensely alive in the past few years as young hip
come crowding in, opening restaurants, shops,
d book stores. It had the best weather in the
strict, which had the best weather in the city.
ound the chunky, tough-faced owner in the base-
ng out trash.

d? Apartment five, second floor. Won't get him
t, though. He works in some Polk Street leather

out his roommate? Jeff Simson?''

Ferdinand ain't got a roommate. Just enough
g through his place to start a men's room. Try
er midnight.''

toward the empty doorway of his office and said, in a half-irritated voice, ''What is it? I told you I didn't want . . .'' He let it trail off, then after a moment he said, ''Oh,'' and turned back to the phone. ''Dan, I've got a call from Sacramento on the other line.''

''Sure, Johnny. And thanks again. See you Monday.'' Kearny chuckled. ''In court.''

Delaney hung up and gave a tremendous racking belch. He popped three more Tums, checked his watch and got his coat to head for Rocca's for one quick one even though it was only 11:38 A.M.

Dan Kearny stabbed the OFF button of his phone recorder after hearing the conversation through for the third time. He frowned and chewed his lower lip. No. No slightest sound of the secretary's voice in the background announcing Delaney's Sacramento call. No sound of the door opening or closing.

So Delaney had been faking the other call. Whenever anyone started faking things, especially an attorney, watch out. But Hec felt that letter with Kathy's signature, unless they could suggest it was not genuine through the testimony of whoever else had been in the office that day, put them in an untenable position. They had to go with the hope that Delaney was dealing in good faith. He punched Giselle's extension on the phone—until a few days ago, Kathy Onoda's extension. Hell, don't let's start that again, he thought.

To Giselle he said, ''Draw a check for Pivarski on the DKA general account—*not* the trust account—in the sum of . . .''

Meanwhile, Heslip and Ballard had just returned with a couple of soggy footlongs from the Doggy Diner up on Van Ness. There was a call waiting for Heslip from DKA's police informant who had been checking out the lead furnished by the wrong Jeffrey L. Simson: the *right* Jeffrey L. Simon had picked up so many parking violations that a warrant was out for him.

Their informant was a black cop in Accident Prevention whom Bart had developed after their previous contact, a mean old Dutchman named Waterreus, had gone up on Department charges and had hastily retired. He said, when Heslip picked up, "This is Malcolm X."

"Soul, brother."

"Your boy Simson got tagged eleven times on the 3800 and 3900 blocks of Twenty-fourth Street, daytime on the meters there, over the past four months."

"Latest when?"

"Ten days ago." He reeled off the addresses and times of the tickets, as well as the make and license of Simson's car. Heslip wrote it all down and went next door to give Ballard the information.

"But no way of knowing which shop or store or restaurant he's been visiting."

"I wonder, visiting," said Heslip. "Look at the times on those tickets."

"I see what you mean. All of them before noon."

"Like a guy being a little slow getting up in the morning."

"I'll go looking tonight," said Ballard.

"And I'll go looking for a pimp name of Johnny Mack Brown."

"Or black, as the case may be."

Heslip chuckled. "At least we know the Mack part is right."

When Ballard rang the bell, the door was opened by a sloppy white girl with bell-bottoms and an embroidered vest over a man's blue work shirt. She had round cowlike eyes. An infant was balanced on one hip. "His name is Journey," she said. "Milf's at work if—"

"I left a business card a day or two ago . . ."

"In the mail box. Yeah." She was barefoot, and when she rubbed one bare sole against the inside of the other leg, it made a dusty mark on the pantleg. The bell-bottoms were frayed from being walked on. "We figured, since we didn't know you, it wasn't for us."

"Sure." Ballard gestured. "Why Journey?"

"Because he's a trip!" she e
"I'm trying to get hold of a fc
"The fruiter. Yeah." She roll
repaint the bedroom. Him and h
purple." She thought for a mon
sorta like some sorta perversion
into Jesus. Jesus an' CB."
"Jesus and CB. I like it. Wh
"Green Realty over on Missi
It was just a block away, sc
realty office was on the groun
building where the upper floors
bottles decorated two corners
realty was small and crowded
store that sold religious articles
The Chicano woman behind
heavy body encased in black,
alive and snapping, her utterly
gray of years at the temples
English with a liquid vowel
twinge of memory about Mar
hell she was now that she was
"We're trying to get in touc
of your rental properties on
named Jeffrey L. Simson."
"He now lives out on For
she said instantly, without loo
"Has someone else been a
She shook her head, then s
It is that one he roomed wi
That one, he is damned, God
it."
Ballard nodded. Diamond
toward Simson. "The addres
nues is no good."
"Diamond is not that other
he wears a diamond in his n
And he wears a robe as A
paused. "Damned."

"You h
She ga
fourth Str
money, he
been pilin
Jeffy'd ha
had moved
The ho
had been c
had come
people had
clothing a
Mission D
Ballard
ment clea
"Diamo
until tonig
shop."
"How a
"Queen
guys passi
tonight. A

Ten

Corinne Jones worked for a travel agency on Sutter and Stockton. Visit exotic lands. See the pyramids across the Nile. Whopping discount on all air fares, so she could see the world cheap with a companion of her choice. Except he would never take a vacation. First Bart had been a professional fighter, now a private eye. In four years he'd taken one week off. Total. Still, he was her man, and that was that.

Some dude in a gold Eldorado convertible honked at her as she was walking up Sutter Street after work. From the corner of her eye she could see he jumped sharp in a powder-blue Edwardian-cut and wore a big-brimmed crimson pimp's hat. He honked again. She refused to turn her head. She was a beautiful woman and knew it, with *café-au-lait* skin and a profile right off an Egyptian wall painting.

"Hey, baby, whut's *happenin*?"

She speeded up, heels clop-clopping with an angry sound. Heads turning, mouths laughing. It was almost a rout. And then as she came up to the 450 Sutter Building's garage, the Eldorado bulled right across the sidewalk and stopped where she almost walked into the side of it. The top was down.

"I swear, baby, you the hardest mink I *ever* see to give a ride home to."

She stared in amazement at Bart Heslip's grinning face

under the wide-brimmed hat, then jerked open the door and got in. "You bastard. Oh, you rotten bastard!" she exclaimed.

Heslip had backed out into Sutter Street again, ignoring the angry horns and shouted curses behind him. He wore four-inch clogs and a pink ruffled shirt with froths of lace at the wrists.

"This's class, right, baby?"

"You just pick this thing up?"

"O'B grabbed it three days ago. Dude's out of Dee-troit, owes fourteen big ones on it."

"If Kearny finds out you're driving around in it . . ."

Heslip took a left down Grough, heading toward her apartment. Corinne relaxed against the pale leather upholstery, stirred by faint envy of whoever had been driving it.

"What about those clothes?"

"The Apeman lent them to me." The Apeman was a dealer who lived upstairs from Heslip and spent most of his bread on clothes.

"Bart Heslip, you're *working!*"

"I gotta get a line on a pimp calls himself Johnny Mack Brown."

Corinne, an old-movie buff because of so many nights alone in front of the tube hoping Bart could come over, had to laugh. "You can't be serious!"

"*He* is. Used to work out of Oakland, now he's dropped out of sight. Maybe working some girls in the topless joints out in North Beach. First I gotta find him, then I gotta ask him some questions. And the only dude he's going to tell anything to—"

"No you don't!" she yelped. She'd seen where he was headed. Much too late, of course.

When Ballard pulled into the lot of the Mint Condition, that all-night place on Duboce and Market a little ways from the old government mint, it was nearly midnight, and he'd checked out Queen Ferdinand's street for the car and apartment for him or Simson three times already. And realized he'd missed supper.

Only as he turned into the lot, he was looking right at

Simson's car. He could hardly believe it, but there it was: 1974 Gremlin, white, with the license number Bart had gotten from their tame cop. He tried to remember Simson from last year's DKA Christmas party. All he could come up with was a sort of slender guy with brown hair.

How about phoning inside the restaurant from one of the pay phones out here? He could see through the window, and . . . But what if the state people had warned him against talking with anyone from DKA? Better try to spot him on a casual walk-through.

He'd never been in the Mint Condition at night before. It was a revelation. All races, shades and shapes of gay were there now the sun was down. The most common shape was slim, hipless as a teen-age girl whose breasts have not yet developed, clothes skin-tight, pants without pockets because pockets destroyed that seductive line of thigh and buttock, tops mainly striped $40 French tank tops or tailored shirts with plunging necklines.

Ballard took a turn through the place. Voices high and hyper with excitement, tinkling laughter; most of them beautifully groomed, the skin a little too tight over the cheekbones, the eyes a little too glittery with ready passion, the hands a little too ready to touch and caress. In the bar, absolute contrast: three hackers in studded black leather, obvious rough trade, drinking their beer and waiting for someone to buy the hard night's sodomy they offered.

Nobody quite like his vague memory of Simson. But in the booth on the far side of the circular dining room, Ferdie Diamond. Queen Ferdinand indeed. A sari of gleaming white picked out with gold thread. A BB-sized diamond at the edge of one nostril awink with a turn of the head. A dozen glittering red rhinestones pasted along the outer edge of each eyelid, accented with red eyeshadow. Jammed hip to hip with five others in a four-person booth.

Ballard went back outside. No use making a play in there, Ferdie probably knew everyone in the place. Obviously he was driving Simson's car, so equally obviously he knew where Simson was. Ballard drove out of the lot and parked in the yellow zone across the street from the restaurant.

From there he could see Ferdie in the booth, and could see just the trail of the white Gremlin around the edge of the building.

He settled down behind the wheel and turned the radio to KNEW-91. His dashboard clock showed a new day had begun. He waited.

As he drove, Ferdie Diamond kept casting covert glances at the shuddery brute beside him. Where had the scary darling *been*, that he'd met him only tonight? A bear of a man, with a gravelly voice, and cheeks that would always need a shave, and a mop of coal-black hair growing low on his forehead. Deep-set eyes, a straight bar of brow above them. Positively Neanderthal.

A little shiver of delight ran through Ferdie under his sari. He felt suddenly weak as he thought of being under the Neanderthal man in bed. He backed into the open parking space three doors down from his apartment house. Another parking ticket in the morning, because he just *knew* he wouldn't be up early.

"Here we are."

Neanderthal didn't speak, he rumbled. "You're very kind to offer me a nightcap."

"Let's hope it's an . . . experience neither of us will forget."

"It will be."

That was too much for Ferdie. A little moan of anticipation escaped him as he turned blindly toward the big, rough-voiced man. Their mouths met as a thick-fingered hand slipped up Ferdie's thigh under the togalike robe toward his groin. The hand tightened. And tightened. Ferdie's moan of pleasure turned to one of pain.

"Aw, Jesus H. Christ!" Ballard burst out aloud.

Queen Ferdinand and his boyfriend were parked across the street, four spaces up, and they were *kissing*, for Chrissake!

But then the door on the rider's side opened and the black-haired guy got out with Ferdie right behind, still gripped tenderly in the big man's grasp. Writhing in passion even after they were out of the car into the deserted midnight street. Passion? Or pain? From where Ballard set, the embrace looked more like a choke-hold.

Diamond was getting mugged. Right there on the street. Ballard started his hand toward the horn, to scare the guy off, when the two men turned in abruptly at the Queen Anne and disappeared into the shadows beneath the building.

Ballard was out of his car, eight-inch Stillson wrench from the floor of the back seat in hand. He stood on the sidewalk, breathing quickly and shallowly, trying to pierce the shadows with his gaze. Back there in the dark the big guy could be wringing Diamond's neck as easily as he would a chicken's. Ballard ran silently and obliquely across the street. The narrow concrete passageway under the house was ripe with garbage but otherwise empty. At the far end, a staircase of narrow rough plank stairs.

Sure. Up to Diamond's apartment, clean him out, leave him trussed up and broke. Or broke up. Or dead.

Ballard went up the stairs to the second floor. The door there opened into an interior hallway. No time to think, because if he stopped to think he'd call the cops. That guy looked mean. But, he told himself, Ferdie was his only link with Simson.

Okay, then. Down the silent carpeted hallway to Apartment 5. When he pressed an ear against the door, he could hear the rumble of the big guy's voice.

"... cut it outta your nose, fruiter-boy, unless ..."

Ballard got a flash of the bastard sawing through Ferdie-baby's nostril with a big Bowie knife. Another flash of the same knife sinking up to the hilt in Ballard's gut. Oh, wonderful. Just what he needed right now was a vivid imagination.

He dragged the head of the Stillson wrench down the door with a clawing noise on the wood. The voice stopped.

"I saw you, Ferdie, with that gorgeous hunk," Ballard trilled. "Let me in. Let's share."

Ear back to the door. Furious rumbling whisper. Ferdie's terrified voice from beyond the door. "Go away!"

Ballard dragged the wrench down again. "Stop teasing," he said. And stepped quickly back across the hall. Braced himself. Watched the doorknob until it turned.

His shoulder hit the door and smashed it wide. He ran right across the room and knocked over the portable bar with a terrific crash of glasses and bottles. At the same time he caught one confused glimpse of Ferdie reeling back, his nose spread all over his face by the door, and the black-haired guy, unhurt, coming toward him like a cat.

Ballard whirled toward him, letting the wrench lead his movement. It caught the black-haired guy on the right arm. The knife went flying as the elbow shattered like glass. The man screamed, doubled over holding it, every aggression washed away by pain. Ballard tapped him on the back of the head with the wrench, although every nerve and fiber screamed to bury the wrench in the skull up to the handle.

The big guy went down, hard, on his face.

Ferdie was sitting in the middle of the floor, his gown up around his waist like a two dollar hooker in an alley showing a prospective trick what she had. What Ferdie had was male genitals and no underwear.

"Cover yourself up, you disgusting creep," said Ballard.

Ferdie was beyond modesty or coquetry. Blood from his busted nose leaked from between the spread fingers held up to his face. "By dode," he moaned. "By dode id brokend."

The tough-looking landlord from that afternoon appeared in the doorway, a dangerous glint in his eye and a baseball bat in his hand.

"Call the cops," said Ballard.

The man's eyes took in the scene as his nose twitched to the raw stink of the broken liquor bottles. He nodded and disappeared.

"By dode," moaned Ferdie.

Ballard looked at him and blew out a long disgusted breath. And said coldly, "Where's Simson?"

Eleven

The man weighed over two hundred pounds and little of it fat, with a luxurious brown mustache and straight brown hair fanned out across the shoulders of his fringed buckskin jacket. Except that he waved a flashlight instead of a Colt Peacemaker, he would have been Wild Bill Hickock. He pointed the flashlight at the worn plush curtain. "*The daughters of sin, come in! The daughters of sin, come in!*"

Four college types in warmup jackets accepted the invitation and followed the beam through the curtains to the unknown delights.

"*Gorgeous female models in . . . the . . .* nude!" cried the barker. "*The daughters of sin, come in!*"

A gold Eldorado convertible stopped in front to disgorge two daughters of sin. The blond white girl was taller than the afro'd black girl, but both were striking in their revealing Frederick's of Hollywood party dresses.

"*It's all right inside, folks!*"

They trailed cheap perfume past the barker as they went in. The black girl also trailed lingering fingers along his jawbone. "Ti-i-i-ger!" she purred.

As they disappeared inside, the driver got out of the Caddy. He was a very black dude in a wide-brimmed pimp's hat.

"*Gorgeous fee-male models in . . . the . . .* nude! *The daughters of sin, come in, come in . . .*"

The women stopped inside the door to let their eyes adjust to the gloom. On the stage to their right, bathed in red light, a topless dancer gyrated to the soul beating from the juke box. She had more breast and buttock than was to either woman's taste, but it wasn't them she had to please.

"Oh mama, shake that stuff!" yelled one of the college types.

The woman on the platform did not respond in any way. She was green as a Martian at the moment, courtesy of the spotlight.

"Jesus!" said the blond *sotto-voce*. The black girl threw back her head and laughed loudly, as if at a very funny remark. Then she said, "Git-down time fo' us girls."

They sauntered on. It was one-thirty of a Saturday morning, and there were a number of tables open below the raised platform where the dancer jounced and quivered her talents. A scantily clad waitress appeared, tired of face and bare of breast apart from pasties.

"We want a table, shugah," drawled the blond. She was smoking a cigarette made to look forearm-long by its holder.

"And what to drink?"

The black girl simpered. "We was hopin' maybe some kind gen'mans take care of that little item fo' us."

"Sure, sure. But while you're waiting for Mr. Right."

"*Misters* Right, baby, cause we two togethah is *dy-no-mite!*" She waved a peremptory hand. "Two Scotch-and-waters."

The waitress turned away.

"An' we wants to *taste* the Scotch, shugah," called the blond.

The dancer—yellow at her finale—finished, and a black girl of about the same dimensions took her place as the jukebox flipped sides.

"Boogie on me, baby!" yelled a college type.

The blond at the table caught the eye of a hard-faced fiftyish man sitting with a red-headed man at a nearby table. She winked. The redhead intercepted the wink and leaned forward to say something to his companion. They laughed loose and dirty laughs.

"Rattle those milk cans!" shouted a college type at the dancer.

"Chocolate milk!" called a third, to loud laughter.

The curtain was swept aside and the girls' pimp entered. Over his Edwardian suit was a knee-length white fur coat. He sauntered back to the L-shaped bar past the black topless dancer, who was now turned to gun metal by the blue spotlight. The newcomer found an empty stool at the arm of the bar habited by other black males as outrageously colorful of dress as himself. He swept back his fur coat to sit. "Scotch-and-water," he told the bartender.

A very tall, lean man detached himself from the group and moved with a dancer's grace between the tables. He did a sudden expert dance step to the music, finished with some bumps and grinds, yelled "Shake dat moneymaker, momma!" at the dancer, and sat down at the girls' table. "You a fine-lookin' stallion," he told the blond. "You got a old man?"

"You tryna take my application, jiveass?" she said.

"Now, momma, we jus' talkin a little shit here. Your ol' man black an' beautiful?"

"At de bar, mack man," said the black woman.

"You jivin' me?" He turned to look at the bar. "I know all them players. . . ."

He stopped as his eyes lit on the newcomer in the white fur coat. He looked back at the girls again, then stood up and strolled to the door, pulled aside the curtain and stood talking with the barker outside. The hard-faced man and his red-headed companion stood up and went over to the girls' table.

"Park the frame, Red," said the blond.

As they sat down, the lean black man let the curtain fall and returned to the bar without another look in their direction. The red-headed man had Huck Finn freckles on a debauched Huck Finn face. His hard-eyed companion smiled at the black girl. "Do you think we should buy you ladies a drink first?"

"No need." In the background, the blond and the redhead laughed loudly together. "We just have to talk price."

At the bar the tall, lean pimp was buying a round. "An' fix up de brother here, too," he added.

The man in the white fur coat turned to look at him. Not even his heavy white coat and beautifully tailored clothes could disguise the breadth of his shoulders or the hard muscularity of his body. He nodded and smiled and stuck out a palm to be slapped. The lean man did. "I see by yo short you jus' out here from Dee-troit," he said.

The new man laughed. "That too fas' a track back there fo' this sucker."

"Bein?"

"Black Bart."

The tall man put out his palm to be slapped. "Ready Eddie." He looked over at the two girls, just getting to their feet with the men who had picked them up. "That gray woman could open my nose fo' me, man."

"That be my bottom woman."

"You bringen her out here fum Dee-troit?"

"Both of 'em," Black Bart said. "Johnny Mack *tol'* me my ladies'd bring me plenty cookies in this town."

"Johnny Mack *Brown*?"

"He's de one."

"That nigger in Dee-troit now?"

"If I'm lyin, I'm flyin."

The pickup foursome was just disappearing through the front curtain to the street.

"Looks like they gonna break luck. I could get behind some partyin' tonight to celebrate our firs' night in this town."

Ready Eddie looked at his watch. "Me an' my partners goin to de jam house fo' a little blow after the man cuts us aloose here."

"Mmm-hmm! Say it loud, brother!"

Out on Broadway, the two hookers and their tricks had walked to the parking lot just off Rowland Alley. The hard-faced man gave the white-jacketed attendant his ticket, the black girl hanging adoringly on his arm. Behind them, the blond and the red-headed man were giggling together. The attendant returned with a four-door LTD hardtop, and they got in. The hard-faced man waved away the change from his five and they drove out into Broadway's bumper-to-bumper bar-close traffic.

"Where now?" demanded Corinne Jones. "The night is yet young."

"And I'm not," said Kearny from behind the wheel. "How in hell Bart dreams up these scenarios . . ."

Giselle was disentangling herself from O'B in the back seat to begin repairs by her compact mirror. "Wait'll I tell Bella."

"We had to make it look good," said O'Bannon.

"Not *that* good."

"I'm still not totally clear on what this accomplished," said Corinne.

"It established Bart's bona fides," said Kearny. "You girls, and us picking you up, were his credentials with those pimps so he can try to find where Johnny Mack Brown went with Verna Rounds."

"Remind me never to become a prostitute," yawned Giselle.

Kearny looked in the rear-view mirror to catch O'Bannon's eye. "Want to take a drive down to L.A. over the weekend?"

"With the hearing coming up Monday?" asked O'B, surprised.

"Larry got a direct lead to Jeff Simson from his ex-roommate, and I want to get a statement from Simson myself. So I'm going down to talk to him while Larry goes north to get hold of Rose Kelly. She apparently was on the switchboard that night."

Corinne said abruptly, "I wonder what Bart's doing right now."

Bart Heslip took from his vest pocket a crisp new hundred dollar bill folded longways. He said, "I like the way you got yo crib freaked off, man," unfolded the bill and extended it toward Ready Eddie. They and several other players from the bar were at Eddie's apartment on Page Street in the Haight.

Eddie dipped a tiny gold pocket spoon into the hundred dollars' worth of cocaine the folded bill held. "You one bad nigger," he said, lifting the spoon daintily toward a nostril. The other players followed suit.

Heslip nodded. "Y'know," he said, "I gotta get my string expanded now I'm here. Johnny Macks was tellin' me 'bout a sweet little ho he had here, whut was her name . . ." He frowned in thought. "Was it Verna?"

"Verna. Sure, hey, cat, I remember Verna. But I thought that sucker took her with him, man."

"You jivin' me?" demanded another. "Man, that Johnny Mack is a *boss player*, not no simple pimp. That little girl, she was a *dope* fiend, wouldn't no Johnny Mack take her back east with him."

"Boss player!" snorted Eddie. "Lissen, mother, I don't know as he had such a heavy game. Whut 'bout that Sally he had in his stable, got a crib over there on Hickory just off Webster? Now, there's a ugly, nothin'-ass bitch I ever see one. She an' that Verna was mighty close, I come to think 'bout it."

"Well, shit, mother, that Johnny Mack was jus' playin the short money game with both of 'em." The pimp started to laugh. "She prob'ly got the claps anyway, that Sally."

"The *Texas* claps?" asked Heslip, to cover the fact he had not snorted any coke himself. Then he chanted, "Them bugs at night is big and bright, clap, clap, clap, clap, deep in de heart of Texas . . ."

And the conversation drifted to other things. Heslip had what he'd come for: Sally, 600-block of Hickory Street. But Kearny was going to wig out when the expense voucher for $100 worth of cocaine came in. Labeled, of course, "payment to informant."

Twelve

The house at 15321 Redwood Highway in Santa Rosa was so thoroughly empty that Ballard wondered if it was waiting for the wrecker's ball. Few of these little frame houses remained; now it was high-price motels, gas stations, shopping centers and the sort of businesses that line freeway access roads.

He stood in the bright morning sunlight going through the Rose Kelly file. *One* damn reference listed. A Jack Gunne at 301 Second Street, Eureka. Not even a phone number. He could see it all now. Eureka, 235 miles north. Was Dan Kearny going to expect him to drive all the way up there to talk with this Jack Gunne? Dan Kearny sure as hell was.

One of the boxy little postal vans with the steering wheel on the wrong side pulled up beside the mailbox, then started off.

"Hey, wait a minute!" yelled Ballard. He came up to the open window. "I'm looking for Rose Kelly."

"She moved."

"I know. You see, I'm her brother and I came up from Riverside expecting to spend the weekend, and—"

"Got married," said the postman.

Ballard retrenched quickly. "Thing is, I've been to sea with the merchant marine for half a year. After I spent a couple of days with my girlfriend in Riverside, I thought I'd come up and see Rose. I didn't know she was going to marry him so quick. Uh . . . what's her new name now she's married?"

"I figger a brother'd just know that."

And off he putted. Ballard muttered a naughty word under his breath and looked around for other informants. Local store? The shopping center half a mile down the road. Neighbors? Closest to the south was a motel that covered four acres, had a pool, a sign forty feet high, and free color TV in every room. Sure. They'd know their neighbors the way Ballard knew conceptual nuclear physics. What about up the road?

MADAME AQUARRA KNOWS ALL. SEES ALL. TELLS ALL.

So what else was there to do at eleven o'clock on a Saturday morning in Santa Rosa? Listen to the sun shine?

Madame Aquarra knew, saw and told all in a stucco box of a house from the thirties. High-peaked roof with green shingles, narrow windows, the front door with an old-fashioned brass thumb latch instead of a knob. Set back from the road in an unkempt lot with a couple of fossil automobiles buried in the summer weeds. A sign above the thumb latch, ENTER. Ballard did.

The street noises were instantly gone, replaced by a faint scent of incense. A foyer was created by thick ceiling-to-floor plum-colored curtains on three sides. Those on the right parted.

"What wisdom do you seek?"

Maria Navarro ceased to exist. Raven wings of utterly black hair framed the face. Hurt liquid eyes as black as the hair, eyes that looked right through his blue ones to the back of his head. Small mouth and full lips, slightly tipped-up nose.

"Madame Aquarra knows all."

Cloud castles came tumbling down. A gypsy—and the gyps, the *rom* as they called themselves, were 100 percent bad news 100 percent of the time to the *gadjos*, non-gyps.

"Does she know a forwarding address for Rose Kelly?"

"Madame Aquarra knows all."

She stood aside and he entered past her. Part of him

reacted to the touch of her breast against his arm, the rest of him wanted to put a hand on his wallet to keep her from lifting it. She was dressed in a faded floor-length ivory-colored gown with lace over the tight bodice. The room behind the drapes was cool and dim.

"Look, do you have a forwarding for the woman or—"

"Quiet . . . please."

The girl sat down at a round table in the middle of the room which had the first real crystal ball on it Ballard had ever seen. Black plush reached from the table to the floor all around. Ballard sat down across from the gypsy girl.

"The crystal concentrates the inner sight." She spoke without looking up, her hands tented against her forehead to shadow the eyes. When they did gleam blackly up at him, they were like the eyes of an animal trapped in its burrow. "I see . . . flowers. Not sad flowers. Happy flowers." Her eyes dropped again. "I see . . . yes. White. A . . . some sort of ceremony . . ."

"Do you see the postman in there?" asked Ballard. "He told me Kelly got married before she moved out."

The girl raised her head. "That will be fifteen dollars."

He stood up in disgust and headed for the door. She was there before him. "That will be fifteen—"

"Send me a bill."

"You mocked my inner sight. You destroyed the vibrations of the third eye. You—"

"You tried to tell fortunes without a license," he intoned. "How about it? You have anything on the chick lived next door? I'm a private investigator hired by an insurance company to find her."

The girl suddenly started to laugh, a laugh full of what sounded like genuine gaiety. Ballard mistrusted it because she was a gyp, and all investigators learned to never trust gyps.

"She moved out on May fifth. We never knew the name of the man she married." The gypsy girl shrugged. "Check the bars. She drinks a lot."

Ballard went by her into the foyer. She put a hand on his arm as delicately as a cat seeking attention.

"You are a detective? Truly?"

"Sometimes I wonder," he said. "Who are you when you aren't being Madame Aquarra?"

"Yana."

"Yana what?"

"I am always here." She opened the front door, so Ballard could do nothing but go through it. To his back she said, "Rose had a brother in Carlotta named Roy Shelby."

He turned back to her, utterly surprised, but the door was shutting in his face.

"Remember Yana," said her voice through it.

The door was shut. Firmly. He trudged back to his car, still dazzled by the black light of those eyes. What had that been all about? Something to think about during the 235 bloody miles north to Eureka to get hold of Jack Gunne at 301 Second Street. Unless Carlotta, where her brother lived, was . . .

No. A flyspeck on the map only about twenty miles south of Eureka—and several miles off into the boonies. Before starting north, he used a pay phone at the shopping center to confirm what he'd already felt in his bones: neither Jack Gunne in Eureka nor Roy Shelby in Carlotta had listed phones. He started driving.

Bart Heslip parked and carefully locked his car. Even at two in the afternoon you didn't leave your car open in the Western Addition. They called Hickory a street, but it was really an alley that ran for six blocks between Oak and Fell. The middle couple of blocks had been pretty badly chewed up when they had put the skyway in years before, but where he was, just off Webster, was residential.

If dilapidated single-car garages and the backs of rundown apartment houses were residential. Ghetto-land, baby. Ninety-nine percent black, so old Redevelopment probably was eying it and licking thin whitey lips. Man, they'd *houses* there, an' *people*, an' everything. Quick, tear it down.

Old Redevelopment, he liked them empty weedy lots.

His shoe skittered an empty beer can across potholed

blacktop. A startled rat dashed from the noise into a garage. Heslip went up sagging wooden stairs to 578 Hickory. The door was unpainted, slicked here and there with spots and splotches of old varnish. Where the bell should have been was a perfectly round hole with a couple of taped-off wires hanging out of it.

The door rattled under his fist as if a little more force would put a knuckle through it. He heard the protesting creak of bedsprings. Something female yelled something unintelligible, then cleared its throat with a long dragging sound like a power mower starting up.

"Johnny Mack sent me, Sally," he called through the door.

More creaks. A series of grunts. The door was tugged open a foot, and a broad ebony face, almost ferocious in its ugliness, looked out. He could see a fuzzy once-pink robe below it.

"Why that snotty bastid sendin you around?"

"He said you could hip me to where Verna's at."

She stared at him for long moments, then finally dragged the door wider. She had small, nasty, bloodshot eyes and a nose flat enough to have been hit with a board. Her mouth was wide and very pink when she opened it. "Well, c'mon in. You look big enough to handle it."

Heslip had to step around the edge of the once-expensive opened-out hide-a-bed to do it without touching her. A burst of stuffing at one corner suggested a live-in cat or a long-ago stabbing. The place stank of sleep and cheap wine. In one corner was a pile of laundry ripe enough to culture yeast.

"You ain't interested in no Verna, is you, baby?" she simpered. "You tryna turn me out, ain't you?"

Heslip sat down at a chrome-and-plastic chair by the breakfast table jammed into a corner of the room. "Verna," he said flatly.

"Then whut you comin' round runnin' a game on me this time of the mornin'?"

"It's two in the afternoon."

"Mornin' to me." She jerked a thumb at the door. "You cute, but I ain't in the mood."

Heslip laid a $20 bill on the table besides the remains of a pizza someone had used as an ashtray. Sally wet her lips. Somehow the pink robe had fallen open. "I'm *gettin'* in the mood, baby."

In the dim light he could see the heavy sag of dark-areolaed breasts, the rounded swell of soft gut and the darker pubic triangle between the pastel edges of soiled cloth. They excited him like watching traffic signals change.

"Verna," he repeated.

Humanity abruptly contorted her face, surprising in its intensity. "Verna ain't gonna cop no trouble fum you? You swear you ain't de heat?"

Heslip flicked the $20 bill so it drifted to the floor. Sally looked at it, avarice gleaming in her yellow-balled eyes.

"If I was a pi-i-g, momma," he said contemptuously, "would I be comin' around with no cabbage like this?"

The eyes stared beadily at him for a moment longer, then she stooped and snatched up the bill. Heslip made no move, so she shoved it in the pocket of the robe and went to the closet. She talked as she rummaged. "Knew you wasn't from no Johnny Mack, not when you started askin' me bout Verna . . . She talked him into goin' back east somewheres to fin' someone . . . Sent me this here card . . ."

She returned with a picture postcard of a church. Heslip checked the postmark for time and city of origin.

"January. New Orleans." His eyes followed the childish scrawl. *Jonny got me a room im workin, this heres a nice town. Aint found still looken. Write, love Verna.* He looked up. "Answer it?"

"I been busy," she said almost defiantly.

"Sure."

Heslip doubted he would be chasing Verna Rounds anymore. Dan Kearny just wasn't going to need her that bad. Not all-the-way-to-New-Orleans bad.

Thirteen

Kearny was driving east on York Boulevard in the Eagle Rock area. O'Bannon was beside him, leathery face twisted in concentration over the unfamiliar Los Angeles street map. Kearny turned the LTD into Avenue Fifty and O'B started checking street numbers.

"On the right," he said.

It was a multi-unit setup with shrubbery and redwood chips and an iron-gated walkway through to an inner court where a couple of tons of weekend-idled flesh broiled around a blue-glinting pool. Kearny twice ran his finger, without success, down the rows of plastic-protected names on the buzzer board beside the gate.

"Landlady is Mrs. Theron Johnson," said O'B.

Kearny shoved the buzzer and a tinny voice spoke to them from the squawk box. The gate was buzzed open. They found Mrs. Theron Johnson to be a wide-hipped woman in red stretch slacks of the sort that are almost a uniform in certain portions of Los Angeles. She wore horn-rimmed glasses and her hair ten years out of date. "That one? Jeff Simson? Moved out last month owing two weeks back rent. Why do you want him?"

"An insurance matter."

She stepped out into the empty concrete breezeway. Beyond the decorative greenery, someone hit the pool with a loud splash. Water glinted in the air. People laughed. Mrs.

Johnson leaned closer and in a hoarse, furtive whisper said, "Simson, he's one of *those*."

Kearny reared back in amazement. "*No!*"

"Yes. A young fellow named Tommy Cannacova, lived upstairs in 319, he moved out the same time as Simson. They were awfully close. Of course I'm not *sure*, but . . ."

"This Simson, no forwarding on him?" asked O'B.

"Like I said, he stuck me with two weeks' rent. Of course I had a security deposit and all, but . . ."

"Cannacova?"

"He didn't move owing, but no forwar . . ." She interrupted herself. "Say, I do believe my boy Alfie used to deliver the morning paper to that Cannacova boy's mother when he had his route. She was remarried, had a different name, but . . ."

Alfie Johnson was a tow-headed thirteen, tall and rangy and betraying his youth by a still high-pitched voice and an Adam's apple that jumped nervously as he talked. He had the standard California public school mumble which swallowed so many word endings that it was almost a speech impediment. "Sure, uh, Tommy Cannacova, uh, sure . . ."

He couldn't remember the mother's remarried name, or the address, but after two Big Macs and half an hour of cruising the streets around Occidental College he pointed a youth-grimy finger. "That one. With the brown trim."

It was a small bungalow set back from the street behind a green postage stamp of lawn as meticulously barbered as a TV personality. The windows were down on the five-year-old Duster in the driveway, so Kearny reached in and flipped open the glove box for a long few moments. He slammed it shut and straightened.

"Paul and Zelma deSouza."

The front door opened and an overweight boy with braces on his teeth stood looking at them as they came up. "You from the finance company?"

"Just get your ma," said Kearny. The house was small enough for them to have to speak over the noise of a vacuum sweeper inside.

The fat boy disappeared. Kearny shook out a cigarette, offered the pack to O'B. They lit up. The vacuum stopped.

A very buxom woman wearing an apron came to the door. She had reddish hair and a face which was jolly the way a pig's face is jolly. The eyes were pig's eyes, also. O'B moved forward with his ready charm.

"We're from the Apartment House Protective Association," he said, coining a phrase. "We carry the fire and liability on the apartment complex on Avenue Fifty where your son Tommy was—"

"If they claim Tommy tore up that apartment..."

"Quite the opposite, Mrs. deSouza. When Tommy left there he apparently overlooked a substantial cashier's check, made out to CASH, in the dresser drawer. Mrs. Johnson held it the thirty days prescribed by law, then brought it to us. Naturally—"

"How much is it for?" she demanded quickly.

"Your son can tell us that to establish ownership."

"I can take it for him..."

"We can only give it to your son direct, after he gives us a Hold Harmless letter," rumbled Kearny, moving in. "Now, if we could just have his current residence address..."

It was not yet dark enough for headlights when O'B brought the LTD off the San Diego freeway at Wilshire and turned right into Veteran Avenue. They found a narrow concrete alley that started as an access road to a Bank of America drive-in window, then changed its mind to bisect a pocket of small, neat California ranch-styles at Fort Point Street. Houses from just after the war, getting a little seedy despite their aluminum sashes and sliding patio doors.

"With the double garage," said Kearny.

O'B stopped in front of the open overhead door. Inside was a jumble of old lawn furniture, a freezer and a busted trike, a power lathe and a jigsaw wearing naps of sawdust. A back-wall door was open to show a little barefoot girl teasing a scruffy puppy with long floppy ears. A woman in old-fashioned pedal-pushers, pushing forty in a crudely handsome way, came through the door. "It's Saturday, Hank is napping. You guys want a game, go—"

"Want Jeff Simson," said O'B.

She gestured indifferently out the open door past the little girl. "The bungalow out back." With the mileage showing in her eyes, Kearny wondered what sort of game Hank dealt. "You boys don't look the type."

"Closet," explained O'B.

"Simson's home, his roommate just left in tears a while ago. They had such a *spat*."

The bungalow was a frame building which probably had been bootlegged as a rental unit in the postwar days before tightened building codes. Shrubbery masked the windows, but lights went on inside just as they got to the door. Kearny knocked. It was jerked open and Simson stared out into the dusk. A long set of parallel fingernail scratches decorated his left cheek. "Tommy, if you think—"

"Hello, Jeff." Kearny pushed by him into the living room. It was obviously rented furnished, mostly to UCLA students.

"Hey, wha . . . oh. Mr. Kearny . . ."

O'B slid in behind Simson and shut the door and leaned back against it, thus becoming a jailer. Kearny paused in mid-room. "We want to talk with you, Jeff."

Simson was much straighter-looking, except for the clawed cheek, than when his sexual preference had still been in the closet. Or the bus depot men's room. "Talk about what? I want to warn you, I now am studying to be an attorney, so if you think—"

"An attorney? Terrif!" exclaimed Kearny warmly.

He walked over to the formica breakfast table, pulled out a tube-steel and plastic chair, and sat down. Simson was still on his feet, a wary look on his face. O'B walked by him and took a chair across from Kearny, who kicked back the chair between. Still wary, Simson very slowly lowered himself into it.

"If you're studying law," said Kearny, "you know the sort of trouble DKA could be in on this licensing flap."

"I understand the attorney general's boys have been around talking to you about it," said O'B.

"Me? N . . . Nobody's, uh . . . said anything about . . ." He essayed a watery smile. "Uh . . . what's it all about?"

Kearny told him with the economy of thousands of field reports written during three-plus decades in the manhunting game.

"Well, uh, yes, I *was* in the office that evening, but—"

"Who else?" demanded Kearny.

"Who . . . uh . . . Kathy. And . . . uh . . . the man. The subject."

O'Bannon was taking notes. He looked up, felt-tip in hand. "Pivarski?"

"Yes. Him."

"Just the three of you?" asked Kearny. "What about Kelly?"

Sweat sheened Simson's face. "She was in the outer office. On the switchboard."

"What did Pivarski say when he gave Kathy the money?"

"Say? How am I supposed to remember?"

"Cash? Money order? Personal check?"

"Cash. It was cash I took to the bank."

"Nothing unusual about the transaction, then," said O'B.

"Just a normal collection," agreed Simson eagerly.

Kearny nodded and beamed, as if entirely happy with Simson's answers. "Five minutes for you to say that at the hearing on Monday, Jeff, and that will be that. Our treat on expenses, of course."

"The hearing?" Consternation showed in his face. "But I can't testify at the—"

"Why not? What you've been telling us is your best recollection of the truth, isn't it?"

"Sure, but . . ." His words suddenly tumbled out very fast. "But I've got classes that day. I'll do anything I can to help you guys out, but I just can't miss my Monday classes."

"We can sure understand that, Jeff," said Kearny in sympathy. He snapped at O'B. "Give him a couple sheets of paper and that felt-tip, O'B. He can write up his statement in his own hand, just as he gave it to us, and sign it, and we'll be on our way."

"Hey, I didn't mean—"

O'Bannon had shoved pen and paper under his nose.

"In your own words," said Kearny, "just as you remember it."

Kearny's massive jaw was underlit by the red glow of the dashboard lighter he was bringing up to the tip of his cigarette. He turned right into Wilshire; his usual L.A. motel, the Del Capri, was a short mile away.

"He obviously never heard of that attorney letter Pivarski is supposed to have gotten Kathy to sign," said O'Bannon.

"Which explains why the State was around talking with him."

"I don't follow that."

"The State isn't going to want him testifying as to what's in this statement." Kearny patted his breast pocket. "Just a routine collection and all of that. I bet they told him to stay lost."

"Then why'd he give us the statement?"

"He's weak," said Kearny indifferently. "He was more scared of us, here now, than of the State last week. I sure hope Larry gets hold of Rose Kelly, and she has something to help us out." He laughed mirthlessly. "Can you imagine what a sharp attorney would do to this guy on cross-examination if anyone was hard-up enough to put him on the stand?"

Fourteen

Ballard woke on Sunday morning in a motel in Eureka on California's great northern redwood coast, population 24,337 and falling, due to the decline of the logging industry. He woke with somebody's used sweat sock in his mouth and all five fingers of his right hand rammed into somebody's monstrous gooey eye.

''*Help!*'' he yelled, jerking upright in bed.

Then he relaxed. The sweat sock was his tongue, courtesy of Jack Gunne, the listed reference in the Rose Kelly file. Gunne hadn't been at his Second Street address, which turned out to be a skid-row bar. Gunne was due back today. The gooey eye he was now licking off his fingers belonged to the Colonel: a lemon-whipped cream tart he had been too full to eat after downing the Colonel's Extra Crispy 5-piece Jumbo Dinner the night before.

Shaving, Ballard realized that he hated Eureka and had always hated Eureka. If it wasn't raining, it was foggy in Eureka. You had to drive through endless miles of endless redwoods dripping endless gallons of water down the back of your neck to get to Eureka. He contemplated the empty rumpled bed as he dressed, and wished Yana the gypsy queen were in it so he wouldn't have to face the Eureka Sunday morning coming down.

Coming down, he learned as he made a dash for the coffee shop, by the bucket. And still coming down as, around 10 A.M., Ballard ducked from his car to Gunne's run-down joint on Second Street. It was jammed with skid rogues of both sexes eagerly pulling at the hair of the dog. Gunne was a mild-mannered Englishman who wore a white shirt with a patent-leather snap-on bow tie, old-fashioned patent-leather hair and a Charlie Chaplin mustache.

"Haven't seen Rose for a month of Sundays, old boy. Had to eighty-six her last time she was in."

"Really?" Ballard shuddered as his first gulp of cold beer jumped up and down in his delicate stomach on the two over-easy from the motel coffee shop.

"Wonderful, jolly gal until she's had too many whiskeys. Then she's a holy terror. Must run close to two hundred and fifty pounds, you know."

Ballard remembered her then. Almost six feet tall and built like one of the Raiders' front four.

"Fred Burchard, he's your man. The Pavilion, Third and C."

Fred Burchard's Pavilion looked very much like a barn, and, Ballard thought as he stood inside the front door dripping on the floor, it smelled very much like one. The crowd was smaller but noisier than Gunne's, yappy as a dog fight, and Fred Burchard was drunk as the rest of them at a corner table in the rear. He was shamelessly cheating himself at solitaire as a couple of equally stewed cronies watched.

"Married? Rose? Hadn't heard that. What you want with her?"

"I want to sell her a tractor," said Ballard.

"Went back to farmin', did she?" He shouted across at the bar. "*George*." He turned back to Ballard. "George'll know where Rose is. He used to plow her field for her now and then." He dug a sudden elbow into Ballard's ribs and winked grotesquely.

George looked too drunk to know where he himself lived. Red suspenders with a black stripe down them held up his gray wool pants. He had a four-day beard, the shakes, and a breath to pickle specimens.

"Feller here wants to sell Rosie Kelly a tractor."

"Rosie don't need no tractor," shrieked George, "Rosie *is* a tractor."

He doubled up at his own wit, slapped his knee, and fell on the floor. He landed on his side in a fetal position, jerked his shoulder a couple of times like trying to pull up the covers, and started to snore. Burchard looked at him with a practiced, calculating eye. "Nope. He's gone off. You want Rosie, better come back . . ."

He stopped talking because he had lost his audience. Ballard had turned around and marched back out into the rain. Burchard stared after him a moment, then turned to his cronies.

"Abruptest goddam John Deere salesman *I* ever see," he said.

California 36 cut off 101 at Alton, twenty miles south of Eureka. The rain had become a cloudburst brisk enough to swamp Ballard's wipers as he pulled up in front of the Carlotta General Store. He ran through sheets of falling water to find the front door locked. Floundering through a calf-deep carpet of pine needles to the living quarters behind, he surprised a red Douglas squirrel on the back stoop. It gave a giant leap into a sodden thicket of huckleberry and was gone.

A stooped gray-haired man opened to Ballard's knock. Mild blue eyes watched the water from the eaves pour down Ballard's neck. "Roy Shelby? Sure. Stay on the blacktop here for another five miles or so, you'll run into a dozen shacks along the road. Ain't any of 'em been painted in a while, so you can tell Roy's cause it's got a new door."

There was no car in front of Roy Shelby's shack—three rooms and made of unpainted wood—and nobody answered Ballard's knock. Cutting across the sloping ground to the next shack through the wind-torn sheets of rain, Ballard slipped and landed on his butt and rolled all the way down to the next house in the mud. He felt like an old war-movie character as he cursed his way up to the front door.

A mid-twenties woman in a bathrobe and smelling of Herbal Essence shampoo answered his knock and listened to his tale about being a friend of Roy's and having a flat tire and . . . "Well . . . Roy, he's still driving for the lumber camp, you know. They're working today even though it's Sunday. You ask for my husband—that's Chuck Farber—you ask at the loading dock there, and he can tell you where Roy's working at."

The lumber camp was two more miles further in, on a dozen cleared acres deep in the redwoods. There was a sawdust burner with a screened stack to keep sparks in, and a sawing shed full of wet, rough logs. Chuck Farber was a massively-muscled man in a stained lumberjack shirt spattered with fresh wet sawdust, as if he'd been in a wind tunnel. "Roy's been havin' some personal troubles lately—"

"Not from me, he hasn't," said Ballard.

Farber bought his story. Yet another two miles down the road, past the gas station and the two-story hotel. Up the hill, and the first gravel road to the right. After the bridge a mile in, left.

Ballard took a good look at what the logging trucks had done to the muddy road down into the deep woods beyond the bridge, and decided to hike in from there. Within a few yards he was making tracks like Bigfoot because of the great mud boots his shoes had started wearing. *Damn* Dan Kearny, oh, just *damn* Dan Kearny.

When one of the huge, grumbling logging rigs came up the track by him, he yelled "Roy?" at the driver. The truck stopped. The driver said in a wary voice, "Who's asking?"

"I'm trying to get in touch with Rose. It's important."

"You come all the hell back in here to ask about *Rosie*?"

Ballard told his story and Shelby, a wiry black-haired man with quizzical eyes, loosened up considerably. "She married a wop this time around, name of Angelo Palermo. But are you sure you gotta see her in person? Mail gets delivered three times a week up to their place."

"Gotta see her."

"Okay, then there's two ways in. Either through Bridgeville—ten-twelve miles further down the road here—or all the way back up through Eureka to Arcata, and then in through Kneeland. You got four-wheel?"

Ballard shook his head.

"Then go in through Kneeland, cause it's mud all the way from Bridgeville. Last week you could of made it but we been gettin' some moisture these past few days."

"I hadn't noticed!" shouted Ballard above the roar of falling rain.

Fifteen

The hearing, scheduled for 10 A.M. on the second floor of the State Office Building at 400 Golden Gate, was postponed for an hour because the Hearing Officer had gotten stuck in heavy traffic on Interstate 80 from Sacramento. When Kearny, Giselle, Heslip and O'B did walk the three blocks from the office, they found Hec Tranquillini leaning against the wall outside the hearing room with his nose buried in a legal-size manila folder.

He looked up at them. "What do you have for me?"

"Simson's handwritten statement."

"In one sentence."

"See no evil, hear no evil, speak no evil," said Kearny.

"The letter?"

"Never heard of it."

"Good. We need every break we can get because the Hearing Officer, who's from the Consumer Affairs Bureau up in Sacramento, is somebody new. I don't know how good his law is, and I—"

"This just isn't fair!" burst in Giselle. "The accusation is made by the Bureau of Consumer Affairs, and the accusation is heard by the Bureau of Consumer Affairs. What sort of—"

"At this stage the State is treating it as a routine administrative matter.'' He laid a calming hand on her shoulder. ''Take it easy, nobody's laid a glove on us yet.''

''That *bastard!*'' exclaimed Kearny.

They followed his gaze to the hearing room door ten yards away. Johnny Delaney was just entering, attaché case in hand, accompanied by a short, stout mid-thirties man wearing a brown suit and a Western string tie and a tan shirt with Texas longhorns stitched into it. His clothes were wildly at odds with his thinning black curly hair and black goatee.

''Norbert Franks,'' said Kearny bitterly. ''After Hawkley—''

''I expected Franks,'' said Tranquillini. ''They'll use him to try and establish that letter Kathy is supposed to have signed. I'll take care of Franks.'' He tapped Simson's folded statement against Kearny's chest. ''This statement helps, but what we need is an eyewitness.''

''He says he and Kathy were alone in the office.''

''Just in case,'' said Heslip, ''I've been trying to run down the file clerk, Verna Rounds. Last address, New Orleans.''

''What about the switchboard? Wasn't some Irish girl—''

''Rose Kelly,'' said Giselle. ''Larry was supposed to get her statement over the weekend, but we haven't heard from him yet.''

Ballard had been a wise-ass, trying Bridgeville instead of Kneeland as Roy Shelby had instructed, and so had been stuck in the mud since 4 P.M. Sunday. When Giselle wondered aloud on Monday morning where he was, Ballard had covered some ten miles afoot from his car. Ten soggy miles, on toward Rose Kelly (now Palermo) instead of back toward Bridgeville, because he was sustained by the certain knowledge that next time he'd have a spade in the car to dig out with. A spade with which he already would have beaten Dan Kearny to death.

''You lost, mister?''

The voice jerked his head up. Hey. He'd reached the top of the hill and the rain had slacked off; he'd almost passed right by the narrow gravel track going off to the right between white plank fences toward a prosperous-looking farm with old-fashioned red barns. A diminutive middle-aged man with thick gray-shot curly hair was resting his forearms on the top rail of the fence.

"Are you Angelo Palermo?" asked Ballard.

"That's right."

"Then I'm not lost."

Rose Kelly-Palermo was mucking out the cow barn when Ballard came in. She was dressed in bib overalls and a Pendleton shirt. Her chin was fleshy and belligerent, her nose strong and hooked, her blue eyes quite mad. She threw aside her pitchfork at sight of him. "Larry Ballard!" She gathered him to her immense bosom, cantilevered out like a Frank Lloyd Wright roof. "C'mon up to the house for some breakfast. You too, you wop bastard," she added fondly to her husband.

Breakfast was impossibly bountiful, and Ballard ate everything in sight. After all, twenty-eight hours had passed since those coffee-shop eggs the previous morning. As he drank a fourth ambrosial cup of her coffee, and watched Palermo canonize her with his gaze, he decided old Rosie had to have something, all right.

"I'm surprised you found this place," said Rose. "I haven't exactly been leaving calling cards since my ex-, that Mick bastard, swore to shoot poor Angelo here." She turned from the stove where yet more bacon sizzled. "Now I'm wondering why you bothered."

Ballard told her. Rose was indignant. "Jesus, last *November?* You realize how long ago that was? I didn't even know this wop bastard yet." She tousled the graying curls. "Picked him up in a motel bar just down the road from the place in Santa Rosa."

"Yana, next door to that place, gave me the lead to your brother."

She put aside the bacon to drain. "Poor Yana. Married to a real mean gyppo bastard. She saw in her crystal ball I was going to meet Angelo—"

"Married?" Ballard's hopes, barely articulated, fell.

"Since she was about twelve or some damned thing." She dropped into the chair across from Ballard's. "Anyway, I don't remember any bohunk bastard named Pivarski."

"Irene Jordon says you were on the switchboard that day."

"If Irene says I was working, then . . . *wait a minute!*" She slammed an open palm on the table, making Ballard's empty plate jump a foot in the air and overturn in his lap. He grabbed his cup of precious coffee in mid-bounce. Rose was already at the sideboard, rummaging in her purse. "November. Early Novem . . . YEAH!"

She waved a flat packet of birth-control pills in triumph, and stabbed a fat red finger at the prescription label.

"Sure, I've got it now. I had my checkup that Friday, because my prescription had run out. So I wasn't on the switchboard after all for that extra hour."

"Who would have been?"

"The spade chick, I guess. Verna Rounds. Kathy would have kept her late to fill in."

The hearing room was like a miniature courtroom, with a raised desk to serve as a bench for the Hearing Officer, a witness chair, a smaller table below for the court reporter—a colorless man with horn-rims who was just opening his transcription machine—two counsel tables and a dozen chairs for spectators.

The Hearing Officer himself was a not very judicial-looking thirty, but Tranquillini liked his crisp, decisive delivery: it would give clear-cut specifics later if he had to appeal. "We will open the record and come to order. This is a hearing before the Director of Professional and Vocational Standards, Consumer Affairs Bureau, State of California. We are here in the matter of the Accusation against Daniel Kearny Associates, Inc. Note the appearances of John E. Delaney, Deputy Attorney General, representing the Complainant, and Attorney-at-Law Hector C. Tranquillini for Respondent-Corporation. Inasmuch as this is an Accusation, the burden of proof is upon the Complainant."

Delaney began. Tranquillini seemed at first disinterested. "We will submit at this time the moving papers, already examined by the Respondent," said Delaney. "They consist of the Accusation, Statement to Respondent, Statement of Service by Certified Mail, a signed copy of the Notice of Defense, a Notice of Hearing, and a Statement by Certified Mail of the Notice of Hearing."

"These will be received as the pleadings," said the Hearing Officer, "not as evidence. They will be marked Exhibit A."

Delaney cleared his throat. "We would like to bring to the attention of this hearing two facts which we feel materially affect the nature of these proceedings."

"This is material not contained in the submitted documents?"

"That is right, Your Honor."

Tranquillini shifted on his chair like a fighter on his stool before the bell for round one. What the hell was this? He waved an arm in airy dismissal. "No objection."

"Proceed."

"Over the weekend, Respondent Corporation has paid, by check, the sum of $226.30 plus costs and interest to Kasimir Pivarski through his attorney, Mr. Norbert Franks, here present. Respondent Corporation also paid Mr. Franks' legal fees for his representation of Mr. Pivarski."

"Noted," said the Hearing Officer, looking puzzled.

Delaney cleared his throat again. "The State feels, Your Honor, that these payments constitute *prima facie* evidence of guilt on the part of the Respondent Corporation."

Tranquillini's face had gone very white and he had gotten entirely still. Back in the spectator section, Giselle whispered to Kearny, "Dan, does that mean what I think it does?"

"Yeah. Delaney suckered us into making a payment which he now claims is an admission of guilt because we made it."

Tranquillini said, "We wish the record to reflect, Your Honor, that Respondent acted under advice of counsel. Respondent was not competent to understand the legal ramifications such payments might entail." He turned to Delaney and said, very distinctly, "You shouldn't have done that, boyo."

"What was that?" demanded the astounded Hearing Officer.

But Tranquillini had sat down. After staring at him hard for several seconds, the Hearing Officer turned to Delaney. "Proceed with your presentation, Mr. Delaney."

"Your Honor, the State feels that these payments have altered the circumstances of this case, and that judgment should be rendered against Respondent Corporation at this time."

"Is that a motion?"

"Yes, Your Honor."

"Noted and denied. Proceed."

The State's first witness was Norbert Franks. He was sworn and qualified as an attorney. Tranquillini stipulated to his qualifications and Delaney started his presentation. "Now, I understand that you filed an action against Daniel Kearny Associates on behalf of Kasimir Pivarski. What was the nature of that action?"

"Preliminarily, to resolve whether a Complaint filed by Daniel Kearny was a valid Complaint. Secondarily, to prevent further attachment of Mr. Pivarski's wages. Finally, to endeavor to recover certain monies received by Daniel Kearny from Mr. Pivarski."

"I see. Previous to the attachment of Mr. Pivarski's wages by the Respondent, had he come to your office?"

"He had."

"And what was the purpose of his visit?"

"He wanted our office to examine the documents that were filed against him by Daniel Kearny, to see what recourse could be had. I determined that a demurrer to the Complaint would apply, and therefore filed one."

Delaney was pacing, nodding as if given great enlightenment. "Yes. I see. I see." He stopped abruptly. "And did you tell Mr. Pivarski that he had a meritorious defense against Daniel Kearny?"

"Objection."

Delaney looked at Tranquillini with apparently genuine surprise. "*Objection?*" His voice made the word unthinkable.

"Of course the witness is going to advise his client that the suit he plans to file is a meritorious one. That doesn't make it so."

"Mr. Hearing Officer," said Delaney in a pained voice, "I wish to draw from this witness what he advised his client to do just before that client went to Kearny's office. This will bear *directly* on what Mr. Pivarski had in mind when he talked with the Respondent."

"An attorney has a conversation with his client," said Tranquillini, "and after the conversation the client goes somewhere and does something. What is important is what he did, not what his attorney told him to do. I think my objection is good."

The Hearing Officer said coldly, "You will proceed, Mr. Delaney. There is no question pending."

Tranquillini shrugged and sat down. Delaney went on. "Do you recall the date that conversation with Mr. Pivarski took place?"

"There were two or three conversations preliminarily. In the initial interview, my client told me—"

"I will object to any conversation that has no direct bearing upon the actual crux of this case."

The Hearing Officer said, "Mr. Franks, please limit your answer to any conversations between yourself and Mr. Pivarski just prior to his visit to Respondent's office."

"Well, of course, that visit took place on November fifth of last year. But the demurrer to the Kearny complaint had been filed on October eighteenth, and on November twelfth that demurrer was sustained without leave to amend because opposing counsel did not appear. I notified . . ."

He paused because Tranquillini had suddenly leaned forward to begin a furious scribbling of notes. Franks shot a look at Delaney for support, who said in a syrupy voice, "November fifth only, Mr. Franks."

Tranquillini was still scribbling. When he finally straightened up, the Hearing Officer looked at the watch laid out on the bench, and called the noon recess.

Sixteen

It was not a buoyant lunch, even though the Rathskeller's knockwurst and sauerkraut and steins of rich heavy dark beer were up to the usual standard. One trouble was Tranquillini: he was so sore he could hardly eat. "Oh, I imagine that zinger Delaney tried about our payment to Pivarski originated with Greenly up at the Licensing Bureau," he said. "But I'm still going to burn his butt for it."

"Did he really think he could make it stick?" asked Giselle.

"I doubt it. Even if DKA admitted outright that they owed Pivarski the money, that would not be an admission of any impropriety. I imagine he hoped to influence the Hearing Officer's mind subconsciously against us."

"That explains Delaney," said Kearny. "But why would Greenly suggest it in the first place?"

"Padilla Drayage?" O'Bannon, slaking his usual massive thirst, was on his third stein of beer to everyone else's first.

"The thought has to cross your mind," said Tranquillini.

"No," said Kearny around a mouthful of potato pancake. "The big boys from the East who are behind Padilla Drayage owe me, personally, a favor. A big one."

"Such as?"

He looked at the others and sighed. It was time. "Remember the Chandra case a couple of years back?"

Tranquillini spooned dark mustard onto his plate. "I wasn't your attorney then, but sure, I recall it."

"A guy named Phil Fazzino, the local Mafia honcho, had killed his own superior to take his place, and then killed an old dance teacher named Chandra because she overheard the hit being planned."

"Frank Padilla was who got it." Heslip added almost dreamily, "Remember that scam we ran on his widow, Giselle?"

"Black is diz-guz-ting," she said.

"But there wasn't any *proof* Fazzino had hit Chandra," said Kearny. "Nothing a cop could use to convince a D.A. or a D.A. could use to convict in front of a jury."

"So Fazzino went free," said Giselle in a bitter voice.

"Only he didn't." The tone of Kearny's voice told them what he meant. "Yeah. I pulled the plug on Fazzino and his wife Wendy to the mob. Told their local attorney, Wayne Hawkley, all about it. They didn't need proof. Whether they ever caught up with Fazzino . . ."

"They owe you," Tranquillini agreed crisply. "No wonder you accepted that Hawkley wasn't behind the State's move."

"Yet it's his nephew—a member of his law firm—who's nailing our tails to the wall of that hearing room."

Tranquillini gave his sudden cocky laugh. "All the odds haven't been posted on that race yet."

"You mean we aren't doing as bad as I think we're doing?" asked Giselle. "This afternoon they'll bring up that letter, and—"

"And we can't stop them." lamented O'Bannon from behind his fifth tankard of strong waters.

"We don't plan to stop them," said Tranquillini. He looked at his watch and got to his feet. "We let them get it in as *hearsay*."

They started up the stairs toward the street level.

"I guess I'm dumb," said Heslip, "but even as hearsay, isn't that going to hurt us?"

"Sure. But we can't keep it out. And we have a hearsay

of our own that *they* won't be able to keep out once theirs is in."

"Simson's deposition?"

As Tranquillini nodded, the headwaiter called after them, "Phone call for you, Mr. Kearny. A Mr. Ballard."

"*Now* you're talking!" exclaimed Tranquillini. "Get me an eyeball from our side of the fence to back up Simson's deposition, and if they try what I think they will with that letter, we'll knock them right out of the park."

The court reporter's fingers moved over the keys of his machine like hooked pale ghosts as the Hearing Officer said, "Mr. Franks was on the stand. He already had been sworn." As Franks moved forward, Kearny bent over Tranquillini's head at the counsel's table. "Ballard's been in a ditch in the boondocks for the past twenty-four hours," Kearny whispered, "but he found out Rose Kelly *wasn't* on the switchboard that day. Verna Rounds probably was."

Tranquillini tapped his lined yellow legal pad with his felt-tip pen for a few seconds, scowling. "Dammit. Okay. Get Bart Heslip on a plane to New Orleans."

"He's already on his way over to Oakland to talk with the girl's mother. Then he'll fly out to New Orleans direct."

"If counsel please—"

"Sorry, Your Honor," said Tranquillini. "Ready for the Respondent."

Delaney started in again. "You were about to testify concerning the events of November fifth, last year."

"Yes, sir. I had spoken with Miss Onoda previously to arrange for Mr. Pivarski to go to the Kearny office between five-thirty and six o'clock on that day. I prepared a letter for him to take, along with the two hundred dollars, to Daniel Kearny Associates. He was to present it to them for signature at the same time he tendered the money to be held in trust until—"

"Objection."

"Sustained."

"Sorry, Your Honor. Mr. Franks, tell us about the letter."

"I told my client to surrender the two hundred dollars

only if Miss Onoda would sign the original of the letter, which he then was to return to me. Here is a copy of that letter."

With a dramatic flourish, he presented Delaney with a piece of paper from the thin attaché case he had been holding on his lap. Delaney turned to the Hearing Officer. "At this time, we would like to present in evidence—"

"Objection," said Tranquillini. "My client tells me he has no information with respect to this letter, that he never saw it and no one in his office has ever called it to his attention. As you know, Miss Onoda is deceased. My client has no way of knowing if any signature on that letter is Miss Onoda's or not. I will object to its introduction unless Mr. Pivarski is here to testify that he delivered it, and to whom."

The Hearing Officer stared at Tranquillini for a long moment, as if the feisty little attorney were half a worm in his half-eaten apple. Then, with a sigh, he leaned toward the witness stand. "Mr. Franks, do you have any information as to whether this letter actually was given to anybody at Kearny Associates?"

"Yes, I do."

"On what is your information based?"

"On what was reported to me by Mr. Pivarski subsequent to his visit to Kearny Associates."

The Hearing Officer sat back and drummed his fingers on the desk. He looked over at Delaney. "Is Mr. Pivarski here present?"

"He is not, Your Honor," said Delaney in an aggrieved tone, "nor will he be. He is not a party to this action, which is a purely disciplinary charge brought by the State against the Respondent. We submit this letter as our Exhibit next in order."

"My objection is on record," said Tranquillini.

"The objection is sustained at this point," said the Hearing Officer. "I'll mark the document as Exhibit B for Identification only."

Delaney began, "But Your Honor—"

"If it is later established by direct testimony that this

letter was indeed delivered to the Respondent's office, then it will be accepted in evidence at that time. All we have in the record so far is hearsay, and I cannot base findings on hearsay."

There was a strangled silence while Delaney tried to figure out a new way to get the letter in as evidence rather than as a mere Identification Exhibit. He finally stepped forward again.

"Mr. Franks, you have testified that before Pivarski left your office, you discussed with him the *conditions* under which he was to pay over this two hundred dollars." He cast a look at Tranquillini. "*That* fact is not in dispute, I take it. Now, then, what exactly was your advice to your client along these lines?"

"That the money would be paid to Miss Onoda to be held by Kearny Associates until the determination of the demurrer seven days later, on the twelfth. In the meantime, Kearny would not further attach wages and cause Mr. Pivarski to lose his job."

Tranquillini stirred. "We're right back where we started from, Your Honor. This is not direct evidence of what actually happened, yet this is the crux of the case against my client."

"The Hearing Officer notes, for the record, that any conversation this witness had with Mr. Pivarski when no representative of the Respondent was present is clearly hearsay."

Delaney was unable to control himself when he heard this door too being slammed in his face. "Well, it's *not* hearsay, Mr. Hearing Officer! It may not be direct evidence on the issues, but it's certainly not hearsay. The witness is reciting his own conversation."

"With a third party," said Tranquillini.

"That's not hearsay."

"In my book it is," said the Hearing Officer. "Proceed."

"The witness is reciting what he himself said," Delaney persisted almost desperately.

"I have made my ruling, counsel. It will be received as hearsay in the record."

The remainder of Franks' direct testimony was put on the record merely for form; Delaney's heart was not in it. The court hearing Franks' demurrer on November 12 had entered judgment in Pivarski's favor. Franks had then filed suit against DKA for $226.30—the $200 paid Kathy Onoda, plus the $26.30 collected by the sheriff under Kearny's original attachment. On February 18 the court had entered judgment in favor of Pivarski for the amount asked, plus interest and costs.

"And since February eighteenth, despite numerous demands made upon Respondent by you, the money has not been paid back as ordered by the court. Is that correct?"

"Until this morning's mail," said Franks.

"That is all, counselor. You may step down."

But Tranquillini was on his feet as Franks started to rise. "I have a few questions *on voir dire*."

Franks slowly sank back into the witness chair. Tranquillini leaned an elbow on the witness stand and from less than two feet away stared at the other attorney. Franks began to fidget and look away and clear his throat and, finally, took a handkerchief out of his pocket and mopped his face. Tranquillini stepped back abruptly when, from the corner of his eye, he saw Delaney starting to his feet to make an objection.

"You said on direct testimony, Mr. Franks, that you instructed Mr. Pivarski to get Miss Onoda's signature on the letter. Did he also get a receipt?"

Franks cleared his throat. "I have no knowledge of such."

Tranquillini laid a copy of Kathy Onoda's receipt to Pivarski on the Hearing Officer's desk. "Respondent wishes at this time to introduce his Exhibit A, a copy of the DKA receipt to Mr. Pivarski on the day in question."

"*Objection!*" burst out Delaney. "This—"

"The Hearing Officer will note that this receipt plainly states 'Two hundred dollars received on account from K. Pivarski, November fifth, 5:48 P.M.' Nothing about money held in trust or—"

"This is purely hearsay evidence!" cried Delaney with an apoplectic face. "Mr. Franks has no way of knowing—"

"Pivarski does," said Tranquillini.

"The State has no intention of producing Mr. Pivarski."

Tranquillini paused. For the first time he realized that Delaney's reluctance to produce Kasimir Pivarski went beyond a desire to avoid putting a witness on the stand who would be thoroughly mauled by opposing counsel. He needed time to think about that reluctance. This was not the time to push it. He shrugged eloquently.

"Respondent amends the submission to Respondent Information Exhibit A, with the request that this exhibit be put in evidence if direct testimony so indicates at a later time."

"Noted."

In turning back toward Franks, as if it were an afterthought, Tranquillini picked up two Xerox copies of Simson's affidavit, and dropped one on Delaney's table and slid the other across the bench to the Hearing Officer. "Respondent also wishes at this time to present Respondent's Exhibit B, a holographic, signed, and witnessed deposition by a witness, Jeffrey L. Simson, as to events on the day in question."

"How did you find . . ." Then Delaney, scanning the affidavit, yelled, "*Objection*, Your Honor! This is not only a purely hearsay document, it is presented out of order—"

"We are not a formal court here," said Tranquillini blandly. His spur of the moment idea was working, by God. "As you pointed out this morning, this is a disciplinary action, not a trial."

The Hearing Officer looked up from the document. "That's all very well, counselor, but this *is* being presented out of order. Why wasn't it among the Respondent's documents presented to and filed with the Bureau of Private Investigators and Adjusters last week, preliminary to this hearing?"

"If you will note the date, Your Honor, this document was not obtained until this past weekend."

Tranquillini glanced over at Delaney, expecting an objection, but there was none. Instead, he looked almost pleased. Which wasn't right or reassuring. Something more to worry about after the session was finished.

"This is obviously a hearsay document, not connected up at this time," said the Hearing Officer. "However, since I already have admitted two other hearsay documents and a good deal of hearsay evidence, I will accept this as Respondent Information Exhibit B. Please proceed."

Tranquillini had, for the first time, been examining his copy of the letter Pivarski was supposed to have given to Kathy Onoda.

> This is to acknowledge receipt of Two Hundred and no/100 Dollars to be held by you on behalf of the account of Kasimir M. Pivarski. In return for this payment you have promised not to attach the wages of Mr. Pivarski at this time. Your signature on this letter will constitute a receipt for the Two Hundred and no/100 Dollars.

He read it again, stared at it, unable to believe what was there. Or rather, what wasn't there. He turned to the waiting Franks.

"Counselor, would you tell this hearing whether there is a space at the bottom of this letter where Miss Onoda was to sign on behalf of Daniel Kearny Associates?"

"Well, yes, but . . ."

"I see no such signature there, yet this purports to be a true copy of the original letter, does it not?"

Delaney was on his feet, his face scornful. "Objection, Your Honor. Obviously, this is merely a Xerox copy of Mr. Franks's office carbon of the letter. If counsel insists on Mr. Franks producing the original with Miss Onoda's signature, it will delay proceedings considerably and . . ."

Tranquillini went after Franks before the Hearing Officer could rule on the objection. "The original letter with Miss Onoda's signature, offered as an exhibit, would have been direct rather than hearsay evidence, would it not, Mr. Franks?"

"Objection," said Delaney again, quickly, realizing his witness was in trouble. "Calling for a conclusion from the witness."

"Witness has been qualified as an attorney-at-law."

"Even so," said the Hearing Officer, "I must sustain."

"As you wish, Your Honor." To Franks, Tranquillini said, "Why didn't you give the original letter with Miss Onoda's signature on it to the State for submission into evidence?"

Delaney started up to object, then, frowning, sank back again. Franks was silent for so long the Hearing Officer said, "The witness may answer."

"Uh . . . I don't have the original."

"Then Mr. Pivarski still has it."

"I . . . don't know."

Now? Tranquillini asked himself; then rejected it. No. Not yet. Instead, he veered sharply in his attack. "You have testified that opposing counsel was not present at the hearing of your demurrer on November twelfth of last year—a hearing at which judgment was rendered in favor of your client."

"That is correct."

"Prior to that hearing, you of course served Respondent with the necessary notice?"

"My office served Respondent's attorney. I didn't personally wait around in a doorway to—"

"Quite," said Tranquillini drily. He turned. "Your Honor, at this time I wish to be sworn so I can testify under oath that no such notice was ever received by my office."

Franks said, very quickly, "We didn't serve *you*, counselor. We served a Mr. James."

"I have been attorney-of-record for Respondent Corporation for the past twenty-two months. Mr. James has not represented Kearny Associates for nearly five years."

There was a moment of uneasy silence. No one doubted that Franks had known he was serving an attorney who would not pass on the service to Kearny or to Tranquillini, and that thus Franks would win his case by default. As he had. And now was the time to push again. Tranquillini turned to the Hearing Officer. "I once again, at this time, request on behalf of the Respondent that Mr. Pivarski be brought into this court, under subpoena if necessary, to testify as to the events of that day in November."

The Hearing Officer nodded. "Noted," he said. "I feel this hearing should be adjourned until Wednesday morning at ten o'clock, at which time the Hearing Officer will have had a chance to study this question of Mr. Pivarski's possible appearance. Frankly, at the moment all I have before me is hearsay evidence."

Tranquillini, starting to stuff papers into his attaché case, did not bother to lower his voice as he said to Delaney at the next table. "Your witness is lying his ass off, Johnny-me-bhoy. The question remains—why?"

Seventeen

"Sign here," said the uniformed property clerk.

"Yessir," said Sammy Rounds. He didn't add any smart-ass remarks, either. His night and day in a holding cell had scared all that jive right out of him. He could write little else but his name, but he wrote that gladly, and gladly submitted to the embrace of those massive mammy arms which went around him as he emerged from the meshed enclosure.

"Samuel . . ." said the fat black woman.

He was even crying and not caring until, among the indifferent loungers in the basement of the Oakland Municipal Building, he saw a face which was not indifferent.

He pulled away. "Whut he doin' here?"

The fat frantic black woman in the cheap cotton dress and black cloth coat turned to look, still snuffling, one pudgy hand still clutching her son's arm as if afraid he might be ripped away. "Wasn't for Mr. Heslip, you'd still be in there."

Sammy snuffled defiantly. "Don't need no he'p."

Heslip got them up the stairs and out to the car and drove them home. It had taken him a number of hours to find out Sammy had been busted during a drug-store burglary the night before, locate Mrs. Rounds trying to make her quasi-hysterical way through the legal complexities of getting her fourteen-year-old son out of city jail after he'd convinced the authorities he was eighteen.

"Samuel," the fat woman exclaimed as they came through the door of the run-down frame house, "you go straight to your room and get down on your knees and give thanks to God that you are home."

"Aw, ma—"

"I don't need no sauce from you, boy. *Now!*"

Sammy *now*ed. Her powers had miraculously returned as she had entered home territory, and Sammy knew that tone of voice and that glint in those usually loving brown eyes. He *now*ed. As she stared down the hallway after him, big tears started running down her cheeks. "Whut'm I gonna do?" she moaned. "Ain't got no man to set him straight. The street's gonna get him, same as Verna. Once we was a family. . ." She heaved a vast sigh. "That boy's fourteen, can't barely read, can't write much 'cept his name."

"At least he's out of jail," said Heslip the pragmatist. What the hell, it was a start, wasn't it?

She looked at him with shrewd eyes, and then led the way to the kitchen. "Thanks to you. And now de note comes due, don't it?"

Heslip sat at the battered wooden table as Emmalina Rounds brought over steaming cups of coffee. Ham hocks and lima beans simmered on a back burner of the aged gas stove. Ghetto smells familiar to him from his childhood. He leaned forward to lay his DKA I.D. on the table. "I'm from Daniel Kearny Associates. Where Verna used to work? We're in trouble with the State and we need Verna's help."

Her mouth set in a tight line. "Whut a little nigger girl—"

"Hey, I'm on your side, okay?" He pocketed his I.D. "I didn't turn her into a prostitute."

"You know 'bout that?"

He drank his coffee. It was thick, and rich with chicory of all things. God, he hadn't had chicory coffee in nearly ten years, since his mother had died. Emmalina was wiping her eyes. "I'd hoped that job'd be Verna's chance. That Japanese woman she worked for, Verna liked her jus' fine. But—"

"She's dead now," said Heslip. "That's why we need Verna."

"Dead?" She was shocked.

"Of a blood clot at the age of twenty-nine." He felt a sympathetic tightness in his own chest. "Died in her sleep." He paused for a moment. "Do you know where Verna is, Mrs. Rounds?"

She stared at him from deep-set eyes infinitely sad; the bones of her face were somehow starkly apparent despite the heavy overlay of flesh. "Verna ain't anywhere you can reach her." She leaned forward with a shocking swiftness to hiss, "*Dope*." With a vast effort she added, "Heroin," and then burst out, "Whut'm I gonna do?"

Hope she dies young, Heslip thought. A black junkie whore had maybe as little future as anyone except a terminal cancer patient could have. A Big Ben alarm clock on the refrigerator ticked away the seconds as Emmalina Rounds took the cups over to the stove for a refill. She returned to carefully lower her yardwide bottom into her chair. She sighed as if she'd heard his silent reply.

"All I really know is that she was with a pimp name of Johnny Mack Brown, who was workin her out of some motel—"

"The Bide-A-Wee on MacArthur. She left almost a year ago."

"Come home cryin for money . . ." Her right hand unconsciously massaged the inside of her left elbow. "Like somebody had hit her in the arm. But the bruise couldn't hide them needle marks." She heaved a shuddery sigh. "Stole my purse when she lef', her own mother's purse who raised her in fear of de Lord . . ."

Heslip stood up and finished his coffee on his feet. "I have to catch a plane for New Orleans, Mrs. Rounds. Your daughter was there in January, looking for someone. Do you know—"

"New Orleans?" Her face was confused. "Lookin' for someone? That's where her daddy lef' me, most fifteen years ago when Verna was 'bout five and I was big with Samuel . . ."

Involuntarily, looking down at her own vast bulk, she burst into full-throated, indomitable laughter. Heslip, writing Corinne's name on the back of his business card, had to join in. "I don't know where I'll be staying, but this woman at this phone will always be able to reach me." He handed her the card. "Anything you can find out about your ex-husband would help, because he's probably who she went looking for. He can probably tell me where she is, if he's still in New Orleans."

Ballard was still in Santa Rosa, where he had no business being, and in a steaming tub which had turned him lobster red, where he'd been for over an hour. He'd decided his night in the ditch had earned him a night of recuperation at a motel with a forty-foot sign outside. The fact that the motel happened to be a few hundred yards down the Redwood Highway from Madame Aquarra's fortune-telling scam was nobody's business, certainly not Kearny's.

"Dammit, Larry," Kearny burst out when Ballard rang the DKA San Francisco number which didn't go through the switchboard, "where in the devil are you?"

"Santa Rosa. I'll be in first thing tomorrow morning."

"How sure is Rose Kelly that she wasn't on the switchboard?"

"I saw her packet of birth-control pills myself. Dated November fifth. If she missed work for the doctor's appointment, she wouldn't be apt to mistake the time of the appointment. Why?"

"Jeff Simson says she was on the switchboard that night."

"If their stories don't agree, my money is on Rosie."

He hung up and tried to talk himself out of what he knew damn well he was going to do. Married to a mean gyppo bastard, Rose Kelly had said. But God! Those eyes! That mouth! Beautiful and sad, and who could resist a combination like that? Not Ballard.

He got out of the tub and got dressed and drove the five blocks to Madame Aquarra's. The place looked shut up tight, but when he touched the bell a gypsy woman as sleek as an otter opened the door. She was gaudy in a parrot's reds, yellows, blues, and greens—and jangled as she moved. A mustache downed her upper lip. Oily black hair coiled in heavy braids around her head.

"Madame Aquarra knows all."

The mother-in-law, obviously. And beside her a massive mongrel about the size and apparent temperament of the Hound of the Baskervilles in that Christopher Lee movie that popped up on Creature Feature every once in a while. Ballard built an instant role. "We've been getting beefs about fortune-telling being done without a license at this address."

She didn't ask who "we" was: his suit, his stance, his dark car with the long aerial all spelled cop. Her eyes went flat and uncomprehending and her Romany accent thickened to near unintelligibility. The dog at her side growled softly. "But ve haff been doing noddinks dat—"

"Complaints are against a..." Ballard turned to read from a blank page of his pocket notebook by the dim streetlight. "Female gypsy in her early twenties who—"

"Dere iss no vun here by dat description."

The door started to shut, but Ballard thrust out his jaw and one foot. The jaw stopped her, the foot stopped the door. The dog gave a vicious snarl, but Ballard's voice crackled with ice. "Trot her out here, lady, or I'll make this mitt camp so sick it'll need an iron lung to stay alive."

He turned and swaggered down the steps to stand with his back to the place, hands shoved deep into his suitcoat pockets in a cop's stance of habitual arrogance. Yana's voice spoke behind him with practiced hesitancy. "Officer, my mother-in-law tells me I have broken the law..."

He turned. "Hello, Yana."

"You must be crazy!" she exclaimed in recognition. "Do you know what will happen if—"

"If your husband comes out? I'm a cop interrogating a suspect."

"My husband and father-in-law are traveling with the carnival now. But *that* one..." She made a gesture toward the house. It was a despairing and forlorn gesture. At the same time, she brushed up against him. "You are now threatening to take me down to the station. I am trying to excite you with the promise of what I might give you."

Ballard put his hands on her shoulders and thrust her away. Her flesh was arousing under his fingers. "You really think she's watching?"

"She is watching."

"Can you get away for a while?"

"You think I am easy because I am a gypsy?" she asked coldly.

"A drink. A drive. A movie. A hamburger. A pizza," he said irritably. "How the hell do I know?"

"You must take me with you, then." She made pleading gestures. Ballard shook his head. She moved in to lay a suggestive hand on his chest. "I will go in and tell her you are taking me away, but that I will try to seduce you enough on the way so I will not be arrested or booked."

Ballard jabbed a dictatorial finger at the house. Yana dropped her hands in resignation and, head lowered, retreated sadly back up the stairs. Ballard made a tough-guy silhouette again and wondered if six gypsies would come bursting out to hold him down while the Hound of the Baskervilles bit his balls off. But Yana returned.

He shoved her unceremoniously into the Cutlass, thankful for the police-like CB antenna and the car's plain dark color. He drove half a block without lights so the rear plate wouldn't be illuminated in case the mother-in-law wanted to get his license number.

"Where to?" he asked, braced for more defensiveness. But she laughed deep down in her throat and stretched her arms high above her head to emphasize a marvelous bustline.

"Why, your motel room, of course," she said.

Why, ah . . . of course. Oh Ballard, you devil you!

Eighteen

Benny Nicoletti looked like a good pro linebacker gone to seed. He sounded like your Aunt Ethel getting ready to faint over a mouse. Only the eyes said cop. His 230 pounds overflowed Kearny's client chair. It was Tuesday morning and Kearny was not at all happy to find him on the doorstep. He said in total delight, "Congrats on the promotion, Benny, and what the hell do you want?"

"Can't an old friend drop around to say howdy?" asked Nicoletti in his reedy voice.

"When he's just been put in charge of the Police Intelligence Unit? No."

To Kearny's surprise, Nicoletti looked almost embarrassed. "Do you owe me any favors, Dan?"

Kearny said nothing. Nicoletti sighed and drew himself erect. He had a cop's slightly seedy hardness, not so much of conditioning as of having dished it out and taken it for a couple of decades.

"I didn't think so. But I need one."

Kearny pushed Giselle's intercom button, then realized it was the first time he'd thought of that signal as Giselle's instead of Kathy's. "Could you bring down some coffee for the three of us?"

"On the way, Dan'l."

Her voice sounded sprightly. Kathy had begun her inevitable fade from everyone's consciousness. Nicoletti grunted to his feet when Giselle entered with an insulated pot and three plastic cups. "When are we off for that weekend together, babe?"

"When you hadn't gotten married to a wonderful woman and had those four great kids."

He shook his head sadly and sat down to sip his coffee. "It's my middle-aged charm." He slapped his belly. It sounded like a board being struck. "And this ten pounds I picked up since I ain't got time for handball any more." He sipped and sighed. "Now your witness is here, Dan, you ready to go?"

Kearny feathered smoke, unembarrassed. "I start to get wary when you bureaucrats show up."

"Bureaucrats!" Nicoletti snorted. "And the hell of it is, you're right. Anyway, remember that Mex dude got blown away down on Fisherman's Wharf last November fifth?"

"Everything that happened that particular day is engraved on my brain," said Kearny. "Yeah, I remember. Espinosa, was it?"

"That's him. Adán Espinosa. This coffee's pretty good."

"Larry kicked up such a fuss about the instant that we got a Mr. Coffee," said Giselle.

"His real name wasn't Espinosa." Nicoletti's specialty was mob activity in California. "He was actually Phil Fazzino."

Fazzino! Kearny felt as if he'd been kicked in the stomach. The man he'd fingered to Hawkley two years before. He said, with a poker face, "Good old Flip?"

"Good old Flip. Coroner tells me he was an easy autopsy."

Giselle almost choked. Abstract approval of Kearny's phone call to Hawkley was one thing; somebody being an easy autopsy because he'd been blown all over the front of a motel dresser was something else. She said, "Why was it kept out of the papers?"

"It wasn't easy. But we had witnesses. A woman, a kid, a linen-truck driver who started running the same afternoon. He had to know something, because he didn't even stop to deliver his towels. We caught up with him when he phoned his wife from Canada on her birthday. The kid didn't see the killer, just his car. The woman just saw the corpse and lost her lunch. So we needed the driver." He reached for the coffee pot. "This guy, he's a survivor, he wants to keep on living. So we had to pry him open."

"How?" asked Kearny.

"Yeah, well, we're a little ashamed of that." Nicoletti sounded as ashamed as a cardinal at a canonization. "We told him we were putting six uniform people, four shifts around the clock, on his wife and kids. They don't go to the bathroom, one of our people is holding their hand, get it?"

"No," said Giselle. Kearny was silent. He got it.

"Then we told him that we'd let drop on the street how he was fingering the Espinosa hit man, and then we'd pull the protection and give odds on how long his family lasted."

"You *should* be ashamed!" burst out Giselle.

"Yeah, well, it opened him up. What he seen was somebody he knew. The triggerman. Well, didn't really know. By sight at the union hall, like that. You're in paying your dues, you see a guy around. But the big thing is, we got a face he can recognize."

"So he went through the mug books and—"

"No way," said Nicoletti, "this one is under the hat because, way we figure it, we nail down the hit man he's gonna have to start trading—otherwise he's got himself a death penalty without the jury leaving the box, and they ain't gonna keep stalling executions in California forever. So we got a list of all the members of the Teamsters local our linen-truck driver belongs to, and had DMV pull all their driver's license photos, and we copied 'em and couriered 'em up to Canada. And our witness come up with a make."

Kearny saw it first. He stood up and solemnly reached out to shake hands with Nicoletti. It took them right off the hook. But Giselle said, puzzled, "So who was the hit man?"

And Nicoletti said, "Kasimir Pivarski," and shook Kearny's hand all right, but also added, "Only you don't understand. The one thing our three witnesses agree on. Time. It went down at 5:55 P.M. on Friday, November fifth, last year."

Giselle said. "Oh, no," and Kearny sat back down again as if his bones were old and brittle.

"*Could* Pivarski have been in your Oakland office earlier than five-thirty or so?" asked Nicoletti.

Kearny shook his head. "Kathy always wrote her receipts and stamped 'em while the subject was still in the office, and this one is time-stamped at 5:46 P.M."

"And there's Jeff Simson's affidavit to get around, too," said Giselle. "He covers the time element of Pivarski's visit."

"Pretty definite, ain't it?" Nicoletti had been thumbing through a copy. "He was in your Oakland office when Flip was getting wasted fifteen miles away."

"What about his background?" asked Kearny.

"Absolutely clean. We worked it over pretty good after we got our I.D. and before we found out about the time conflict. But when we tried to waltz him around a little, here's his attorney, Hawkley, who does a lot of legal work for guys in the Teamsters. He slapped a show-cause on us, and we had to vacate our material witness warrant without even getting a chance to serve it. We had a screwed-up time element, and only a questionable I.D. from a DMV photo, right? Not even a formal line-up. So I got one interview with him in Hawkley's office, and that was it."

"What kind of guy is he?" asked Kearny. "I haven't laid eyes on him either."

"Seemed like a big dumb Polack, and I'd by Jesus swear that's *all* he is. Divorced, no kids . . ." He shrugged. "Just a truck driver."

"What was Fazzino doing back in San Francisco?" asked Kearny. He didn't like knowing that whoever had pulled the trigger, it had been Dan Kearny who had sort of pointed the shotgun. "I would have thought this was the last place he'd show up, knowing . . ."

Nicoletti got animated. "Money. The Feds have traced him and Wendy back to a little Mexican village, Zihuatenejo, where they laid low for a year while trying to buy Argentinian citizenship. Once that came through, they flew up here as Adán and Elena Espinosa. Flip went to a safe deposit box at

Golden Gate Trust, drew out a satchelful of what hadda be cash.''

"And they were watching the box?'' asked Kearny. "After a year?''

"A bank v-p named Nucci had a NOTIFY flag on it. We can't prove nothing, but Nucci probably made a phone call to somebody when Flip checked out the box. Whoever he notified blew Flip away and took the money. And just so nobody would make any mistakes about why the hit was made, a penny was shoved up . . .'' He looked over at Giselle and actually colored slightly. "A penny was placed on Fazzino's body. An old mob trick to mark a betrayer.''

So live with it, Kearny thought to himself. He deserved to die and the State couldn't touch him. So live with it. But to change the subject, he said in a dry voice, "Have we come to the favor yet, Benny? I've got to be in the hearing again tomorrow, and the work I've got piled up on my desk as it is . . . .''

"It's about the hearing, as a matter of fact.'' Nicoletti cleared his throat. "Y'see, Dan, we figure Hawkley must know we got a witness somewhere to that Fazzino hit, can maybe I.D. the triggerman. So he's been keeping Pivarski under wraps so we can't get a formal line-up on him—''

"But he also has to know Pivarski *isn't* the triggerman,'' said Kearny. "The time element won't let him be. So why wouldn't he just let your witness see Pivarski and get it over with? The witness will say, hey, that isn't the guy, and—''

"What if our witness says, hey, that *is* the guy?''

Giselle said suddenly, "That's what I'd say if *I* was the witness. Then they wouldn't have any more reason to try and kill me.''

"We still want our witness to see Pivarski,'' said Nicoletti stubbornly. "He's agreed to come down from Canada for it, on our promise he won't have to testify in open court . . .''

"And you want him at the hearing, posing as one of our field men, if the Hearing Officer rules that Pivarski has to testify,'' said Kearny sourly. Then he shrugged. "Okay, Benny, I'll let you know if Pivarski's going to show up.'' His voice thickened. "But if he does, for Chrissake don't let

a bunch of rosy-faces from the FBI come sucking around. Hawkley'd spot them from across town."

"Right you are," said Nicoletti. He was suddenly on his feet in an easy movement that belied his appearance of soft bulk. He nodded, and slid open the glass door. "Thanks, Dan."

And was gone. Giselle stood up, ready to go upstairs and get back to work. "I still don't see why Hawkley wouldn't just let the witness I.D. Pivarski and get it over with," she said.

"Hawkley likes to play games," said Kearny thoughtfully. "And until this license hearing, I doubt he had any way of proving that his client *wasn't* over in San Francisco shooting Fazzino. Which makes me feel that, somehow, he's behind the State's move after our license. I just don't see how he could have set it up."

"And I don't see what good it would do us even if he is," said Giselle. "We're still in a lot of trouble."

Kearny nodded. "What we need is an eyewitness who'll support the version of events that's in Simson's deposition. And at the moment, that's Bart Heslip's problem."

Nineteen

New Orleans—Nawlens, as the locals called it. The sinking city, built on a marsh so they had to bury their dead above ground. Heslip's folks had moved to San Francisco from Baton Rouge, the state capital, a couple of years before he'd even been born, but his ma had talked about Louisiana a lot and until the day she'd died had put chicory in her coffee.

Coffee. Ballard should be here, not me, he thought. Man would go insane over this coffee. Hot and black, like a good woman. He chuckled to himself, and drained his cup. Old Corinne catch him thinking about hot black women, she'd take his head off. 'Cause she could never get it through *her* head that she was the only woman he ever thought about. Now, here he was on a trip like she always was after him for them to take, and she wasn't along! Damn, he missed her.

"More coffee?"

He smiled up at the white waitress. He was in a chain drug store on Canal Street, without even a motel room yet because he didn't know where, or if, he would want to stay.

"Can you tell me where the topless places are located?"

She filled his cup. "Y'all fum outta town. Ah can tell by y'accent." Heslip smothered laughter. "Most places ah on Bourbon Street. In the Vieux Carré? But most of the Nigra gahls dance in the cheapah places. On the sahd streets."

A Nigra gahl was who he was looking for, in a cheap topless joint, after talking with the old black lady, Mrs.

Delbert, who ran the broken-down rooming house from which Verna had sent her postcard to Sally. It was just a few blocks from Canal Street where he now was, by the Superdome, next to the William Guste Housing Project. Heslip had posed as Samuel Rounds, Verna's brother and a deacon of the Four Square Gospel Church of Oakland, California.

"Your sister was here from around Christmas to early March, Deacon Rounds. Went off 'thout any forwarding. Left with a man . . ." She stopped suddenly at the implications of her own words. Deacon Rounds cast his eyes heavenward.

"I know my poor sister lost her way," he said piously. "Like to broke our poor mother's heart. Uh . . . was she using . . ." He found the word. "Anything?"

"You mean drugs? Could have been, now you mention it, Deacon Rounds. I never saw no indication, but then I wouldn't . . ."

"She ever mention he . . . our father? It was here in New Orleans that he abandoned Momma and us kids, fifteen years ago."

Mrs. Delbert shook her head sadly. Then brightened. "One thing was, around mid-February she all of a sudden told me she'd got a job. She was happy 'bout that." Her eyes misted with remembrance. "She was a *good* girl, Deacon Rounds. Such a good girl in her heart."

"What was the job?"

Her face clouded again. "Topless dancing in one of those clubs over there in the Old Quarter. Told her a job at Woolworth's was a lot better than showing her body to lustful men—"

"Better than *giving* her body to them, Mrs. Delbert," said the Deacon. "You wouldn't remember the name of the club where she worked, would you?"

The old black lady shook her head regretfully. Heslip thanked her and shook hands with her and started down off the stoop. When he reached the sidewalk, she called suddenly after him. "Fleur."

He paused on the cracked, uneven concrete. "Fleur?"

"The girl who got her the job at that topless place. Fleur. Skinny little thing with freckles all over her face, light enough to pass, almost . . ."

So here he was, drinking coffee and bracing himself for a long night of ducking in and out of topless joints, asking for Fleur or Verna, trying to dredge up a lead. But it sounded as if Verna never did find her father—if that was indeed who she'd been looking for—and Johnny Mack Brown had moved her on elsewhere.

He looked out and saw he'd coffee'd away the daylight; ornate streetlights had begun to glow on the center islands of Canal Street. He signaled the waitress. "How far is Bourbon Street?"

"Just two blocks down—toward the river."

Bart Heslip turned a corner and was suddenly engulfed in the raucous gaiety of Bourbon Street after dark. Masses of shirt-sleeved and cotton-dressed tourists wandered the street from sidewalk to sidewalk, since striped police barricades interdicted the street to auto traffic.

From open honky-tonk doorways poured hot jazz. The topless joints and strip houses had their doors open to give passers-by quick glimpses of the meat on display inside. Heslip was starting early to hit as many places as possible before the lines waiting for the next complete show started building up. At a po'boy stall he got a beer in a paper cup—glasses were forbidden outside on Bourbon Street—and a sandwich; ate and drank standing at the curb, happy with the warm night and the festive throng.

And then it was time for work. He angled across the street toward the nearest topless joint where two dancers sprawled in chairs just inside the open doorway, their loose, meaty, naked thighs spread wide to catch the cool breeze and indiscriminate male pedestrians. Heslip slipped into the empty chair between them. On his passage across the street a pair of mirrored shades had appeared on his eyes. "You lovely ladies are as sweet as a mother's love, I swear."

Neither girl answered, so he leaned over and pinched one gently on the thigh.

"Hey, listen, shithead," she snarled, sitting up straight, "you just look, you don't touch."

"Praise de Lawd. I thought you wuz daid."

"Oh you're funn-n-ny. Ha. Ha. Ha."

"Little Verna, *she* thinks I got my game uptight. What time she come on?"

"No Verna here, black boy," she said with a lifted lip.

"Fleur?"

"No Fleur, either." She raised her voice toward the dim interior. "Hey, Chuck, this Nigra . . ."

Heslip was up and out, sliding away nimbly through the crowd, an eye to storefront windows reflecting the street behind him until he was sure Chuck wasn't following his scent. Then he slowed and turned into the next topless joint. No girls on display outside this one, so he threaded his way through darkness, noise, smoke, and the jazz beat of the band next to the raised stage where a girl in a frayed, filmy negligée moved in approximate time to the music.

He slid onto a stool and ordered a beer. As he paid he flashed a Stepin Fetchit grin at the bartender and said. "Hey, my man, if you can tell me what time Verna comes on . . ."

Back into a 4 A.M. street, dimly lit and alive with ghosts, stepped Heslip, zipping up, after depositing the most recent two hours of beer in a littered doorway. He'd lost track of the number he'd drunk, as he'd lost track of the number of near-naked women he'd looked at in the last seven hours with only negative results. They'd all run together in his mind—a single fat, skinny, beautiful, sad, ugly, happy, alcoholic, straight, spaced-out, drunk, coked-up, sober woman with an indifferent body who smelled of perspiration and tired feet.

He checked his watch: 1:30 A.M. in San Francisco. Here, only blown trash and rumbling garbage trucks and early delivery vans and the lonely sound of his solitary footsteps, but there, his fragrant, elegant lady asleep in her bed. Was it too late—too early?—to call her and tell her how he missed her?

Far down the street, on the far side next to an alley, light and jukeboxed jazz spilled from an all-night bar. He looked in the window when he got to the place; in the back, near the restrooms, was a pay phone. He went in.

Stale beer. Sweat. Dime-store musk. Seven male patrons, two with women of their own, watching the almost naked black girl on stage display her ineptitude. A tall blond with the strident tones of a drag queen was using the phone. Heslip sat at the nearest table and leaned back and shut his eyes. Tired. The music stopped to a smattering of applause. A new record started.

"Yeah, what'll it be?"

"The phone," said Heslip without opening his eyes.

"Gotta order."

He opened his eyes. The waiter was short and black and had led with his nose against a fist or a bottle many years before.

"Beer," he said, as his eyes looked beyond the waiter to the stage where, now, a small skinny girl with breasts a midget's hands might cup and the body curves of a high school sprinter, gyrated with great energy and no talent. Heslip added sharply to the waiter's back, "Hey."

When the waiter turned, he was holding out a ten-dollar bill. The girl on stage had freckles and skin light enough to pass.

"And tell the little lady that Santa Claus is black and early this year."

He shut his eyes and drifted again. The music stopped. Started. Stopped. Did it all again. Dusting of applause. Finally, one of the chairs squealed being pulled back from the table.

"Jingle Bells?" It was a little voice willing to be playful.

He opened his eyes. A good face, small and serious behind all the cosmeticked garbage.

"Hello, Fleur," he said. "Where's Verna?"

Twenty

"Will Delaney have Pivarski here or not?" asked Kearny as they got out of the elevator.

"Hell no," snorted Tranquillini. "Neither would I if he was my client, now that I know what Hawkley has Pivarski ducking. He can't be sure, if this witness comes up with a positive I.D., that the State wouldn't go after his client for Murder One anyway. And you can never tell how juries will react in murder-for-hire cases."

"But if he was in our office fifteen miles away at the time—"

Tranquillini stopped abruptly outside the open door of the hearing room. "He would have to prove that. And they're having their troubles right inside this hearing room proving it to satisfy the referee. What would they have to do to convince a jury, in the face of a positive eyewitness?" He shook his head. "I figure Delaney will stall today and then, if ordered to produce him, will do it next Monday. By that time, Benny Nicoletti's witness will have gotten cold feet and gone back up to Canada. My guess is that today Johnny-boy will have a very nasty surprise for us."

"Be seated and state your full name for the record," said the Hearing Officer.

"Jeffrey L. Simson. S-I-M-S-O-N."

"Your address, Mr. Simson?"

"One-four-seven-two Fort Point, Los Angeles. Fort Point is two words."

The Hearing Officer said to Delaney, "Proceed."

"Mr. Simson, were you employed by Kearny Associates as a collector during November of last year?"

"Yes I was."

"Do you recall the Pivarski account?"

Simson cleared his throat. "Yes sir, I do."

"Do you recall Mr. Pivarski coming into your office on November fifth, and if so, do you recall the purpose of that visit?"

"He came regarding an attachment of his wages."

"Did he offer to pay any money at that time?"

"Two hundred dollars," said Simson.

Tranquillini was doodling on his scratch pad and looking bored.

"To whom did Mr. Pivarski talk when he came in?"

Simson affected to think very deeply. Finally he nodded. "Yes. First myself, then Miss Onoda."

"Can you tell us anything further about the purpose of Mr. Pivarski's visit to the Kearny office?"

"It was my underst—"

"I object to the form of that question," said Tranquillini. "He wouldn't know Pivarski's purpose. He might know what Pivarski told him."

"Sustained as to form," said the Hearing Officer.

"Well, would you state what Mr. Pivarski said?"

"It was my understanding that the money was to be held—"

"I object to his 'understanding' something."

The Hearing Officer sighed. "Will the witness please just relate the conversation as best he can recollect?"

"Yes, Your Honor. Mr. Pivarski told me that this money was to be held in trust by Daniel Kearny Associates until his demurrer was heard, and to stop any further attachments until such time."

Delaney said, "And did either you or Miss Onoda agree to forestall further actions of attachment?"

"Miss Onoda did. Yes, sir."

"Did Mr. Pivarski bring a letter with him to your office?"

"Yes he did. From his attorney."

"Do you recognize this as a copy of that letter?"

Simson looked at it. "Yes. This is a copy of the letter that Mr. Pivarski submitted to me."

"At this time, Your Honor," said Delaney to the Hearing Officer, "we ask that Exhibit B be formally introduced as evidence."

But Tranquillini was on his feet. "I would like the opportunity to cross-examine the witness before the letter is placed into evidence."

"We offer it in evidence at this time," Delaney repeated.

"I am reserving my ruling on this document at this time, Mr. Delaney," said the Hearing Officer. "Proceed with your examination."

Delaney shrugged in resignation and returned to Simson. "Was this conversation you were having with Mr. Pivarski and Miss Onoda interrupted by a phone call?"

"Yes, sir. By a phone call I was requested to make by Miss Onoda. She asked me to call Mr. Tranquillini."

Tranquillini started up to object, then checked himself and sat down again. Delaney wouldn't have asked it if he didn't have it covered. And he did.

"Who actually talked to Mr. Tranquillini?"

"I could get no answer at his office number, and we didn't have his home number in the Oakland office Rolodex."

"Did Miss Onoda tell you why she wished to speak with Mr. Kearny's attorney?"

"Yes she did." Simson had not once looked back toward Kearny during his testimony. He kept his eyes on Delaney. "She told me that she wanted to advise counsel that Mr. Pivarski was in the office with two hundred dollars to be held in trust. She wanted advice on what she should do, since Mr. Pivarski would not give her the money unless she signed the bottom of the letter he had brought."

"What did Miss Onoda do when she could not reach counsel?"

"She took the money and signed the bottom of the letter."

Delaney glanced at Tranquillini. "Was that the only receipt?"

"Yes, sir." Then he suddenly exclaimed, "Oh, while I was waiting for her to make up the day's bank deposit, Miss Onoda made up a receipt for the Pivarski payment on a DKA receipt form."

"But hadn't Mr. Pivarski already departed?" asked Delaney in exaggerated amazement.

"Yes, sir. She ran the file copy of the receipt through the time-stamp machine in the usual manner, and threw the original in the wastebasket. I remember her saying something like, 'If he thinks we're actually going to hold that money for him, he's crazy.' Then she winked at me and—"

Giselle was on her feet in the spectator section, crying, "He's a dirty damn liar! Kathy never would have sa . . . mmmph."

Kearny had dragged her back to her seat. There were furious whispers. Tranquillini did not bother to turn his head, but the Hearing Officer's brow was very dark.

"I want counsel's assurance that this will not be repeated."

"It won't happen again, Your Honor," said Tranquillini.

Delaney, who had turned to observe Giselle's reaction, turned back again, shaking his head as if appalled. He said to Simson, "Did you remonstrate with her for this unethical action?"

Simson hung his head.

"No, sir. You see, sir, I was paid on a commission basis by Kearny Associates. If the two hundred dollars was held in trust as Mr. Pivarski thought it was going to be, I would not have received my percentage of it. I . . . was very tight on money just then, sir, so I . . . I was weak, and . . ."

Delaney's manner dripped sympathy. "We understand, Mr. Simson. Thank you for being so candid with those of us in this hearing room interested in the truth.'' He turned away. ''That is all I have at this time.''

''You may cross-examine.''

''I would like to ask for a recess until after the noon break,'' said Tranquillini. ''Obviously, this testimony has come as a complete surprise to me, and I would like an opportunity to discuss it with my client.''

The Hearing Officer checked the time. He nodded. ''Very well.''

''You don't believe any of that crap about Kathy, do you?'' demanded Giselle rather wildly. They had gone for lunch to the Madonna Cafeteria, at a raised table overlooking a small enclosed garden, which Tranquillini had thought might soothe her angry emotions. So far it had failed to do so.

''Of course I don't believe it,'' he said evenly.

''Then why say you have to confer with your client, which makes it look like Kathy was a dishonest cheat who would falsify—''

''What was I supposed to say? Try to understand, Giselle, we are stalling for time because we don't have any direct evidence to present. *We* know Simson is lying, but—''

Kearny, who was eating chop suey, put down his fork with a clatter. ''You aren't going to have any trouble taking *that* lying bastard apart, are you? It's so damned obvious that he's—''

''Obvious to us, Dan, isn't always obvious to the Hearing Officer. Or, much as I hate to say it, obvious to Johnny Delaney, either.'' He leaned forward to speak earnestly to both of them, noting with satisfaction that Giselle had quit reacting and had begun to use her mind again. ''Let me tell you how it went. On Monday we hit Delaney with the unexpected: Simson's deposition. I'm sure he thought Simson was buried where we couldn't come up with him.''

''Which means,'' said Giselle almost triumphantly, ''that he knew Simson's testimony would support our side of the case. So now, when Simson is saying anything Delaney wants him to, how can you say Delaney doesn't know he's lying?"

"Delaney knew that deposition hurt him," said Tranquillini patiently. "He thought he could get the letter in as direct evidence. The Hearing Officer had excluded it—hearsay only. Now we have a document which suggests there was no letter tendered by Pivarski or signed by Kathy. So Delaney needed direct testimony—and so far it seems that meant either Pivarski or Simson. We know Hawkley would fight any move to bring Pivarski out to testify, so Delaney would send a couple of the Attorney General's investigators down to talk with Simson."

"And ask him to perjure himself," snapped Giselle.

"I'm sure that was Simson's own idea," said Tranquillini. "With an assist from the investigators. You know—you wanta be an attorney, there might be a job in the Attorney General's office after you pass your bar..."

Kearny nodded. "Yeah. Simson's just the boy would go for one like that."

"He'd tell them that the deposition was just to help out an old friend—namely, you—but that testifying under oath was something else." Tranquillini shoved aside the ruins of his pastrami sandwich. "So the investigators would tell him what Delaney needed the worst, and he would tailor his testimony to fit. But I'm sure Delaney believes that what Simson said on the stand this morning is roughly the truth."

"Well, I'm going to send Ballard up to Sacramento to nose around in Tom Greenly's life," said Kearny. "He's the lad brought the charges against us, and I want to see if there's anything to connect him with Hawkley or the organized crime boys he represents."

"What you really want, Dan, is to not feel DKA is helpless in this thing."

Kearny shrugged darkly. "Whatever," he said in a gruff voice.

"And I have to tell you that I don't think Hawkley has a damn thing to do with this. I think Pivarski made a complaint, and I think Franks complained to the State, and I think the State decided they could grab your license and went for it. Both Franks and Simson are lying, but I don't think we'll be able to prove it unless Bart Heslip comes up with a witness on your side.'' He turned to Giselle. ''Have you heard anything from him?''

''Just a message left on the answering machine in Dan's office at two this morning, our time. Verna has left New Orleans, but he's tracked down her best friend, a girl named Fleur who dances topless in a joint called the Iberville Cabaret.''

Twenty-One

Bart Heslip opened his eyes and stared at the ceiling. He could feel the weight of Corinne's head against his bare chest, could feel her feather-soft exhalations against his skin. He cupped his hand around her head, his fingers thrust through her frizzy hair.

He was suddenly out of bed, looking back at it. Corinne didn't have frizzy hair. And sure as hell not that strange shade of orange that very black hair takes when it is hennaed. The girl grunted and sat up. She looked at Heslip from big soft eyes in a funny little monkey face. "You're a strange dude, you know that? You could have made it with me last night, and you didn't even try."

Heslip, scratching his hard fighter's belly through his T-shirt, mumbled something unintelligible. When he'd accepted her five-in-the-morning invitation to use her bed, she'd been in a chair across the room in a bulky nightgown, saying she'd roust him out when she got tired. Now she'd been nude in bed beside him.

Fleur said, "We could make it now, if . . ."

Heslip shook his head. She was sitting up nude, watching him. "You gay or something?"

"Something," said Heslip. "You seen my pants?"

"Hanging over the oven door." She was up on her knees, careless of her nudity, a puzzled look on her face. "Married? Steady fox?"

"Steady fox."

"She's back in San Francisco, right? You're here in New Orleans. So how she ever know if you an' me do a little number here on the bed?"

"*I'd* know." Heslip was in pants and shirt now, sitting on a dinette chair and lacing his shoes. Abruptly, she was off the bed in a flash of warm brown flesh, and into the bathroom. She stuck a freckled brown face around the edge of the doorway. "Man, a long time ago in my life I wish *I'd* said no to me."

She was gone. Water started to run. Then she stuck her face around the doorjamb again. "If I can't seduce you, can I at least feed you?"

They ate facing one another across the tiny formica breakfast table, talking mostly about her life: six nights a week dancing topless in a sidestreet joint, occasionally peddling her butt to a live one when the money was right.

"Think you'll ever get out of it?" Heslip asked.

"Ain't got a whole lot of choices." She buried her teeth in her slice of toast and an eighth-inch of peanut butter, and brought up the subject before Heslip could. "Sorta like Verna, after she was sure."

"Sure of what?" Heslip drank coffee. Hadn't had a bad cup yet. He was going to end up like Ballard if he wasn't careful.

"About the baby."

"You mean she . . ." Heslip dropped back in his chair to cast his eyes to the ceiling. "A baby. Oh, that's terrific."

"I don't see nothing so wrong with it. She wanted that baby, worst way, cause it would be the first thing she'd ever had was hers alone. Wouldn't have no abortion. That was murder, she said."

"A trick baby?" Heslip used the term for babies born to prostitutes who have no idea of whom the father is.

"Or Johnny Mack Brown's. Maybe that's why he stuck with her even after she got hooked on smack."

Heslip asked casually, "Still mainlining when she left here?"

"Ain't that shit so easy to get off of, man."

"Anybody ever point out to her that babies use the same bloodstream as their mother while she's carrying 'em? So if the mother is a junkie, the kid's hooked before he's born. They have to cold-turkey it right there in the hospital. How far along is she?"

Fleur counted on her fingers "Was over two months gone in February, when she quit flat-backin' cause some dude knocked her around and hurt the kid. Quit dancing cause it was startin' to show—"

"So she's had it by now," said Heslip. "She ever find her own father?"

"You know 'bout that?"

"Guessed."

She went back into the bathroom to put on a face. "She sure knew a lot 'bout findin' people. Wrote away to Baton Rouge for his auto registration and driver's license, stuff like that . . ." By the shape of her words, they were spoken around a lipstick being applied. She came out pressing a Kleenex between her lips to get off the excess. "Let's go talk to him."

Heslip was on his feet, draining the last coffee from his cup.

"So she found him."

"She found him. I went with her when she went to see him. Was a mean, ugly dude in a fancy house. Told us to leave."

"Maybe we'll do better with him," said Heslip.

Down in the street, he unlocked his rental car, then stopped to drum thoughtful fingers on the roof as Fleur got in. He was sure he'd left it *un*locked, because that way kids wouldn't break a window to get in and boost it. Would a kid *re*lock it afterwards?

To hell with it. Fleur directed him to Magazine Street and then over to Jackson Ave. which eventually put them on the I-10 expressway. Heslip listened to her chatter, as bright and pleasant as rain on the roof, and wondered what Corinne was doing just then at the travel agency under the Sutter-Stockton Garage.

Corinne was getting a breather on the phone. The heavy voice said, "Fleur. The broad's name is Fleur."

"I beg your pardon?"

"The one in New Orleans. The topless dancer."

Corinne held the receiver away as if expecting it to squirt water at her like the fake *boutonnières* that used to be advertised in comic books. She returned it to her face. "This is a travel agency," she said, "not a massage parlor."

"Heslip. He slept with her last night," said the husky, half-whispering voice. The breathing got heavier. "Lemme tell you what he did to her. First he . . ."

She was so astounded that she actually listened for several seconds before slamming down the phone.

"What's the matter, Corinne?" asked Toni, the other girl in the office. "You sick or something?"

Corinne waved a hand rather weakly. "Just . . . a weird call."

"An *obscene* call?"

"Uh . . . something like that." Then she added very quickly, "Just a breather." Toni was an ardent libber and very behind self-defense: thirty-seven ways to geld a man with bare hands, feet, or sarcasm. "I hung up on him, he won't call back."

She put the incident from her mind, only it wouldn't stay put. Bart *was* in New Orleans, after all. Looking for a hooker. And a lot of hookers hung around topless bars. Fleur. The caller had used a specific name. Would he do that if it was just a crank call?

But it was silly to think that way. What she would do, she would call Giselle at DKA and tell her about it. The call probably had something to do with the license thing. Only when she called, Giselle wasn't there. Nor were Kearny, Larry, or O'B. Probably all over at those licensing hearings . . .

At which Hec Tranquillini was putting Simson on the grill at last, starting gently, hoping to pry him open by careful manipulation. Because that was the only way in the world he was going to be able to keep excluding that damned letter.

"For the record once again, please, what is your name?"

"Jeffrey L. Simson."

"Have you gone by any other names?"

"Yes, sir." Simson obviously had been well-briefed. "Jackson J. Jacoby, that's J-A-C-O-B-Y, and Jeffrey J. Jacuzzi, that's J-A-C-U-Z-Z-I."

"What a lot of names. How old are you, Mr. Simson-Jacoby-Jacuzzi?"

"Objection. Those were professional pseudonyms, not—"

"I withdraw the question in that form. Your age, Mr. Simson?"

"Twenty-five."

"Where do you live?"

"One-four-seven-two Fort Point, Los Angeles."

"How long have you lived there?"

"For I guess a month or something like that?"

Tranquillini saw his opening, but did nothing to show he was going through it. "And before that?"

"Avenue Fifty in Eagle Rock. Near Occidental College."

"What number on Avenue Fifty?"

"Um . . . Gee, I'm not sure . . ."

"How *long* were you at number um Avenue Fifty?"

Delaney was on his feet. "Your Honor, counsel's sarcasm is neither witty nor necessary. The witness is responding as best—"

"I apologize to the witness,' said Tranquillini meekly. "How long were you at the Avenue Fifty address?"

"Well, I guess it must have been . . . maybe four or five months."

"And before that?"

"In San Francisco for two years."

Tranquillini took a chance. "Most of that at a single address, I believe?"

"Yes, sir."

"Could you give us that address, please?"

Delaney had another objection. As Tranquillini had hoped, he obviously was trying to keep Simson's homosexuality out because he thought that was what Tranquillini was trying to get in. "I fail to see the relevance of this line of questioning."

"Is that an objection?" asked the Hearing Officer.

"Yes, Your Honor."

"Overruled."

"Do you remember the address, Mr. Simson?"

"Not the street number—thirty-three-hundred something. It was just a block off Mission Street."

"You had a roommate there, did you not, who—"

Delaney was up. "Objection."

"I withdraw the question. Do you remember which *street* it was, Mr. Simson?"

"Ah . . . Sure! It was Twenty-fourth Street." He smiled in relief. "Thirty-three, uh . . . Yes: Thirty-three ninety-six."

"Thank you very much, Mr. Simson," said Tranquillini in a suddenly significant voice. He looked up from his papers. "When did you work for Kearny Associates?"

"From some time last year until—"

"What was the specific date you *started* working for them?"

"I believe it was . . . ah . . . September? October?"

Delaney was on his feet again. "Does counsel plan to take this man through the last year of his life minute-by-minute?"

"This does seem rather extended, Mr. Tranquillini."

Tranquillini avoided saying what he was doing: establishing the witness's obvious difficulty in remembering detail. Instead, he said, "I request the utmost latitude with this witness because his is the *only* direct evidence against my client which the State has yet produced. Therefore I feel—"

"Counsel is stalling, Your Honor." Delaney was advancing on the bench. "He has no direct evidence of his own . . ."

"If the State would quit interposing objections, I could proceed with my interrogation. But since we are discussing motions, Your Honor, I am still waiting for a ruling on mine of Monday afternoon concerning a subpoena for Mr. Pivarski . . .''

Delaney was shouting. Tranquillini covertly checked his watch. Oh yes. Old time was yet afleeting. Every minute spent this way gave Bart Heslip extra time to look for Verna Rounds.

Twenty-Two

If Zebulon Rounds had been white, he'd have been a good ole boy. But he was black, and what investigative ploy was going to work with a 250-pound black redneck?

Fleur hadn't had the street address out in Kenner where he lived, near the airport, which was upper-crust black and had obviously been white a few years earlier. But she was able to recognize the house, where Rounds' wife was out in halter and shorts trimming an honest-to-God magnolia tree. Also wearing a mouse under one eye and a swollen jaw, neither of which had come from an afternoon bridge game with the girls.

Posing as an insurance salesman, complete with clipboard and clear-glass horn-rims and a fruity manner, Heslip had been led out West End Boulevard to Bucktown and a dazzling white, crushed-shell parking lot near Lake Pontchartrain. It seemed that the uncharitable Mr. Rounds had, like Heslip, been a professional boxer. His career had led him, not to manhunting, but to part ownership of a rather fancy bar-restaurant catering to the tourist trade, which was built out over the water on concrete pilings. When Heslip pounded on the closed front door, it opened on a thin, white, dispirited face with a cigarette dangling from a lower corner of it.

"We're closed," said the face.

"Tell Rounds I'll be waiting in the parking lot," said Heslip. "Tell him it's about his daughter."

Five minutes later a hulking black man with massive shoulders and a strutting stride appeared, his eyes moving suspiciously from car to car until they spotted Heslip leaned against the fender of a Torino hardtop several stalls away from the rent-a-car where Fleur waited. Up close Rounds bore the marks of his former profession on his square, massive face. A flattened nose, thickened lips, scar tissue around the deep-set gorilla eyes. Maybe, Heslip thought, remembering the current wife's battered appearance, Emmalina was lucky Rounds had dumped her years ago.

"I need your daughter's address." Heslip was still wearing the clear-glass horn-rims and carrying the clipboard, but the fruity manner was gone. "Your real daughter. Verna."

Rounds' eyes got even meaner than usual. He went into a half-crouch. "Lissen, Oreo, you got no call coming around . . ."

"Get off it," Heslip snapped. "We know you never bothered to get unmarried from Emmalina, so your children by the woman you are living with now are illegitimate." He curled his lips around the word. "*Bastards*, Rounds. Got it? Now, where's Verna?"

Rage washed across Rounds' features but there was also an underlying intelligence and caution Heslip hadn't expected. This tempered that always smoldering rage, checked it, controlled it. "I ain't telling you nothing."

Heslip made a notation on his clipboard, holding it so Rounds could not see what he wrote. "That's your choice, Rounds." He looked up. "What's your social secur . . . no. The computer has that."

"What . . . what're you writing there?" Much of the belligerence had drained from the big man's voice.

"You'll be . . ." He clicked his pen and pocketed it. "You'll be served with a Summons and Complaint. Your attorney can explain . . ."

"Attorney? Summons and Complaint?"

"If it goes against you, you'll lose the restaurant, of

course. Convicted felons can't be licensed for the on-premises sale of alcohol in this state.''

He turned and started to walk away. Rounds caught his arm.

''Convicted felon? What are you tellin' me?''

Heslip shook his arm free and dissected him with icy bureaucratic eyes. ''We don't force cooperation, Rounds. That's outside our constitutional brief. But when we find evidence of a felony committed by someone uncooperative, we feel no urgency to shield that person from the local authorities . . .''

''But I ain't *done* anything!''

''Bigamy's a felony, Rounds. I would think you'd know that.''

He started off again. Rounds kept pace, hunched and pleading. ''Look, mister, it was Emmalina. She ran off, fifteen years ago. I would have gotten a legal divorce, I swear to you, but I couldn't find her . . .''

''We have her statement to the contrary. The fact that she's listed under ROUNDS, EMMALINA, in the Oakland, California phone book might influence a jury's decision. Add perjury to the other—''

''Look, I tell you where to find Verna, what happens?''

''Our only interest is in contacting your daughter.''

Rounds shook his head in abrupt irritation. He said bitterly, ''I know you bringin' up all this stuff just to force me to talk. I want to know what happens to *Verna* if I tell you where she's at.''

Once again Rounds had surprised him. The huge man's ugly face was set in an agony of indecision.

''Nothing happens to her,'' said Heslip. ''We just need a statement from her.''

Rounds said softly, ''Mister, that little girl got all the grief she can handle. Like to tore out my heart when she came into my home with tread marks on her arms and a pimp's child in her belly.''

''It was our understanding you were hostile to your daughter,'' he said in his cold bureaucratic voice.

''That first time she came to see me, you mean? Man, I

have a wife and family that don't know *nuthin'* about Emmalina or Verna or the boy, Sammy. But she came to see me here, a bunch of times, and we got on fine. I gave her money to go North with that pimp . . ."

"Why North?" Heslip had almost forgotten his role.

"The pimp, he has relatives there, said they'd take care of her while she had the baby. She wrote a few times, it seemed to be working out. Then the letters quit comin'."

"She still on the junk while she was writing?"

"You know anyone gets off it?" he demanded bitterly.

Heslip was tempted to say more, a good deal more, about the fact that a father in her life, instead of just a shadowy, almost mythic figure to be sought out when she was pregnant and needed roots for the unborn child, might have meant she never would have gotten on the junk. But he was there for only one thing. "Not our concern," he said. "We just need the address."

When he got back into the rent-a-car sixty seconds later, Fleur said eagerly, "Did we get anything?"

Heslip had to chuckle at her "we." Emphasizing it, he said, "*We* got an address where she's supposed to be. Or, least, was until about four months ago. One-ten Allerton Street, Roxbury, Massachusetts. Let's find a phone and get me lined up with a flight to Boston, and then I'll buy you dinner wherever you want."

"Just over at Fontana's," she said, "is some of the best soft-shelled crab you ever ate."

Not only the best, but the first.

Ballard had found Thomas Greenly listed in the Sacramento phone book; a $50,000-class house on Bartley Drive near William Land Park, not out of a civil servant's honest reach these days. Greenly was third from the corner of Cavanaugh Way, so Ballard had to hit only those two houses before Greenly's in his role as a census taker for the Polk Directory. The wife was obviously the one he had started with, one of the kids was in college and the other two in high school, all depressingly honest and aboveboard. No meat there for any conjecture of mob contacts, none at all.

Next stop, in on Sixteenth Street to 0, left to the 1000-block. The Business and Professions Building directory told him room 516, which he entered lugging half a dozen bulging legal-size files from the trunk of his car. His view through an open door from the secretary's desk showed him the man from the anniversary photo the wife had proudly displayed. Medium height, lean, stooped, prominent Adam's apple, dark hair receding from an accountant's high brow.

"Hey, I'm really sorry"—scooping the files back up off her desk before she could open any of them—"I wanted 416. Only my second week on the job, I still get lost . . ."

Outside to park where he could see Greenly's green Toyota, again, courtesy the talkative wife, and then he settled down to wait. Nothing on Greenly yet to think about or plan, so he thought about his night at the motel in Santa Rosa with Yana. What a woman! And so many contradictions. She couldn't, for instance, read or write.

"Oh, I can recognize the shape of the letters that make up the name of the city—Santa Rosa, eh?—and I know numbers because we depend on the telephones a lot. But beyond that . . ."

He watched the first freshets of what would soon be a flood of departing civil servants start from the state buildings.

. . . Beyond that, she had loved him and asked for nothing in return. She'd been sold to her husband for six thousand dollars when she'd been thirteen and her father had discovered she was sneaking into school on the sly instead of selling stolen flowers on street corners as she was supposed to be doing.

"I have miscarried seven times in the five years since then, because I have been unhappy. But now I am happy and you and me, we will make a very handsome baby."

Which was not really what Ballard had in mind, but *dammit!* He had just caught a flash of the rear end of Greenly's Toyota as it made a right into N Street off Seventh where Ballard was parked. He bulled across traffic to get seven cars behind it for a sedate inching back to Cavanaugh Way on Fifteenth Street. Ballard parked down the street and bored himself into a near-coma waiting for the house lights to go out.

When he finally left, nobody tailed Ballard to his motel.

When Heslip left Fontana's, somebody tailed him back to Fleur's place. At least he thought maybe somebody did. "You know anyone drives a white Monte Carlo Landau Coupe? I keep seeing the same car behind us."

"Somebody jealous, you mean?" He nodded. "Jealous of a topless dancer?" She gave a great burst of laughter.

"Don't sell yourself short," said Heslip. He stopped at the curb and started to get out to go around and open her door.

"Yeah, I saw the way you couldn't wait to get at me in that bed last night." She grabbed his arm. "Don't get out, you'll miss your plane." Her eyes were momentarily serious. "I'll remember this day jus' fine the way it is." She leaned over and kissed him on the cheek. "That's a lucky woman out there in San Francisco, Bart Heslip."

She was out of the car and up the stairs with a wave of the hand. Quite a girl. He waved also, though she was already gone, then pulled out into traffic. And back to work, keeping an eye out for that Monte Carlo. It was dark, so he wasn't sure until thirty minutes later, when he left I-10 at Williams Boulevard and could get a look at the car again under the streetlights.

Yeah. But *why?* Verna? Then who? And where and when and how had the men picked him up? Last night? This morning when they'd still been asleep at Fleur's? Might explain the car locked when they'd come out. When and where. But *how* in the hell . . .

He went by the row of dilapidated taxis parked on the shoulder of Airport Highway waiting for radioed pickup calls from the terminal, checked in his rental car, and went up the escalator from ground level with the two men from the Monte Carlo so tight behind he was afraid they might try to stand on his step with him.

White, tough, not bright but dogged. How, for Chrissake, had they even known he was in New Orleans? What could Verna have that they wanted? Were they bird-dogging him to her, or trying to beat him to her? And how to shake them, notify Kearny of the tail, call Corinne to say he loved her . . .

Then he got a break. He noted, without seeming to, that his Boston flight would depart half an hour late. Gave him time to shake them. First, to the National Airlines desk on the second floor of the bright new modern building, for a one-way ticket to Miami on a flight leaving in three hours. Next, to an arcade restaurant with a second entrance from the corridor through the men's room. Then, a table by the window to order a steak, pie, and coffee, with a three-minute discussion about the wine he would order.

While waiting for his supper, he went to the men's room. The door, as he swung it open, reflected the images of his two tough-faced tails just settling down at the counter with coffee and pecan pie.

No, not bright. Not bright at all.

At Eastern he picked up the ticket he'd ordered that afternoon by phone, and made it through the airport security and onto the Boston-bound plane with a full sixty seconds before departure time. He slept most of the way to big, empty, echoing Logan International, where he found a pay phone from which to call Corinne. He gave a jaw-creaking yawn as he waited: at least he'd hit Boston clean.

"This is your handsome charming prince checking in," he said.

"*Bart!*" Her voice became elaborately casual. "I thought I'd hear from you last night."

"I'm sorry honey, it's been a couple of hectic days."

"Hectic days with Fleur?" She couldn't keep the sudden venom out of her voice. Heslip's mind raced against frightening thoughts.

"How in hell did you hear about Fleur?"

"So you *did* sleep with her!" she cried in despairing triumph. And hung up. And wouldn't answer repeated rings. Damn, damn.

Twenty-Three

"I have to assume Heslip isn't going to come up with Verna Rounds," Tranquillini told them before the Thursday morning session. "Until Simson, the State had no direct evidence to prove or support their charges. Just hearsay. Now they have a witness whose testimony expands the State's case at every point. There is only one way to keep that letter he swears Kathy signed from being admitted into evidence—which would mean your license would be taken away."

"What's that?" asked Kearny levelly.

"I have to prove he's a perjurer."

When Corinne Jones let herself into the office, her phone was ringing. She picked up.

"Good morning, Far Flung Travel."

"Listen, baby, now don't hang up on me—"

She hung up on him. And burst into tears.

Jeffrey L. Simson did not look ready to burst into tears. He looked cool and calm and collected—and well briefed. Tranquillini hoped he'd been briefed against delaying tactics, not a try for the jugular.

"Now, Mr. Simson, you testified yesterday that you were a collector at Kearny Associates. What were your duties?"

"To call the debtors on the phone and pressure them into paying the money that they owed."

"And you worked there for how long?"

Today, Simson was ready for it. "I started work at the DKA Oakland office on October eleventh, last year, and quit on February thirteenth this year."

"Quit?"

He looked quickly at Delaney. "Was . . . um . . . terminated."

"That was approximately four months. How many people would you say you called up during the average working day?"

"Mmmm . . . I would think about twenty-five."

"It is a pleasure to interrogate a well-schooled witness." Before an objection could be made, Tranquillini went on, "Now tell me, on the first day you worked for Kearny Associates, that would be October eleventh, what was the name of the first person you called?"

Delaney was on his feet. "Mr. Hearing Officer, the name of the first person he called has no relevancy to this case."

"If Your Honor please, I am testing the man's recollection."

"The witness doesn't have to attest to his memory, for God sake!" exclaimed Delaney. "He doesn't remember, how could he? You're just harassing him for no reason."

Tranquillini did his Al Capone jaw-thrust number for the first time during the hearing.

"I will decide what I shall ask him, and the Hearing Officer will decide whether or not I have the right to ask it. He talks to twenty-five people a day, and then claims he can't . . ."

"The objection is overruled," said the Hearing Officer.

Tranquillini went after him. "Mr. Simson, what was the name of the party to whom you made your first phone call on October eleventh?"

"I . . . do not recall."

"Do you recall the name of *any* person that you telephoned during the entire *month* of October, your first in DKA's employ?"

"Ah . . . no sir."

"You were terminated for cause on February thirteenth of this year. What was the name of the *last* person you telephoned while in the employ of Daniel Kearny Associates . . ."

Toni put her hand over the mouthpiece and caught Corinne's eyes. "Bart Heslip."

Corinne shook her head violently. "Hang up on him."

Toni would have loved nothing better, but there'd been an extraordinary note of desperation in Heslip's voice. And she could see that Corinne was really hurting, too.

"He says it's really, really important."

"I . . . oh, damn him, I'll take it." She snatched up her phone. Her heart was beating so wildly she was afraid it was going to jump right up in her throat. "I told you I didn't want to talk to you."

"Where did you hear about Fleur?" His voice sounded icy.

"Do you have to speak her name?"

"Where? From Giselle?"

"Giselle knew about you and that bitch?"

Toni got up hurriedly and went out to get a drink of water from the fountain across the corridor.

"So it wasn't from DKA. Who from?"

She hesitated for the first time. "A . . . voice on the phone."

"An anonymous voice?"

For the first time since those dreadful midnight moments, she felt a stab of uncertainty.

"At first I thought it was an . . . obscene call. A . . . you know, what they call a breather."

"And you believed . . ." A hurt note had softened his voice. "When did you get that call?"

"I think . . . yes, yesterday afternoon."

Laughter suddenly entered his voice. "Fleur is skinny, has light skin and freckles, orange hair, and a face like those Capuchin monkeys we like to watch out at Fleishhacker Zoo."

"Orange hair? Now I believe you didn't have anything to

do with her.'' Bart hated any sort of hair-dyeing. Toni had slipped back in. A great angry tide was receding inside Corinne, leaving only puzzlement behind. ''But then why the phone call to me?''

''Can only mean one thing. They wanted me to make all my calls through DKA about Verna, rather than through you. Now, I want you to get right over to that hearing room . . .''

''Excuse me,'' said Simson. He was sweating, although the temperature had not changed. ''I was thinking of the previous month.''

''So when you say you did all your collection business over the phone, that was a deliberate . . .'' Delaney started to object, so Tranquillini finished, ''Deliberately loose way of speaking.''

''Um . . . yes, sir.''

''So in reality, three or four parties a week came up to the office to pay in person. Can you give me the name of *any of them*, anyone at all, besides Mr. Pivarski?''

Simson cleared his throat. ''I . . . um . . .''

''Now, you testified that Mr. Pivarski came in on November fifth. That was the first time you had seen him?''

''Yes, sir, it was.''

''Very good.'' Tranquillini, from the corner of his eye, saw a truly striking black woman enter the hearing room and head for the DKA contingent. ''Was Mr. Pivarski ever in the office again?''

''Not while I was there.''

''How old a man was he, would you say?''

''Um . . . late thirties or early forties?''

''I sense indecision. How tall a man?''

''Average.''

''Weight?''

''Average.''

''What was the color of his hair?''

Simson cleared his throat. In the spectator section, Dan Kearny was on his feet and leaving with the black woman.

"I . . . don't recall the color of his hair."

"Clothing?"

"Just . . ." He cleared his throat. "This I don't recall."

"But he *was* clothed? He wasn't naked? Wasn't wearing a lamp shade on his head, or a swimming suit, or—"

"Oh no," Simson chuckled. "A suit, I guess, colored shirt, tie—like that."

Tranquillini turned to the bench. "Your Honor, I had hoped to be finished with this witness during this morning's session, as he is missing law classes in Southern California. But . . ."

"Yes, I see we are only five minutes short of the noon recess. All parties will return at two P.M."

It was more like a council of war than lunch, held at the Doggy Diner on Van Ness.

"All right, what has happened?" asked Tranquillini. "You go tearing off with this utterly charming young lady . . ."

"Hector Tranquillini. Corinne Jones."

They shook hands above the table, awkwardly to keep coat sleeves out of the half-squeezed plastic tubes of mustard.

Kearny said, "Corinne came to tell me Bart is in Boston and that someone else is trying to tail him, to get at Verna through him. Someone picked up his trail through the messages he's been leaving on the DKA answering machine in my office."

"A phone tap?" asked Tranquillini, truly surprised.

Corinne did not mention the ugly phone call or her reaction to it. She was ashamed of both. "Bart thinks they picked him up yesterday morning, from the message he left on the machine about a topless dancer named Fleur who works at the Iberville Caberet."

"Do you need me at the hearing this afternoon, Hec?" asked Kearny.

"To testify? No."

"Okay, then I'm going to get hold of O'B and we'll sweep the office for bugs. What I'm afraid of is a butterfly mike—that would have picked up not just phone conversations, but things like Benny Nicoletti telling me about his witness to the Fazzino hit."

Giselle was lost. "But if Pivarski isn't the hit man . . ."

"This guy saw *somebody*," said Kearny bleakly. "*He can identify the killer* whoever it might be. Which means they still might want to try and hit him."

"Are you going to call Nicoletti?" asked Tranquillini.

"Not until we're sure."

Tranquillini nodded and stood up. "I leave it to you. Time for me to get back to work. Thanks for a superb lunch."

"Hell, I thought you were paying," said Kearny.

Twenty-Four

Heslip had slept in his car yet again, this time in front of the address he had gotten from Zeb Rounds, 110 Allerton Street in Roxbury, Massachusetts. The houses were boxcarred down a San Francisco-steep hill, but the architecture was something completely new to him. Aged three-deck frame houses with an outside stairway to the upper floors on the front of the house and landings which were really porches on each floor. Looked like flats, one to a floor.

At 110, no answer on any floor. He went back down from the top flat and out to the narrow, slanted sidewalk. Roxbury was part of Boston, and Boston was damned cold this time of the morning in October, bright sunshine or not. Two houses down, a gray tiger-stripe cat was watching him. The door behind it opened and a black girl wearing an apron came out and picked it up. Her eyes met Heslip's and he gestured at the house he had just quit. "Nobody home. Do you know—"

"Wasn't no answer upstairs at Ethel's place? Third floor? She's Cliff's sister." Heslip had gotten Cliff Brown's name from Zeb Rounds, to go with the address. One of the girl's hands unconsciously stroked the old tom's blunt, scarred head. "Ethel Brown. Gettin' her welfare under that name, so that's the name she keeps even though she's got a live-in man. Probably went shopping, she's got two boys in school."

Half an hour later a slim black woman in a cloth coat

came trudging up from the bus stop with a heavy supermarket bag of groceries. Heslip held them so she could get out her keys. "You must be Ethel," he said with a big grin.

"That don't tell me who you are." She blew out a long breath. "Whew! The Good Samaritan, maybe?"

"I try to be." He broadened his grin. "Johnny Mack said you'd be home, most mornings."

Her Good-Samaritan look faded. "You a friend of Johnny's?"

He took his cue from her voice. "I owe him a little money on the New England-Miami game, and that's the truth. He was sayin' how broke he was. I got some cash right now from Mother's Day..."

Being when welfare checks arrived. Since she'd been shopping, it was a pretty safe bet yesterday had been the day. She reached, stiff-faced, for her groceries. "I don't hold much with gambling."

"Neither do I," said Heslip with his ready grin, "not when I lose. Thing is, he said his woman was pregnant or some such..."

"*That* woman? That *Verna*? Listen, let me tell you about *that* piece of goods. Was months ago she was pregnant, and..."

Johnny Mack had shown up with the pregnant Verna several months before. He'd bunked downstairs with Cliff, Verna upstairs with Ethel and her family. At first.

"Wasn't enough that girl was a whore, but then I started missing things, things you could pawn, y'know? And any money around the house." She shook her head in remembered outrage. "That damn girl was a *junkie!* A junkie whore, he brings her into *my* house, where I'm raising *my* kids! I threw her out, don't know where she went. Johnny Mack moved out of Cliff's place, too—and I don't know where *he* went, either. I know neither one of 'em will set foot in *my* house again."

"Would Cliff know where Johnny Mack is? I really ought to pay him back this money..."

"Me and Cliff aren't that close, mister."

* * *

Tranquillini said, with the manner of a man who's had a twenty-dollar lunch rather than a hot dog out of a cardboard boat, "Did Mr. Pivarski give you the letter, or did he give it to Miss Onoda?"

"He gave it to me. I read it and then gave it to her."

"Did Miss Onoda make any comment upon reading it?"

"She asked me to call Mr... to call your office."

"And you did."

"Yes, sir."

"And what did you say the date was?"

"November fifth."

"And you got no answer at my office, none at all. Did Mr. Pivarski have any comments while all this was going on?"

"He was not present. I'd left him by my desk..."

"Of course. And Mr. Pivarski then was invited back to the private office and Miss Onoda signed the bottom of this famous letter in his presence, and—"

"Objection to counsel's use of the word 'famous.'"

"Sustained."

Tranquillini nodded acquiescence. "Sorry, Your Honor. Now, it was after this conversation, Mr. Simson, that the money was tendered and the letter signed."

"Yes, sir."

"And you knew of this letter from November fifth of last year until this very day, didn't you, Mr. Simson? You have never forgotten Pivarski bringing that copy of the letter from his attorney, have you? Not for an instant."

"I recall the letter," said Simson stubbornly.

Tranquillini addressed the bench almost off-handedly.

"Respondent has previously placed before you as Exhibit A for Identification, an affidavit signed by Mr. Simson. I now would like that affidavit introduced into evidence."

"Any objection?"

"Yes."

The Hearing Officer hesitated. "I take it this is being offered for the purpose of impeachment, Mr. Tranquillini?"

"We object that it does *not* impeach the witness's testimony," said Delaney.

"That's up to the Hearing Officer," Tranquillini retorted. "We will take a half-hour recess while I study this document. I will rule upon it at that time."

DKA was not an agency that specialized in electronics, but being in the detective business they had a certain familiarity with bugs and their detection. As Kearny and O'Bannon moved about his private office, they carried a short-wave radio, very slowly taking the tuner across the spectrum of bands as they did.

"I'm telling you," said O'B, "that the 'Niners have the best defensive front four in football right now."

"Even if I give you that," said Kearny, who lived in Raider territory, "they don't have the offensive punch of the Raiders. I think . . ." With sudden clarity, his voice was also coming from the radio. ". . . that the Raiders are going to the Super Bowl again this year. I don't think"—he switched off the radio—". . . there is a team in pro football who can stop them."

O'Bannon spoke regretfully, "Well, hell, Dan. I have that Crescent Motors flooring check to get out this afternoon. I've been carrying it around for two days . . ."

"I'll get that billing file from your car."

Neither man spoke again until they were outside and standing under the skyway where their voices were half-drowned in the thunder and growl of overhead traffic, just in case someone was getting really fancy and using a shotgun mike on them from some adjacent building. "Infinity transmitter in the phone, like I thought," said Kearny.

Infinity transmitters, sometimes called butterfly mikes, are tiny senders which operate without wires or outside connections. They broadcast not only phone conversations but anything within thirty feet of the phone, once they have been activated by the phone being rung from outside and an electronic signal being sent to them. A voice-activated tape recorder takes down whatever is said.

"Somebody spent a lot of time and money on this one," said O'B. "Think one of our people let them through the alarms?"

"More likely they got a wiring diagram from the alarm company and cut our electricity from outside long enough to go in and plant the thing. Two, three minutes inside is all they would need. I'll be going back to the hearing in a bit, I can alert Giselle, but would you find a pay phone and call Sacramento? Tell them to radio Ballard on the CB and find out where he's staying and tell him not to phone in. No explanations. I don't want our office up there knowing what's going on."

"Will do."

Kearny returned to his office and lit a cigarette and stared at the bugged telephone. Who? Some agency of the State? He rejected that out of hand, as he did anyone from the city cops. So it was the organized crime people who ran Padilla Drayage as one of their quasi-legal fronts. The bug had served them well, alerting them to Benny Nicoletti's secret witness; but that wasn't why it had been placed—that had just been a bonus. What was there in the DKA license squabble with the State that was worth all that time, effort and expense?

There was only one answer: to find out how close Bart Heslip was getting to Verna Rounds, so they could get to her first. But *why*? What could she possibly know that would be of use to them?

Maybe he'd know more after he talked with Benny Nicoletti tonight. In person. Find out when Benny's witness was discovered, when he'd cracked, when Benny had talked with Pivarski at Hawkley's office—things like that. Meanwhile, he had time to catch the end of Hec's attack on Jeffrey Simson.

"Complainant's objection is overruled," said the Hearing Officer. "The document will be received in evidence as Respondent's Exhibit A."

"I believe that is all of this witness," said Tranquillini.

"Any redirect?"

Delaney picked up his copy of Simson's affidavit. "Did you prepare this document, Mr. Simson?" He looked over at the court reporter. "I am referring to Respondent Exhibit A."

"I wrote what is there, yes, sir."

"Mr. Dan Kearny asked you to prepare this document, did he not, on October twenty-second of this year?"

"I believe that was the date."

"Are the words in this document your own words, Mr. Simson?"

"Well, sir, it's . . . hard to answer that just yes or no. Mr. Kearny and Mr. O'Bannon came to my apartment in Los Angeles and they . . . were present at the time I wrote it. As . . . each sentence was written, Mr. Kearny was looking . . . at the wording of my sentences . . ."

You are goofing it, Johnny-me-bhoy, thought Tranquillini as he mentally rehearsed his objection. This line of questioning makes it impossible for you to claim that Simson altered circumstances in his affidavit to help out his old friend Dan Kearny.

"Did he make any comments to you as to what actually must have happened?" asked Delaney.

"Yes, sir," said Simson eagerly, "he made comments and . . ."

"And *suggestions* as to what should go into the affidavit?"

"Need I remind the witness that he is under oath?" asked Tranquillini off-handedly, "and that the witnesses to *this* conversation are still alive and able to testify?"

Simson cleared his throat. "Mr. Kearny . . . um . . . made no suggestions per se, no, sir."

"Mr. Hearing Officer, I have a great deal of difficulty in examining the witness on this document because I don't understand in what way it impeaches his sworn testimony." Delaney's voice was angry and baffled, as if he were just realizing the mistake he had made in emphasizing the prior antagonist relationship between Kearny and Simson due to Simson's dismissal from DKA in February.

Tranquillini was on his feet. "I believe I can explain to counsel how this document impeaches his witness if I could have permission, from time to time, to go slightly beyond the docu—"

''Objection,'' said Delaney.

''I haven't said anything yet.''

The Hearing Officer said, ''I will rule on the admissibility of counsel's statements as they occur.''

''Thank you, Your Honor. After the witness stated that he tried to call my office and got no answer on November fifth, I had my answering service's records searched. No call, none at all, was logged in during the hour and date in question.''

''I would point out,'' said Delaney hurriedly, ''that answering service records are not kept according to the rules of evidence.''

''Noted. Please proceed, Mr. Tranquillini.''

''In his affidavit the witness stated that only he and Miss Onoda were in the office that evening, with Ms. Rose Kelly on the front office switchboard. We now have located Ms. Kelly, who is willing to testify that she was *not* on the switchboard that day and hour in question.''

Delaney had started to rise to object, but he hesitated, then sank back down while staring thoughtfully at Simson on the stand.

''Faulty recollection on the witness's part?'' asked Tranquillini. ''Perhaps. His memory seems very convenient. But his affidavit also states that the Pivarski transaction was 'just a normal collection'—his own words.''

He raked Simson with scorn-filled eyes. ''Four days ago, when he wrote this statement, that was *all he could remember,* Your Honor. Yet now he remembers, under oath, the letter Pivarski is supposed to have gotten Kathy Onoda's signature on. This, even though the State cannot produce this signed letter. He remembers a call to me of which there is no record. He remembers Miss Onoda fraudulently writing and destroying a normal DKA receipt for the Pivarski payment. Yet he cannot remember the address where he lived six months ago. Only with difficulty can he remember the address where he lived for two years. He cannot remember the name of *one* other of the *two thousand* accounts he serviced as a DKA collector...''

Tranquillini waved a hand as if too disgusted to continue.

"Your Honor, I have no desire to go any further at this time. The document speaks for itself. The Hearing Officer will review this witness's testimony in relation to the document, to determine if it does impeach." He turned cold eyes on Simson. "You are excused."

Delaney began, "Mr. Hearing Officer—"

The Hearing Officer cut him off curtly. "At the end of yesterday's hearing, I directed Complainant to present Mr. Pivarski to this hearing. We are now ready to have Mr. Pivarski sworn in."

"I . . . cannot produce him at this time, Your Honor," said Delaney in an uncomfortable voice. "I have been assured by his attorneys that we can have him here Monday morning, but . . ."

After a long pause the Hearing Officer looked over at Tranquillini. "Counselor?"

"Monday morning is acceptable to the Respondent, Your Honor."

Or never, even, thought Tranquillini. It looked as if he had been successful in showing Simson's testimony was tainted and thus, in keeping the letter out of evidence. Temporarily. But on Monday he had to start all over again with Pivarski. Pivarski's direct testimony would get the letter in for sure, unless he was also able to discredit him. He'd gambled that by pushing a subpoena for Pivarski, Heslip would get enough time to find Verna Rounds, so they'd have direct testimony on their side. It looked like he'd lost the gamble. And cost Kearny his license in the process.

"Very well," said the Hearing Officer. "These proceedings are adjourned until ten o'clock on Monday morning."

Twenty-Five

It was eight at night before Cliff Brown appeared at the three-decker in Roxbury; a slight, black man with big feet he pointed out as he walked. His receding poll and horn-rim glasses gave him a spuriously intellectual look.

"Johnny Mack?" He shook his head. He smelled companionably of beer and cigars. Down the hall, a TV blared. "California."

Heslip had a foot in the door. He was wearing shades to get the slightly menacing effect of a hooded falcon. "I heard different."

"You heard wrong." He gestured with his cigar. His voice was high-pitched and breathless, like a jackleg preacher shouting after parishioners on the street. "And if you don't move that foot outta my door you gonna need a surgeon to sew it back on the ankle."

"We heard Johnny Mack was livin' with you."

Brown came out on the porch a couple of feet, and Heslip stepped back. "Okay, that was four-five months back. But he lef', said he was goin back to California."

"What about his woman? Verna take her dollar-a-day habit back to California, too?"

"Never heard of her."

And Brown stepped nimbly back and slammed the door in Heslip's face. Through the frosted glass panel, which was decorated with scrolls and fountains, he could hear Brown's high-pitched sneering laughter. Chagrined, Heslip grunted, and went up the exterior stairway to the third-floor porch outside sister Ethel's place. He had seen her going off somewhere an hour before; maybe her man knew something she didn't.

He turned the knob and pulled the door back hard toward the hinges, then put his shoulder to the shellacked wood framing the glass panel, just where it met the door frame, and shoved violently. The door flew open and Heslip was in a hallway that ran back to the head of interior stairs leading down through the building. Opposite the head of the stairs was a varnished oak door leading into Ethel's apartment.

Heslip knocked. After about forty-five seconds, a heavyset black man wearing a striped shirt and maroon slacks and slippers opened the door. "How'd you git inside this buil—"

Heslip crowded against him and was inside. With a heel he hooked the door shut behind him. He didn't know what degree of crime he was committing, since he knew nothing of Massachusetts statues; but he knew it was some sort of breaking and entering—at night, a dwelling, unarmed. The heavyset man gave before Heslip's shove, then stood against the far side of the hall and let out a long, sad breath.

"After cash, there ain't any. Moveables, there's the TV set and me."

Heslip had his hands thrust deep in his topcoat pockets because he had no gloves and didn't want to leave fingerprints. But he realized that with the shades and his bulky muscularity and those hands which could be holding guns in the pockets, he would pass as muscle.

"No rip-off," he said. He let his head swivel theatrically to check down the hall toward the unlighted kitchen, up the hall toward the living room where a TV murmured, "You sittin' the kids?"

The heavyset man stiffened slightly. His eyes went to the rear bedroom adjacent to the doorway where they stood. "Now you leave them kids outta whatever—"

"*You sittin' em?*"

He sighed again, and nodded. He had a subdued but massive dignity. Heslip liked him but had to reduce him so the thought of resistance would seem remote to the man. "Your wife, Fat Stuff?"

"No need . . ." Heslip moved his right arm slightly. The man sighed again and the stiffness went from his stance. "Church."

"We want a little chat with Johnny Mack, Stuff."

"Is this . . . bad?"

"Don't be worryin' about his soul, if that's what you mean."

The heavyset man thought about it for a while. Heslip let him. He was in as deep as he could get anyway, if anything went wrong. He pushed a little more in the direction he wanted to go.

"No argument with you an' yours, Stuff. Just think of us as a cloud cross the face of the moon."

Another sigh. "He's living with his brother Willy."

"Where?"

"Don't know the exact address. Few streets over on Madison. Ethel and Willy don't get on even more than Ethel and Cliff don't get on."

"Cliff and Willy close?"

"Christmas and Easter—you know."

Heslip nodded and gestured down the hall toward the kitchen. "I'll use the back stairs. Gotta tell my man out back that we has drawn a blank covert." He used a tight grin he figured went with his dark glasses and the theatricality of his entrance. "You go on back an' watch that TV, and tell yourself your phone is out of order for an hour or two. Dig?"

"I got a woman and kids I care more about than pimps and drug pushers. Go with God, brother."

Heslip used his grin again. "Just so I go, right, blood?"

On his way out of the apartment to the rear stairs, he took the key from the kitchen door. It was a simple three-tumbler, not a cylinder lock, and he hoped the key might be joggled around to open Clifford's back door, below.

Ten minutes later, when a commercial sent Cliff Brown down to the kitchen for another beer, Heslip was waiting. As Cliff started in from the hall, Heslip's open left hand collided with his face and sent him windmilling across the room backwards to slam up against the old-fashioned porcelain sink with the slanted tile drainboard beside it.

Heslip advanced, his right hand jammed in the coat pocket, bunched and slightly raised in the best Bogart tradition, one knuckle pressed against the cloth to approximate a gun.

"I told you we had business with Johnny Mack." He let his voice rumble deep in his chest. "Now, without I get brother Willy's address, we gonna have business with you first."

At about the same time, Ballard was making a score of his own, although he didn't know it at first. He hadn't had a decent cup of coffee all day, and his hours in various Sacramento offices—county recorder, tax assessor, vital statistics, registrar—had been fruitless. Greenly was pure, pure, pure. So when the little green Toyota zipped over into a tow-away zone on Broadway just off Twenty-fourth Street, Ballard didn't expect anything except someone getting a ride home. Not even when the someone was a hefty mid-twenties girl with a pretty face and meaty thighs.

But the ride wasn't home. Instead, up onto the freeway at the massive interchange of 99 and 80, then west on Interstate 80. That was when Ballard's hopes started to rise, especially when they went off on West Capitol Avenue where all the rendezvous motels were located. But their destination was a costly anonymous steak house, not one of the hot-sheet joints which flanked it. They had cassis and soda in the lounge while Ballard—who had never heard of cassis and soda—had a Miller's at the bar, and while they ate filet mignon with mushroom caps in the dining room, Ballard had another Miller's at the bar, to wash down two sacks of pretzels.

No hand-holding or meaty thigh-massaging before, during, or after the steaks. Greenly was about as romantic as a doctor treating a virus. And it was short of nine-o'clock when Ballard front-tailed them back up onto the freeway for the run back into Sacramento proper. Still, it was something. And it got better.

Because Greenly stayed on Interstate 80 to where it swung north and cut through the California Exposition grounds, where the state fair was held each year, Ballard was behind him again by the time he took the Arden Way exit to Howe Avenue and, a few blocks north, a modern apartment building two stories high and half a block long, shaped like a motel. The green Toyota went into stall 23 and Greenly and the girl went upstairs.

Ballard was standing in front, in the driveway, when lights went on in a second-floor apartment. He went up and checked the door—Apartment 23—and then down to check mailboxes. Madeline Westfield.

Who held Greenly there for under two hours. The tailjob back to Bartley Drive put Greenly into bed yet again before midnight. And, Ballard was sure, to sleep. He would have spent his sexual energy on Madeline. For the wife, the tale of a late-night budget session or the weekly poker game with the boys. For Ballard, back at his motel, a message to call Dan Kearny at 8 A.M. at a number Ballard didn't recognize. Left for him two hours earlier.

Which meant that about the time Ballard had watched Madeline Westfield's bedroom lights go out, Kearny had been ringing Benny Nicoletti's doorbell. It was an old dark Victorian on Elizabeth Street below Diamond Heights. Kearny had never been there before. There were fancy frosted glass panels on either side of the door with Nicoletti's initials on them. A plain-faced woman answered.

"Come in, Mr. Kearny." She shook hands firmly. "We've talked on the phone enough times so I feel I know you. Benny's down in his shop."

Kearny stopped at the bottom of the stairs in surprise. There was a full woodworking shop—lathe, drill press, circle and band and jig saws, an electric planer, lots of hand tools.

"When the cops retire me, I'll be a cabinetmaker," said Nicoletti. His heavy body was draped in a brown smock and his forearms were speckled with wood shavings. "I'm trying to turn four exactly similar table legs, and if you don't think that's a bitch . . ."

Kearny looked around for an ashtray.

"Use that coffee can for your butts. What couldn't keep until morning?" There was only curiosity, not rebuke, in his voice.

"My office is bugged," said Kearny.

"Bugged?" Nicoletti, who had just sat down on the edge of the tool bench, bounced to his feet. "You ain't suggesting I—"

"The equipment is too good for you boys."

Benny was pacing the pathway of uncluttered concrete between the various power tools by the time Kearny stopped talking. He was even smoking one of Kearny's cigarettes. "So they know who our witness is, and they know we've brought him down from Canada. They know he's pointed a finger at Pivarski's DMV photo, but that don't matter because he *might* be able to I.D. the actual killer if he ever saw him face to face. So my bet is they want him, and want him bad, just for insurance."

Kearny stubbed his third cigarette. "Anyway, I told you about it." He stood up and yawned. "I hope your operation is as leakproof as you think it is."

"Me and two other guys know where he is, that's all." He was pacing again, thinking aloud. "What say we use the bug to feed 'em false information? You game?"

"False information such as what?"

Twenty minutes later Kearny left, to Mrs. Nicoletti's profuse apologies for not getting the chance to pour some coffee down him. From a gas station he called Ballard's Sacramento motel and left a message that he wanted to be called at 8 A.M. The number he left was that of a suburban pay phone a quarter of a mile from his house in the East Bay town of Lafayette. He doubted that even Hawkley's busy little legions had started bugging pay phones at random.

Heslip had fallen asleep in his rented Pinto outside 428 Madison Street, the address he had coerced out of the terrified Clifford Brown. He hadn't wanted to fall asleep, but here it was the wee hours of Friday morning and his head hadn't hit a pillow since those few hours in Fleur Lisette's bed some forty-eight hours back.

Not that he would miss anything. Willie Brown wasn't about to be home during the hours from dusk to dawn, if then: the neighbors had confirmed what Ethel's husband had suggested with his remark about pimps and drug pushers. Johnny Mack would be the pimp in question; Willie, the drug pusher. Johnny Mack was intermittently there—the same could be said of Willie—but Verna wasn't. And no baby had been seen.

He could have gone looking, but he didn't know this town. Didn't have a photo of Verna, not even a good description of Johnny Mack. This address was all he had, so he had to make this address work for him. Couldn't even call DKA, find out how the hearings were going. Couldn't call Corinne except at work, if there . . .

And he fell asleep, even freezing his butt off because he couldn't chance a telltale exhaust that would alert careful dope dealer eyes. People who dealt in dope had careful eyes, or they passed quickly from the street scene to prison, or to the morgue, or into the sad hollow dreams they sold to the unwary.

Twenty-Six

When the phone rang at seven o'clock on Friday morning, Corinne Jones was sitting on the edge of her bed and marveling at what a good night's sleep she'd had once she knew Bart hadn't been fooling around with that topless bitch back in New Orleans. But the phone started it up again. Who called you at seven in the morning? The breather with another serving of filth? Or maybe just Toni to ask if she could open the office again.

"Ah . . . is this here . . . um . . . Corinne Jones?"

Unknown voice. Female. Southern Black.

"Yes. Speaking."

"Your . . . um . . . Mr. Heslip gave me this number, said I could reach you evenings . . ."

"This is morning," snapped Corinne. If Bart had given that topless bitch her unlisted home phone number . . .

"This here is an emergency . . ." The voice paused breathily but it was the breathlessness of extra poundage, not of menace. "Thing is, I done hear from my husband after all these years, an' . . ."

Damn the woman! But at least, with a husband, it wasn't about to be that topless bitch.

"You'll have to tell me who your husband is—and who *you* are."

"Oh! Emmalina Rounds. It's my little girl that—"

"Mrs. *Rounds!* Yes! Bart said . . . oh, and you've heard from your husband in New Orleans?"

"Uh . . . I guess ex-husband, cause he's done remarried a long time ago. Thing is, four men come to see him an' wanted Verna's address. He wouldn't give it to 'em, so they started to beat on him. He was callin me from the hospital, had some busted ribs an' all, but he knocked one of 'em out so the police, they got him. An' he didn't tell 'em nothin bout where my Verna is at."

"That's wonderful, Mrs. Rounds."

"Thing is, he wanted to get word to Mr. Heslip that there was men after my Verna. He had it wrong about Mr. Heslip, thought he was fum some gover'mint agency . . ."

They talked a little longer and hung up. Corinne sat, phone in hand, trying to think of what to do. She had no idea of how to reach Bart. He already knew other men were after Verna, but he didn't know they were going for violence. What frightened her was that her Bart was the kind who would get in their way rather than let them do anything to the little former file clerk.

DKA. She had to let Giselle know, they would have some ideas. But she couldn't call them because the phone was bugged. Maybe her phone was bugged too. Maybe even the office phone. Maybe . . .

The trouble was, you knew one phone was bugged, actually bugged like on TV or during Watergate, and all of a sudden you were sure every phone in the world was bugged. But if she went down the hall and used the Miltons' phone . . .

Giselle Marc was supposed to be up at 7 A.M. herself so Dan Kearny could pick her up out front on his way through from Lafayette. But Giselle was a slow starter, so the phone ringing at 7:45 caught her slopping around the bedroom in pajamas and thinking that when you cut your foot on the shag rug, it was time to vacuum.

"Yes, Ms. Marc," said a clipped vaguely familiar female voice, "This is ACT calling."

"ACT?" What was this, a joke?

"American Conservatory Theater. Sorry to phone you so early, but we *do* have your name on file and we are auditioning for *Macbeth* at 10 A.M. and—"

"*Macbeth*?"

"I *do* have the right Giselle Marc, do I not? You *are* familiar with the words of the Bard?"

"Of course, but—"

"We are casting the three witches on the moor." The voice was suddenly emoting over the phone. " 'When shall we three meet again' . . ."

" 'In thunder, lightning, or in rain' " Giselle quoted back. She had it now. Corinne, doing a great job setting up a meeting in case tape recorders were turning in some anonymous little room. She and Corinne and Larry Ballard on a fog-swept corner outside the hospital where Bart had just come out of a seventy-two-hour coma, quoting that line to one another. "I'm delighted at the opportunity. I will be at the Sutter Street casting office as soon as I can."

"We'll look forward to seeing you."

As they hung up, Larry Ballard was talking from a pay phone in Sacramento with Dan Kearny on a pay phone in Lafayette, and had just gotten the low-down on the bugged office and all the rest. The phone was just down the block from Madeline Westfield's apartment, where he could keep a watch on the bus stop she'd likely wait at. He'd just told Kearny about her.

"Sounds like just a casual lay to me," said Kearny thoughtfully. "If you laid all the cheating husbands end-to-end—"

"It wasn't like that, Dan. He sure wasn't any Casanova to her last night. More like a mailman delivering a letter."

"Probably just normal civil service enthusiasm for his job," said Kearny. "But try to get a run-down on her anyway. So far we don't have anything suggesting any *other* irregularities in Greenly's life, and Monday is it for us."

Ballard waved sweetly to the woman standing on one foot first and then the other outside the booth. To hell with her, he was here first. He said to Kearny, "I can try to bust his home phone bill to get a run-down on his long-distance calls, but I don't know the billing cycle here so the phone company might not have it until the end of the month. If he's on the take, it isn't showing up in the normal circles of his life. I asked retail credit to give me a full profile, not just a rating, and should get that today. But beyond that . . ."

"As a last resort try to bust his bank account with the state investigator gag. If it backfires, DKA'll pick up your bail."

"Thanks a lot," said Ballard drily. "How's Bart doing?"

"Nobody knows. He's flying blind, we don't even have a contact number on him."

The way he likes it, thought Ballard as he hung up. He stepped out of the booth, put a hand on each of the irate woman's shoulders, kissed her on the cheek, and beamed, "I'm *engaged!*" and started off down the street. When he looked back, the woman waved to him with a black-gloved hand. How often, he thought, did you get a chance to make someone's day for them like that?'

And then broke into a run, because he had just seen Madeline Westfield getting into a car which had pulled up in front of her place. A goddam ride instead of a bus! And by the time he'd gotten the Cutlass turned around, he'd lost the other car in traffic.

So. Hell. Couldn't tail her to work. Which meant back to the landlady of her apartment house. He hoped Bart was doing better than he was.

Bart Heslip, to tell the truth, was getting damned sick of living out of that rented Pinto with all his clothes and shaving gear in the suitcase in back. Thirty-six hours all together, the last fifteen here in the 400-block of Madison Street. Pretty soon they'd carve his initials in the urinal of the gas station men's room down on the corner.

It was starting to warm up a little now, with the sun getting high enough to reach down to him between the buildings. As at brother Cliff's, three-deckers. He got out and stretched in the bright warmth. Corinne would be at her desk by now. How about going up to the café on the other corner that had opened at 6 A.M., getting a cheeseburger and fries, and calling her?

After ordering, he went outside to the pay phone, dropped his dime and gave his credit card number.

"Far Flung Travel. May I help you?"

"Toni? This is Bart. Is Corinne—"

"Thank God you called. Hang on a sec."

But the voice that came on was Kearny's, for Chrissake! Who explained about Emmalina Rounds' phone call, and the fact that the search for Verna Rounds, for some unknown reason, had turned very nasty indeed.

"But what can Verna tell anybody they don't already know?"

"I can't figure it out either, Bart, but be careful. Watch your back-trail."

And the sucker hung up! Just like that, so he didn't even have a chance to tell Corinne how he missed her. He stepped out of the booth, still keeping his eye on the front of 428, up near the far end of the block on the other side of the street. Nobody who fit the neighbors' description of either Johnny Mack or Willie had been in or out, no purple hog Cadillac had shown up in front.

He'd call Corinne again later in the day if he didn't score here before then. Down beyond the intersection a big car backing into a parking space caught his eye for a moment. But it was a Chrysler New Yorker Brougham, not Willie's purple Cadillac. The sunlight glancing off the chrome trim of the tinted windshield momentarily blinded him.

He started into the café for his cheeseburger. The searchers were back there somewhere, all right, but they didn't have Roxbury, Massachusetts. Old Zebulon Rounds had come through in the pinch. They hadn't strongarmed the address out of him, and they wouldn't make another try, not with one of their thugs in police custody. *Jesus Christ!*

He whirled and ran back for the phone booth.

They wouldn't go after Rounds again, hell no, but Fleur the topless dancer knew brother Clifford's address, because he'd told her after getting it from Rounds. And they knew Fleur's address . . .

New Orleans Information had no listing for Fleur Lisette, so he got the number for the Iberville Cabaret. Almost noon there, ought to be someone who . . .

"Listen, lemma talk with the manager, this is an emergency."

"Yeah. Me." He listened to Heslip. "Fleur? Christ man, after what that goddam weirdo did to her, she won't be outta the hospital for—"

"Hospital?" Oh, no, it already had happened. "Which one?"

"John who got his kicks outta cutting, I guess, and . . . which hospital? New Orleans General."

Another credit card call, this time to the head nurse. "I'm Fleur's brother, in the Air Force and just passing through on assignment, can't even come up to see her but if I could speak to her . . ."

"She's in a ward, doesn't have a phone—"

"Anything you can do?"

Head nurses could do a great deal. "But just for a moment, you understand? She's conscious but despite the sedation in a good deal of pain, and . . ."

Fleur's voice came on, weak and pinched.

"Fleur, this is Bart Heslip. I just heard—"

"You bastard! Oh, you rotten son of a bitch bastard!"

"Fleur, I swear to you I didn't know anything heavy like this was going down—"

"You knew they was followin' us. They said they'd hurt me an' I told 'em. Gave that address for Verna. I'm *glad* I told 'em cause maybe you'll get in their way an' they'll do you like they done me."

"Fleur, anything you need—"

"How about a new nose? A new ear?" Her voice was a ragged scream. "*After* I told 'em they done it. For fun. I hope they get you an' cut your nuts off!"

He hung up the dead phone and stood shivering in the sunshine.

Twenty-Seven

Dan Kearny dialed and when a hard male voice answered, asked for Benny Nicoletti. Nicoletti was out. Kearny left his name and number. Seven minutes later the unlisted phone rang—the line wasn't run through the switchboard.

"I got your message."

"Pivarski is going to be there on Monday," said Kearny. "The Hearing Officer made it official."

"Monday!" exclaimed Nicoletti. "I thought this afternoon was when they were supposed to—"

"Delaney conned him into waiting until Monday. Said Hawkley couldn't have his client there until after the weekend."

"Those bastards *gotta* have a pipeline!" exclaimed Nicoletti angrily. "After the weekend! Hell, that's exactly..." He paused. "Look, Dan, not on the phone. Can you come over to the Hall?"

"No way. After Monday I might not have a license, I'm getting out all the billing I can today, so—"

"Okay. I'll be there in ten minutes."

Kearny hung up and looked at his watch and blew out a deep breath. Right on schedule. The bastards had better be listening. When Nicoletti's bulky form filled the open doorway a few minutes later, Kearny actually was immersed in the billing. He looked up. "I don't know why I ever agreed to cooperate with you guys," he said crossly to the big cop. "Shut the door."

Nicoletti did.

Kearny said, "Okay, what couldn't you tell me on the phone?"

Nicoletti leaned forward confidentially. By so doing, he brought his head closer to the bugged phone. "Dan, there's gotta be a leak in the Department. What tipped me was your saying they insisted Pivarski couldn't show at the hearing until after the weekend. See, we got him down here early in the week, told him it'd be a day, two days, for us to set up an eyeball of Pivarski for him. Now all of a sudden it's going on a week. So just *yesterday* he told us that was it, back to Canada Friday night—tonight—if he isn't shown Pivarski in the flesh *today*."

He leaned back and sighed gustily. "I'll do my damndest between now and tonight to talk him into staying until Monday, but I think we're dead. Jesus, what a mess." He stood up and shook hands with Kearny, winked and grinned and said, in a very worried voice, "I'll let you know if we can get him to change his mind."

When he was gone Kearny lit a cigarette. So, if the tapes were turning, this would take the pressure off Nicoletti's witness. And on Monday morning when Hawkley finally brought Pivarski in thinking there was no chance of him being eyeballed by the linen-truck driver, he would get a surprise.

Ballard was singularly unsurprised to learn the resident manager of Madeline Westfield's apartment house could tell him little of the tenant in Apartment 23. That was par for the course. But the manager, Mrs. Garnison, wasn't. She was the rarest of landladies, one who didn't give a damn. She was an imperious, iron-haired fifty-five, with iron in the spine and an open mind.

"Madeline? In a place like this, one of my oldest tenants. She's been here nearly two years, I'd have to look it up if you need an exact date."

"Two years is fine." Ballard had said he was from a bank to which Ms. Madeline Westfield had applied for credit.

"Banks want to know a lot more than they have to." She

was knitting, her large, shapely, capable hands moving with bewildering speed, clicking the needles in a syncopated counterpoint to her words. She never looked down; some inner computer seemed to know when those hands had taken the needles to the end of a row.

"Well, she wants to finance a very expensive car through the bank, and they want to be sure she can handle the payments. Can you confirm where she works?"

"Last I knew..." She was squinting. She started to shake her head, then her face cleared. "Sure. When she took the apartment, she was working for United Parcel Service."

Ballard nodded sagely. "That agrees with our records. Now, how can I put this, Mrs. Garnison? Personal data. Do you know of any personal habits that aren't... well, that might interfere..." He let his tut-tut expression speak for him. "Any special boyfriends or..."

She shook her head vigorously. "Mister, she could run a football team through that apartment for all I know or care, long as their cleats don't scar the floors."

That was that from Mrs. Garnison. He used the same pay phone that he had used that morning with Kearny to call the retail credit agency he'd asked to get a complete rundown on Greenly's credit.

"Oh, hi, Mr. Ballard, I'm glad you called. We just got that data you requested. As we told you yesterday, his current rating is top of the heap. But the computer tells us that as recently as five months ago his credit was very spotty. Bad pay on credit cards and retail accounts, paid the late penalty on his house note for seven months out of an eleven-month period. Classic picture of a man getting into financial trouble. Then he got healthy and has stayed that way ever since."

Ballard felt a rising excitement. Greenly was beginning to come together in a picture very different from the one he presented to the casual observer.

"Anything in the derogs to suggest what his problem was?" Derogs were raw data, derogatory reports collected in the field from friends, associates or neighbors by the retail credit checking firm. They did not go into client reports.

"Um . . ." Ballard could hear papers being shuffled. "A number of informants said he liked poker and the ponies. Gambling."

"Women?"

"Steady family man, by all reports."

More and more, Madeline Westfield was beginning to look like a charade played for Madeline's benefit. Greenly, in financial trouble through gambling, is subverted by mob money for some purpose. What? No idea. But something involving DKA in some way. To get what the mob needs, he has to seduce Madeline Westfield. He goes through the motions, gets what he needs.

So the something has to do with Madeline's job. What in hell could an employee of United Parcel Service have that someone out after DKA could need? Answer: Madeline was no longer employed at UPS. So one of Ballard's jobs was to get her current employment. And in Sacramento he was pretty sure it was in state government. And not in Professional and Vocational Standards, because then Greenly could have gotten what he needed on his own.

Ballard caught Interstate 80 back downtown, and got off at Fifteenth Street. Greenly banked at the Bank of Tokyo on Broadway and Fourteenth. Time to try to fake his way into a look at Greenly's account. See if five or six months ago heavy cash deposits had suddenly begun. See if cash payments to Madeline Westfield had begun. He was sitting outside in the Cutlass trying to work up the nerve to pass himself off as a state investigator when he had an inspiration. One of those inspirations recognized—if not always understood—not only by detectives private and public, but by scholars, researchers, and genealogists among others. The sudden rush of feeling that made you turn around and go back to ask the final question and break the case. The phone call you hadn't planned to make, the public record book you reached for when the one you really wanted was out, the name you looked under in a phone book that had no rational connection with your subject but was the name he was hiding under, all the same.

For Ballard it was a word. *Gambling*. And an absolute knowledge that Greenly, as an accountant himself, would never run dirty money through his bank account. And finally, the fact that it was Friday, and people need extra cash over the weekends.

Thus he was parked on O Street off Seventh at 12:06 when Greenly emerged from the Business and Professions Building. So sure had Ballard been that he'd already fed the meter an hour's worth of change, so he had only to get out and saunter along half a block behind the spare figure moving through the noontime lunchers, strollers, and window-shoppers from the adjacent government offices.

Right into a savings and loan company eight blocks from Greenly's office. Since Ballard's face meant no more to Greenly than a cantaloupe, he was close by when Greenly strode back to the safe-deposit window and read the number off his key to the girl. "Box eleven eighty-seven, please."

"Yes, sir." The bright-faced girl riffled through the signature file, compared it with the name Greenly had written on the slip. "Right this way, Mr. Maling."

Ballard, standing at the closest customer table, wrote "1187" on the back of a withdrawal slip, along with "Maling," and put the folded slip in his pocket. Greenly shortly emerged from the gate into the big, steel-gleaming vault. Several minutes and three blocks later, Ballard watched Greenly, in a quasi-skid-row area a detour away from his office, enter, in turn, a cigar shop and a Chinese laundry.

Since he was stuffing no cigars in his pocket as he emerged from the cigar store and carried no shirts under his arm from the Chinese laundry, Ballard deduced that he had been placing bets with cash gotten from the safe-deposit box. Not a bad trick for a feller whose sole source of income, according to retail credit, came from his salary with the State of California.

The rest of the day was anticlimactic. Out at the huge echoing United Parcel Service warehouse on Shore Street in West Sacramento he learned that Madeline Westfield had left her job as a package sorter nineteen months before, when her Civil Service job as a clerk-typist for the State of California had come through. No idea where she had landed as a clerk-typist, except that it was indeed with the State.

Back downtown, for miles and hours of red tape from office to office, until he was brought to the cubicle of the lady who could tell him where Madeline was now employed—the lady in this cubicle in the Department of Employment on Eighth Street. Only it was empty. Its occupant had left forty-seven minutes early for the weekend and no, nobody else could help him because, see here, mister, this is Friday and we have to clear our desks. Come back Monday, fellow. Who do you think you are?

Nobody, my friend. Nobody at all. Just a taxpayer.

Ten minutes before the streetlights went on, a purple hog with two black men and three white women in it pulled up in front of 428 Madison Street. Heslip came erect behind the wheel of the Pinto, happily jerked from his thoughts by the arrival. They had not been pleasant thoughts because his mind, unbidden, had kept returning to the venomous, weak, hurt, frightened voice of Fleur. God almighty, her nose cut off, an ear gone—could a plastic surgeon fix things like that?

Whatever it cost, DKA was going to pay for it, either out of the health plan or out of pocket.

And then the Cadillac showed up. Behind the wheel was a hard-faced dude wearing a wide-brimmed hat and smoking a cheroot. That would be Willy. The pusher. The other man got out, with one of the girls. Dressed in funky plaid threads and a floppy cap. He would be Johnny Mack. Peanut butter. Off the wall.

The purple hog whispered away as Johnny Mack and the girl, who looked like she was right off the Greyhound, went up the front steps. No hairdo for the girl, a skirt to cover her knees instead of barely covering her pudenda. Yeah. Johnny Mack would be taking her application, recruiting her to his string with a tumble in the sack. As they went through the front door he was all over her, squeezing and touching and loving up.

By this time Heslip was out of the Pinto and halfway across the street. As he reached the sidewalk the streetlights went on, casting his abrupt, moving shadow around his ankles. He looked up and down the street—and froze.

In the next block two bulky men were getting out of the Chrysler. For the first instant he recognized only the stance: the set of the feet, the way the arms were held, the slight arrogance in the tilt of the head. That edge of contempt that physical competence gives one. It is a stance with no innocence. Heslip had some of it himself from his years in the ring, which was why he could successfully pose as muscle when the need arose.

In the next instant he recognized the men—the ones who had tailed him from Fleur's house to the airport in New Orleans. Sure to have been two of the four who attacked Zeb Rounds. Also sure to have been those who slashed up Fleur Lisette.

Here in Boston. Here, now.

Heslip was taking the outside stairs of the three-decker two at a time. He was sure Johnny Mack was taking the girl to the upstairs flat. If the two strongarms caught up with him, they would have Verna next. Johnny Mack would be a slender reed.

Johnny Mack was at the door of the third-floor flat, key in hand and free arm around the giggling, clinging girl, when Heslip kicked in the outside door and came through from the porch. Johnny Mack thrust the girl toward Heslip and backed up against the wall with his hands out toward Heslip, palm first. "You want Willy Brown," he babbled. "I ain't him. Ain't even a friend, jus bummed the borrow of his apartment fo—"

"You," Heslip snapped at the girl. "Out of this." He saw she was stoned on weed. He grabbed an arm, almost threw her across the hall at the interior staircase by which she and Johnny Mack had just come up. "Downstairs, and if you're smart, get a bus back to Podunkville and stay there."

With a drug-tranquilized look, she shrugged and went down the stairs. As she disappeared from sight, she started to giggle. Heslip crowded Johnny Mack up against the door frame and bunched both muscular hands in the lapels of his suitcoat. "Where's Verna? Fast and quick."

"Man, I don't know where that bitch—"

Heslip slammed the back of his head against the edge of the frame so hard he cried out. "There's two men on the way up who cut the nose off a girl in New Orleans for giving them that answer. *Talk*, goddam you!"

Johnny Mack split wide open as Heslip had expected. "I ain't seen her since she had the baby, like three months ago. Only heard she'd been in the hospital after she was gone—"

"Which hospital?"

"Boston Lying-In."

"Doctor who?"

Johnny Mack was almost crying with terror. "Man, how in hell'm I gonna know..."

Heslip slapped the keys to the Pinto into Johnny Mack's hand. More than anything else, he had to keep this dude out of the hands of the strongarms. They'd get the hospital lead and go from there to Verna. "It's a red Pinto on the other side of the street down near the corner. Go through the apartment and use the rear stairs to the alley. Go around to the car. Wait in it for me. If they spot you, take off with the car. Otherwise, wait—or I'll find you and splinter your elbows. *Go!*"

Johnny Mack went. As soon as the apartment door clicked shut behind him, Heslip started pounding on it and shouting. "Open up there!" he yelled. "Goddammit, Verna, I know you're in there. Open that door, or..."

From behind the locked door he heard the distant slam of the rear door. Johnny Mack on his way down the back staircase. Heslip hoped the bastard wouldn't steal his car, but it was better than letting the strongarms get him.

"Verna Rounds, I know you're in there!" He yelled. He smashed his fists against the door. "You and that pimp of yours!"

Silence, within and without. He was silent himself, listening. Nothing. He went to the stairwell, leaned down, listened. Nothing. Had the bastards shucked him, and been waiting at the foot of the back stairs to grab Johnny Mack?

Heslip went up the hall to the outside door he'd kicked in, and out onto the front porch. From there he could see down the three flights of wooden stairs to the street. It had gotten darker while he'd been inside, but he could see the men weren't on the stairs.

At the railing he leaned out to crane down the street and saw Johnny Mack running across toward the parked Pinto, where he stopped to fumble at the unlocked door.

Heslip leaned out further yet to look up the next block at the Chrysler New Yorker. He almost fell over the railing. The Chrysler was gone. *Gone?* But then . . . he *knew* the two men had been the same ones who . . .

He looked back to the Pinto. As he did, it dissolved into a fireball. The thud of concussion sent a shock wave of air against his face. As he stared in horror, frozen for the moment there on the third-floor porch, the realization rose up like vomit in his throat: the killers hadn't been after Verna Rounds. They had been after Bart Heslip.

Twenty-Eight

Heslip came back to his table in the lower-floor cafeteria below the Boston Lying-In Hospital with a refilled coffee cup and another doughnut. He sat down, checked his watch for the dozenth time. It was 7:45 on Saturday morning. Better wait another fifteen minutes for his best shot. It was a scam he'd picked up from Ed Dorsey, who'd quit DKA a couple of years ago after a severe beating by a couple of thugs, and he'd never tried it himself.

To pass the time, he read the newspaper account of his death.

At least he hoped the guys who had done it would assume it had been him in that Pinto. He figured that since it was the weekend it would probably be forty-eight hours before a positive I.D. of Johnny Mack Brown would hit the papers, letting the killers know they'd gotten the wrong man. Until then, he was clean in Boston. Nobody from the other side knew he was alive, *would* know, until Johnny Mack was identified. Unless he blew his own cover.

Which meant no calls, not even to Corinne, not even if she would somehow receive notification that Bart Heslip had been killed in a drug-connected car-bombing in Boston—which was what the newspapers were hinting the hit had been all about. The opposition didn't know he was alive, and didn't know there was a lead to Verna here at the Boston Lying-In Hospital.

He checked his watch again. Eight o'clock. Put down his tip and left. Climbing up the stairway to the broad front entrance of the hospital, he felt good. Rested. After the bombing he'd walked for miles, dazed. Had finally realized what the hit men had realized earlier: that they didn't have to find Verna, all they had to do was keep Heslip from finding her before that all-important—God knew why—Monday morning hearing in San Francisco.

A simple box bomb under the car seat. Anyone sitting on the driver's seat would push down the top of the box, which would thrust a spike down into an acid detonator, breaking the bottle, and WHOOMP!

So Heslip had gotten a hotel room and slept for ten hours, since eight in the morning was the best time for the scam he was about to run.

Inside the front door of the hospital he went into a phone booth and looked up the number of the front desk. On a board opposite were the names of the doctors who worked with the hospital. He picked one that had no flag showing he was at the hospital at the present time. He dropped his dime and dialed. "Boston Lying-In Hospital."

"Records, please."

A wait. "Record Room."

"This is Dr. Robert Cohen's office," said Heslip. "We need the Patient's Number for a Miss Verna Rounds."

"One moment, please." There was a waiting silence. The voice came back, clipped and efficient. "Is the date of admission for the patient July twenty-eighth?"

"That's right." How many Verna Rounds could they have?

"That Patient Number is 471-30-6801."

Heslip thanked her and hung up. While having coffee he had seen that the Record Room was one floor down. Dispatch was on this same floor, right near the rear entrance of the hospital.

Down by the U-shaped Dispatch desk, Heslip found a row of hooks holding the faded green coats worn by dispatch runners. He slipped one on. It was soiled down the front, tight in the shoulder, but it made him anonymous. He took a deep breath and walked over to the desk and picked up a pad of requisition forms and one of the wire mesh dispatch baskets. The sleepy-eyed intern waiting for records on the far side of the counter didn't even see him.

When he had gotten down the corridor and out of sight of the intern, he stopped and examined his prizes. To the bottom of the list of requisitions he added 471-30-6801, ROUNDS, VERNA. He handed the pad in at Records on the next floor down and, in due course, was rewarded with a basketful of beige file folders with red tabs.

On his way back up to Dispatch, Heslip detoured into a men's room for a quick perusal of Verna's record. Attending physician: R. Parton, M.D. He saw something else, too, that struck him like a physical blow. Man, what had *that* done to Verna Rounds? If he ever did find her, she'd be so spaced-out on H he'd probably have to mainline her all the way back to San Francisco so she could get on the stand.

Heslip dropped the records off at Dispatch—Dr. Cohen would probably just put it down as a hospital screw-up when Verna's records showed up at his office—hung the green coat on the same hook from which he'd gotten it, and in the phone booth by the front door once again called the hospital and asked for Obstetrics.

Yes, Dr. Parton would be on duty from midnight.

He left, planning to kill the hours by walking and gawking, maybe some good old double bill at a convenient movie house, maybe a hotel-room TV. Anything to keep from thinking about the fact that Verna's baby had died two days after birth.

It was seventeen minutes past midnight when Heslip looked up from his magazine in the patients' lounge of the second-floor maternity wing at the clack of the nurse's approaching heels. She was slim and elegant-looking and black, and reminded him too much of Corinne. Corinne filled all the holes and cracks in him, fit into them, made him strong where he was weak, stronger where he was strong.

"Mr. Rounds?"

Up close she had a poorer complexion than Corinne, a nose a bit shorter and flatter, lips a little fuller.

"That's right, nurse, I'm waiting for Dr.—"

"Parton. That's me."

Heslip was on his feet. "I goofed that one, didn't I?"

"Because I was a woman you thought that I *had* to be a nurse rather than a doctor?" She shook her head as they started down the hall together. "Everybody operates on whole sets of presumptions. Only when presumptions become pernicious do they become prejudices." She led him down a side corridor. "This time of night nobody'll complain if we talk in the doctors' lounge."

It was a square windowless room with a couch, three chairs, a Formica-topped breakfast table, and a hot plate by a small stainless-steel sink. Dr. R. Parton motioned Heslip to a chair and sat down across the table from him. "So you're Verna's brother Sammy."

Heslip nodded. "I'm glad you remember her. With all the cases you must handle—"

"Verna was special." Then she added, "It's sort of like we were saying a minute ago..." Her eyes narrowed slightly, "about the assumptions we make concerning people. Take you. You sure are the huskiest fourteen-year-old kid *I've* ever seen. Why, if I didn't know better, I'd think you were trying to con me with—"

"Aw, *crap!*" exclaimed Heslip in disgust, "I don't seem to be able to do *nothing* right on this case."

"You can start by telling me just who the hell you are."

He stared at her for a long moment. If she knew, she'd either tell or she wouldn't. Dues-paying time for little detective fellers. "Bart Heslip. Private investigator from San Francisco. I work for the firm Verna worked for as a file clerk before she starting whoring. We need her testimony to keep the State from taking our license."

"Show me."

He showed her his I.D. She handed it back to him. "Who's the manager of your Oakland office?"

"When Verna worked there it was Kathy Onoda. She's dead now, that's why we need Verna's testimony."

She stood up and started across the room. "How do you take your coffee, Bart?"

"Black. And thanks, Doctor."

"Rosalind is fine." She came back with the coffees. She took a lot of cream and sugars in hers, Heslip noted. She sat. "Let me tell you a story."

She told him a story.

Verna Rounds had wandered into the Boston Lying-In Hospital at 2:30 A.M. on a hot morning in late July. She was having labor pains only a minute apart and her water already had burst. "You know the significance of that?"

Heslip knew and told her so.

"Verna was also suffering from extreme malnutrition. She told me afterwards that she'd been scrounging garbage pails and stealing once she'd gotten big enough with the baby that damned few johns except the freaky ones were interested in her. What money she got went to feed her habit, not her. She'd been afraid to see a doctor about her pregnancy because she knew a doctor would see she was an addict and commit her. She'd heard about methadone but didn't believe it existed. Sometimes the appalling ignorance . . ."

Rosalind Parton fell silent, her brown eyes sad as they saw beyond the walls of the room. Around them was the hospital silence of a creature asleep but with its instincts to preserve life still operating, so it could wake in an instant if life was threatened.

"Verna had her baby on a gurney in the corridor. I got there in time to snip the cord, not very much more. Maybe that's when I started feeling responsible for her."

"She was still on heroin then?"

"Suffering the beginnings of withdrawal. She had so much wrong with her that she made the sort of clinically interesting case you would like to read about in a CPC. Gave birth four weeks prematurely. Suffering from heroin addiction, withdrawal and malnutrition. Had two separate venereal diseases and a yeast infection."

"I saw her hospital records," said Heslip. "The child . . ."

"You must be a pretty damned good detective and no,

don't tell me how you did it." She sighed. "The child. What can I tell you? He wasn't malformed, which was a surprise, but he was so weak he didn't really have a chance. Four weeks preemie, weighed—I can't remember—but not over a couple of pounds. A few hours after birth he was suffering classic withdrawal symptoms. Tremors, crying incessantly, hyperreactions to all the physical sensations—light, sound, the touch of blankets or swaddling clothes to the skin, anything at all was agony to him. Watery stools, of course . . ."

She'd tried them all, maybe even a few not in the book: paregoric, chlorpromazine, even phenobarbital. None of them helped much. "And we know so damned little. I was sure there'd been *in utero* damage, I'm sure there *always* is for the child of a heroin-addicted mother—but how bad was it? And what did the damage consist of? So, two days after birth, he died."

"Of what specifically?"

"I guess you could say extreme malnutrition, but take your pick. A respiratory infection had developed that would have progressed into pneumonia. But when Verna learned her baby was dead, *she* knew the cause of death."

"What?"

"Not what. Who. Verna Rounds. God had given her a life to care for, and she'd murdered it."

"That's her mammy talking."

"God love that fat old woman. Verna talked about her a lot during withdrawal."

Heslip was stunned. "You mean she's kicked the habit?"

"The coldest turkey you ever saw. From the moment I told her that her child was dead, she was off the stuff. And never at the worst moments during withdrawal was there any talk of suicide. That would be a second murder before God. And God! did that girl want to live. To atone, to make up for that murder. It had to start with getting clean."

The first week of withdrawal had been at the hospital, the next two weeks at Rosalind Parton's apartment. She took her vacation so she could be with Verna around the clock. Take someone through a heroin withdrawal, and one got scared to take an aspirin or administer any drugs to patients who needed them.

"I almost lost my job over the whole thing—the vacation, Verna at my place . . ." She smiled thinly. "It was lucky I was black. I just yelled *discrimination!* everytime anyone tried to open his mouth about anything, anything at all."

"She's still clean?"

"Fabulously clean. Oh God, Bart, you wouldn't believe how clean she is. What a . . . person she's become."

She fell silent and yawned and rubbed her eyes. Heslip said softly, "End of story?"

"I know where she is," said Rosalind Parton. "You want her. You tell me, Bart—should I give you her address?"

"No."

"Why not?"

He told her. Everything, every single thing that had gone down since Kathy Onoda had died of a blood clot two weeks before.

"Okay, now I'll tell you where she is." Her dark eyes were clear and untroubled. "There isn't anything in this world that is going to flatten Verna Rounds after what she's been through. And I don't think there are very many thugs in this world would be able to get through you to get at her." Heslip was speechless. She added, without pause, "Have you ever heard of Harris House?"

He hadn't so she told him about it. It was in Harlem, as far as she knew the only place like it in the world. It took care of about fifty children at a time who had been born to heroin-addicted mothers, keeping them there until the mothers were off drugs, rehabilitated, and had a job with which to support the kid and a home to take it to.

"You got Verna a job there," said Heslip.

"Didn't *get* her a job. Just sent her up there to talk with Mommy—her name is Clare Harris, but everyone just calls her Mommy. She and Loretta, her daughter—who's got a Ph.D. from New York University and who handles the business end of things—took one look at Verna and hired her on the spot . . ."

The beeper in the pocket of her white smock started to

beep. Rosalind Parton got to her feet and stuck out her hand. "I've got to call in, Bart." She gave him the address of Harris House. "I'll call Mommy in the morning, and tell her you're coming and why. After that, it's up to her and Verna."

Heslip agreed. He would let Verna call the shots, and he would play it her way. And his own, and to hell with what Dan Kearny might think. Playing it his own way was the way he did it best, anyway.

Which included, many hours later in New York, after five troubled hours of sleep on the express bus, finding a florist who was open on a Sunday morning and telegraphing fifty dollars-worth of red roses to Rosalind Parton, M.D., at Boston Lying-In Hospital, from *a friend*. It was the least he could do.

Twenty-Nine

Benny Nicoletti's Sunday brunch was held in the Chief's deserted conference room at the Hall of Justice on Bryant Street because the Chief didn't work on Sundays but his secretary did, and he owed Nicoletti a couple of favors. No record was kept of the meeting, and there was no way anyone could have bugged it beforehand. Kearny came in the front entrance of the Hall fluttering a traffic citation, then left the elevator at the wrong floor. Nicoletti came in from Harriet Alley through the police garage. Tranquillini used the rear entrance off Harrison Street by the Coroner's office.

Last to arrive was Johnny Delaney, who knew only that he and his wife had returned from a movie the night before to find a uniformed patrolman waiting on the front stoop. Delaney was merely asked to meet with the head of the Police Intelligence Unit at the Chief's office the next morning. Being no fool and a bit ambitious, Delaney had expressed total delight at this opportunity to blow his Sunday. "Inspector Nicoletti? Johnny Delaney of the Attorney General's Office. Pleased to meet you."

As they shook hands, Nicoletti said, "I have a favor to ask. I think you know Dan and Hec."

Delaney, seeing them for the first time around Nicoletti's formidable bulk, stopped dead. "What the hell is this?" he said angrily.

"First you listen, then you talk."

"First I walk," snapped Delaney, turning back toward the door.

"Your ass is on the line," said Nicoletti to his back.

Johnny Delaney swiveled slowly, his lips drawn back into a truculent sneer. "According to who, Nicoletti?"

"Information received, as the feller says."

"You exceeded your brief, Johnny-me-bhoy," said Tranquillini in his irritating way, "when you conned Dan into paying Pivarski so you could try to use it against him at the hearing."

"There was nothing illegal about that," said Delaney defensively. Without realizing it, he had turned back and was pulling back a chair from the conference table.

"How about ethical?"

Delaney colored slightly.

"The point is, Johnny," said Kearny, "that *I* know DKA ain't guilty of anything. So I've had my men out, checking around."

The easy anger of his Irish heritage thickened Delaney's voice. "On me?"

"On Greenly. Who's on the take." Delaney said nothing, so Kearny continued, "Unless you've got another way of explaining how he could be behind in his house payments from gambling up to five months ago, then suddenly turning into A-1 pay—without quitting gambling. That he keeps a safe-deposit box under a phony name and a mistress on the side. That he's dropping markers with bookies all over Sacramento."

Delaney finally sighed, like a man who had just laid down a heavy load. He hadn't been sleeping too well because of going along with Greenly; he was almost glad to hear the man was dirty. "Dan, I want you to know that I made that offer in good faith. And urged Greenly to drop the charges if you paid. But he said . . ."

"If Dan didn't believe that," said Tranquillini coldly, "you wouldn't be here."

"How about you, Hec?"

Tranquillini shrugged, his face devoid of emotion. "I

always felt it was Greenly's idea. But I told you at the hearing what I felt about it. I'm going to bust your ass for it, John. Not today or tomorrow, maybe. But sometime . . . in some courtroom . . ."

"Meanwhile," said Nicoletti, "let me tell you about this favor I want to ask."

Bur first he laid everything out for Delaney. The hit on Fazzino, the fact that Pivarski had been I.D.'d from a driver's license photo as the hit man, the fact that he couldn't be because he'd been in Kearny's Oakland office at the time of the murder.

"And we're even more sure of that now than we were before," said Nicoletti, including Kearny and Tranquillini in his remarks. "I've had men out digging. Pivarski was delivering plaster that day to a subdivision site down in Fremont. He delivered his last load there just in time to get out to Concord to Hawkley's office, then down to the DKA office by about five-thirty. We checked on the deposit Simson made to the bank. They don't log-in deposits, but they do have a rule that any deposit made after five o'clock is recorded as a transaction on the following banking day. The one Simson made on November fifth was recorded the following Monday—the eighth."

"So where do I come in?" asked Delaney.

"I want you to meet Hawkley and Pivarski at the Golden Gate entrance of the State Office Building tomorrow morning, rather than inside, and maybe take them up the street to a coffee shop to discuss Pivarski's testimony ahead of time."

"I'd do that anyway," said Delaney. "But why—"

"My witness is in town even though we're sure Hawkley thinks he left for Canada on Friday. We want him to get an eyeball of Pivarski."

"Why? If you're sure Pivarski isn't the man—"

"Mainly because Hawkley has worked so hard to *keep* us from getting an eyeball of him."

Delaney was silent for a time. Finally he shrugged. "Okay. As long as you guys all understand that I think

DKA is guilty as charged, and that I'm going to do my damndest tomorrow to take away their license to operate.''

Nicoletti made a grandly dismissive gesture. ''Fine with me.''

Kearny looked glum. Tranquillini nodded.

''And as long as *you* understand, Johnny, that I'm going to roast your witness's butt in a way you wouldn't believe.''

Harris House was a five-story brownstone in the 100-block of West 122nd Street in Harlem. Bart Heslip had gotten off the bus from Boston at the Port Authority Bus Terminal on Eighth Avenue, had wired his flowers to Rosalind Parton, and then had walked the Sunday-sparse streets up to 122nd just to get the kinks out. At the front door he was told that Mommy Harris was off at church with the older among her fifty charges, and that he should come back at eleven.

As he was finishing a cup of coffee around the corner, he saw a fiftyish-looking slat-thin black woman, followed by a Pied Piper gang of kids, trooping by the direction of Harris House. He finished his coffee and followed.

Ten minutes later he sat with Loretta Harris, the woman's daughter, in her paneled, crowded office of the ground-floor hall of Harris House. Through the half-open door could be heard the muffled confusion of half-a-hundred kids freed by the Lord's day from weekday restraints. ''Bart Heslip, sure. Rosie Parton called this morning. Thinks she's tough, that one, woman of science, detached, medical.'' She gave a rolling peal of laughter. ''Soft as butter. My mother will be either out in the kitchen seeing what the cook's up to for Sunday dinner, or on the second-floor babies' suites.''

Going up the stairs to the nursery after striking out in the kitchen, Heslip felt a growing sense of anticipation. In the past ten days he'd come to have a puzzled regard for Verna Rounds. Started out as an ignorant little file clerk, so ignorant she got recruited into whoring, got knocked up and clapped up and on heroin—and could you get any dumber than that? Then quit the profession, lost a baby, cold-turkey'd her habit, and now was an assistant in the damndest orphanage Heslip had ever seen.

An orphanage where the kids had living parents who were off straightening themselves out, kids who'd been born junkies, kids who now got love and attention from a sixty-five-year-old black woman he was about to meet. He thrust his head around the doorjamb, "Mrs. Harris?"

The thin woman he'd seen on the street had as warm a smile as her daughter's fleshier one. Her face had the tremendous dignity certain black faces got with age and righteousness, yet was youthful and humorous despite the network of wrinkles around the deep-set eyes. "Call me Mommy, most everyone does."

"Bart Heslip."

"About Verna. Yes. Come on in, let's walk and talk a bit."

They walked and talked the length of the babies' suite, which ran the length of the house. At the front were cots for the two- and three-year-olds being made up or changed by a couple of chattering assistants. Heslip had noted all the assistants were black.

"The girls who work here, are they. . ." He paused.

"Ex-addicts?" Mommy shook her head. "Ex-addicts have been through detoxification and withdrawal, but they still have to live in residences where they can get constant advice and attention and see a psychiatrist when they need one—at least once a week. We just don't have time for that around here. The kids take all our attention." She gave a sunny smile. "And all our love."

"Then Verna must be different," said Heslip.

"Oh, she is, she is. Her baby had died, for one thing, and she needed someone to care for outside herself, bad as a body can need. Also, she didn't need any rehabilitation. She'd done that for herself, along with Rosalind's help."

At the rear of the house was a bright, sunny room where the very small children who still needed cribs slept. The walls were vivid with nursery wallpaper; the floor was atumble with toys and stuffed animals and dolls. Some toddlers were going down a small, bright, metal slide in the middle of the room. Others played with toys, one was crying, a little girl was bashing a little boy over the head with a big red sausagelike balloon, both of them crowing gleefully.

Keeping minimum order was a slim black girl with big warm eyes and a patient face and her hair worn in the sort of bun that Mommy wore. Mommy stopped to hug a little girl who was trying a variety of dresses on a brand-new-looking doll, one after another without first removing the previous one.

"My, isn't that a pretty doll?" Mommy marveled.

"That fum my *mama*," said the girl.

"Just as beautiful as can be. But not as beautiful as *you*." They went on. Mommy said to Heslip, "Her mother quit the street, and has a job as a secretary while she studies window-decorating. In another year she'll be able to take Elaine home with her."

"They look pretty much like any other kids," said Heslip.

"Oh, the *kids* aren't the problems. It's the mothers. They don't know how to take care of children, and I think drug addiction dulls the maternal instincts, burns out the ability to reach out toward someone else. Even your child. We not only have to train the mothers to *care* for their kids, we have to teach them how to *love* their kids, too."

"That makes Verna even more unusual."

They were beside the slide where the assistant was making the children take orderly turns.

"Why don't you ask her yourself?" said Mommy Harris. "Verna, this is Mr. Heslip from San Francisco, who I told you about."

They were drinking strong, fresh coffee at one of the long tables where the children and the help ate all their meals family-style. Heslip had laid out the whole thing for both women, but Verna did not seem to have assimilated what he had said. When she spoke, it was only of kids under her care. "Oh, I have the terriblest time knowin' whut to do, and that's the very truth," she said. Her adoring gaze rested on Mommy's face for a moment. "But I'm learnin'."

"Big trouble is," said the older woman, "around here we

get thinking these kids *are* like other kids. But they aren't. Not emotionally."

"Highs an' lows," said Verna. She had a habit of fixing her gaze on Mommy Harris even when speaking to Heslip. "They ain't—aren't—as *even* as other kids. Don't get somethin' they want, *off* they go. Cryin', carryin' on somethin' awful." She added, in quick defense, "Cain't blame 'em none. Not after what they been through. They ain't ever had nuthin'. Not ever, long as they've lived."

Heslip had trouble believing this girl had ever been a whore and a junkie. She didn't have any of the ghetto brashness other black girls of her background had. But he sensed a steel core inside that he'd sensed in her fat old mother out in Oakland, and that was the salient feature of Mommy Harris. Who smiled her abrupt brilliant smile and stood up.

"Time for chores, my goodness." But when Verna started to rise also, she put a hand on the younger woman's shoulder. To Heslip, she said, "I'm just a bug for a clean house, and when you have fifty little ones a clean house is hard to come by." To Verna she said, "Take all the time you need, honey," and shook hands with Heslip and was gone.

There was a moment of constraint between Verna and Heslip. Then he said, "You love it here, don't you?"

"Ain't leavin' till they th'ow me out." She drank the last of her coffee and shook her head. "The urge fo' that shit, it still get so strong sometimes when I'm lyin' alone at night. But I get up an' go into that babies' suite, an' I walk up an down lookin' at them little tots wouldn't have *no* chance wasn't fo' Mommy bein' there for 'em like Doctor Parton was fo' me, an' then I go back to sleep like a baby." She met his eyes and sighed. "So you figure it's somethin' I know 'bout that Friday afternoon? Mos' a year ago?"

"That's the only thing that makes sense," said Heslip. "Friday, November fifth, last year. Do you even remember it?"

She remembered it, and went through the whole thing without a word of prompting from Heslip. Her memory was so vivid because it was her first time on the switchboard and she made a mess of it. And she remembered Pivarski ("that dude Pee-somethin') because she couldn't pronounce his name.

"And you saw the whole transaction?" asked Heslip.

"Was standin' in the doorway blowin' bubbles."

"Did Pivarski give Kathy anything? A—"

"Give her two hundred dollars."

"Anything else? Oh . . . an envelope or a letter or—"

"Wasn't anything like that, Mist' Heslip. He paid her, she give him a receipt, he got up an lef'."

"Where was Jeff Simson all this time?"

"Out at his desk where he b'long."

Heslip drank the final gulp of cold coffee, then sat frowning at the bright gold and white curtain beyond Verna's head. Afternoon sun poured into the room, backlighting her face. Jesus, nothing there. Nothing at all. A totally routine collection. Did it justify jeopardizing her life by asking her to go back with him? Why didn't he just stand up and walk out of there and go back himself and tell them he couldn't find her?"

"All of that he'p any?" she asked. "That gonna be of any use Mist' Kearny an' Miss Giselle an' all, to keep their license fo' 'em?"

Heslip didn't answer, poised on the knife-edge of decision.

"Cause I gotta a lot of work to do, an' if I ain't up there, Mommy Harris, she just pitch in an' do my share herse'f."

Heslip stared at her. And finally said, "What do *you* feel you ought to do, Verna?"

The Last Day

Ballard had planned to be waiting outside the proper window in the Department of Employment office when it opened at eight-thirty on Monday morning, so he could find out where Madeline Westfield worked. But when he came out to get into his car at six-thirty, he had of all things a flat tire. Fixing it involved him in commuter traffic, especially once he was on Interstate 80 beyond Bay Bridge, so it was nearer nine-thirty when he thrust his head through the opening and asked his question of the woman who had left forty-seven minutes early on Friday. She answered with one of her own.

"This Madeline Westfield is a civil service employee of the State of California?" She was a flattened-down-forty, with dark hair and a bright nylon scarf knotted about her muscular neck. She asked her question as if expecting to catch him in an indiscretion.

"That's my understanding, yes, ma'am."

A minute of page-turning and she had it. And told him.

What? his mind shrieked. She worked *where?* In *which* section?

He lit out running for a phone, before remembering that he couldn't phone because of the bug on the DKA phone. He checked his watch. Nine twenty-six. The hearing started at ten. If he drove like hell, he surely would be there before Pivarski had testified and departed. Wouldn't he? Hec Tranquillini planned a minute cross-examination. Man, so inevitable, so logical, when you thought it through. It was the only place she *could* have worked for Greenly to have had to seek her out and subvert her.

Hawkley stepped to the Golden Gate curb from his nephew's car at 9:31 A.M.—tall, lean, aged but not frail, skin like tough old leather. Looked exactly like the folksy cracker-barrel attorney whose image he tried to create. He and Delaney shook hands.

"A pleasure I assure you, Mr. Delaney. My nephew Norbert has been telling me wonderful things about your conduct of the State's case in his hearing." He turned slightly to the second man emerging from the back seat. he was big, muscular, square of body and of head. "Mr. Delaney. Mr. Pivarski."

Christ, thought Delaney, the guy looks like a Polish joke. "Delighted, Mr. Pivarski."

"Yeah." The voice grated like a diesel changing gears.

Delaney turned back to Hawkley, who was just ordering Franks to put the car in the Civic Center Parking Garage and return. He said, ''We've got a half-hour before the hearing, Mr. Hawkley. I'd very much appreciate a chance to take Mr. Pivarski through his testimony before his appearance on the stand, and to do it where the opposition won't disturb us.'' He gestured down wind-blown Golden Gate at the Larkin intersection a long half block away. ''We could go up the street for a cup of coffee . . .''

''An excellent suggestion,'' said Hawkley.

Norbert Franks pulled out into traffic, making a battered six-passenger Checker Cab wait, as the three tall men, two bulky and one thin, started down Golden Gate Avenue toward the coffee shop.

''You get a good look at him?'' demanded Benny Nicoletti from the back seat of the Checker Cab.

The linen-truck driver, a much paler and thinner man than he had been a year before, nodded. He was facing backwards in the jump seat opposite Nicoletti. There were three more large and competent men in the car besides them and the driver. Nicoletti clicked on the safety of the riot gun lying across his knees as the car turned downhill on Hyde Street. ''Well?''

''Yeah.'' The linen-truck driver's eyes were rimmed with fatigue and something else that was probably long-standing fear.

'That's a positive make?''

The driver said formally, ''That's the guy I saw coming out of the motel room with the shotgun and the satchel.''

''That's him but that can't be him,'' said Nicoletti. ''Okay, maybe he's got a twin brother,'' he added drily. He raised his voice. ''Mike. Drop me at Market Street, will you?''

''Hey, what about me?'' yelped the witness. ''You promised—''

''You're on your way to the airport,'' said Nicoletti as the cab started slowing to let him out. ''You don't need me to wave good-bye.''

He stood on the curb watching the cab drive off, then he started wandering. He had to think. It had all been too easy. The big cop began strolling along with his hands in his pockets. Hawkley wasn't dumb. What if he'd noticed that suddenly his tap on Kearny's phone dried up of anything useful *except* that Nicoletti's witness was going to leave on Friday and wouldn't be around on Monday for a look at Pivarski in the flesh? What would that mean?

He walked a little faster, his feet keeping pace with his brain. That would mean Hawkley *wanted* them to I.D. Pivarski as the killer. Did that make any sense at all? Sure, if the *real* killer looked a lot like him and . . .

Nicoletti was striding right along now, unmindful of the fall nip in the air despite the bright October sunshine. Then he slowed.

Then why pick somebody like Pivarski, who had an airtight alibi? Because Pivarski was the only one available? But Hawkley couldn't have known the witness would identify Pivarski from his driver's license photo. Nicoletti had slowed to an amble. Of course Hawkley had fought damned hard to keep Pivarski off the stand at the hearing. But he hadn't fought to keep out the fact that Pivarski had been at DKA's Oakland office at the time Fazzino had been hit, so what good did keeping Pivarski himself away from the hearing do? If he indeed had actually wanted Pivarski I.D.'d by the witness?

Nicoletti realized he was standing mid-block on Fulton Street beside the old Federal Building. Standing stock still. Probably ought to go on up to the hearing, see what happened up there.

He started walking slowly along, hands in pockets, slouching. Now, what if Hawkley really *hadn't* wanted to keep Pivarski from testifying at the hearing, but had merely *seemed* to . . .

So of course Ballard got stopped by the Highway Patrol.

"May I see your operating permit, please, sir?"

Ballard extended his wallet.

"Please remove it from the plastic cover and hand it to me."

Silent manipulations by a seething Ballard, silent perusal by the CHP officer of that sacred ikon of modern life, Identification.

"I'm sure, Mr. Ballard, that you realize this is a fifty-five-mile-an-hour zone by state law. Your vehicle was clocked by our radar as traveling in excess of *seventy* miles an hour . . ."

While Johnny Delaney got down to business. "Mr. Pivarski, I would like you to cast your mind back to the events of last November fifth."

The square, ugly face was made uglier by concentration. "The day I went to dem collection agency bastards in—"

"Mr. Pivarski, please do not anticipate counsel's questions." The Hearing Officer's face was distressed, as if he had a gas pain.

"Uh . . . okay, Your Honor."

Delaney started again. "You left work early that day, did you not, Mr. Pivarski, to see your attorney?"

"Yeah, that's right." He pointed at the Complainant's counsel table. "Mr. Norbert Franks. Him. Right there."

"And he instructed you . . ."

Kearny sat listening while the big dumb bastard methodically and ponderously, like a fat man going to the toilet, took away from him his license to practice his profession. Sentence by sentence. He was too dumb to be lying yet he *had* to be lying.

"Yeah. So I took my two hundred simoleons and that letter he give me, and I went to them collection agency bastards in Oakland. Daniel Kearny Associates."

"To whom did you speak there?"

"Some queer."

Delaney looked at the Hearing Officer and raised his shoulders slightly. "Um . . . a Jeffrey L. Simson?"

"I dunno his name. He took me back to the slant broad."

The Hearing Officer looked at the ceiling and then down

at his hands. He cleared his throat. ''By 'slant broad' I take it you mean an Oriental female, Mr. Pivarski?''

''A slant or a Buddha-head. They all look the same to me.'' He looked back at Delaney. ''She took my two hundred bucks and signed my letter, and I left.''

''This is the letter you have testified previously your attorney gave you to—''

''Dat's right.''

''Would you recall the name of the Oriental lady who . . .''

Hec Tranquillini listened with something akin to awe. He had been able to show Simson's testimony was tainted, but *this* big ape's? The trouble was, he was *too* dumb. Trying to dig his fingers into a crack in that dim-witted testimony would be like trying to get a handhold on polished marble. He was almost too dumb to be true.

''No, no, it wasn't no collection, I'm tellin' you. It was just money for them to hold, like . . . uh . . . a guy holdin' your dough in a bet in a bar, y'know? Till we see which way all the court stuff come out. Just to keep 'em off my back for a while.''

Previous testimony in this court indicates that you never returned the countersigned letter to your attorney, Mr. Pivarski.'' Delaney beamed solicitously at him. ''Is this true?''

The hulking witness looked uncomfortable for the first time. ''Yeah, well, y'see, I figgered wasn't no use runnin' all the way out to Concord with it, y'know, I mean, he charges by the hour, sets a timer the minute you walk through the front door . . .'' He looked doggedly over at Franks. ''So I figured to mail it to him. But . . . well . . . I'd folded it up in my shirt pocket, y'know, a' then I went bowling an' the next day I sent the shirt to the laundry an' . . .'' He looked around sheepishly at the Hearing Officer. ''Guess I should of hung on to it, huh?''

''Just two more questions, Mr. Pivarski,'' said Delaney. ''First, what time did you arrive at the Kearny offices?''

''Maybe five-thirty, around there.''

''Leave?''

''Like quarter to six, ten to six, like that.''

"Thank you, Mr. Pivarski." He turned to Tranquillini. "Your witness, counsel."

And thought, let's see you discredit this baby, Hector, as Tranquillini bounced to his feet and strode to the bench.

"Your Honor, there is a point or two in this witness's testimony upon which I would like to confer with my client. If we might have a brief recess . . ."

The Hearing Officer looked at his watch. "I hope we can conclude these proceedings before the noon recess, Mr. Tranquillini. So I can give you no more than ten minutes."

"Ten minutes is fine, Your Honor." Tranquillini beamed.

And almost took Dan Kearny's head off in the hall, which is where they had to confer since there was no time to go elsewhere.

"Dan, what the hell am I supposed to use to open this guy up? He's lying, he's got to be, unless Kathy Onoda just pulled a monumental goof, in which case we're dead. Get me some goddam ammunition!"

"For Chrissake, Hec, don't you think we're trying?" snapped Kearny. "You can't get information where there isn't any. You can't find people when there isn't any trail to follow."

"What the hell about Ballard up in Sacramento? It can't be too tough to find out where some chick is working, for Chrissake."

Kearny looked uncomfortable. "Larry was supposed to be back down here forty-five minutes ago. Something must have—"

"What about Heslip and this file clerk? Unless we get *something*, you can kiss your ass goodbye as far as operating an investigation agency in this state is concerned. We can appeal, and keep appealing, but do you have any idea what that's going to cost you?"

"The last time we heard from Heslip was—"

"Who dat takin' my name in vain?"

And there was a fatigued, travel-worn Bart Heslip beside them, his clothes wrinkled and his face unshaven, but Bart Heslip all the same. And he was not alone.

''Bart!'' exclaimed Kearny. ''How in the hell—''

''Red-eye special into San Jose. Didn't want any welcoming committees, the way these boys have been playing. May I present—''

''Verna Rounds!'' cried Giselle, coming from the ladies' room just in time to embrace the black girl she had hired as file clerk over a year before.

''Miss G'selle,'' mumbled Verna at the floor. ''Sure mighty good to see you.''

Tranquillini was moving in on her like a mother hen getting a wing over a frightened chick. ''Oh, little lady, are you beautiful!''

''What she's got to say oughtta save the DKA license,'' said Heslip. ''Pivarski got a receipt, he didn't have any letter, the money was applied to the account in his presence, and Kathy even worked out a payment schedule for the rest of his delinquency.''

Tranquillini was already moving her toward the hearing room. ''That's all I have to know,'' he chortled. The rest, except for Heslip, followed. He held back.

''I've gotta call my Corinne and let her know I'm home and that I'm okay. I'll be in after a couple of minutes. That poor lady hasn't heard from me since . . .''

But the pay phone at the end of the hall was busy, so he went down to the McAllister Street entrance where he knew there was a bank of pay phones which couldn't *all* be busy.

. . . Concluded

Tranquillini rose as the Hearing Officer returned to the bench.

''Your Honor, I have no questions of Mr. Pivarski at this time, although I would like the right to recall him at a future time if it seems necessary. Instead, we have a ''

''I believe I stated I would like to conclude this hearing by the noon recess, counselor,'' said the Hearing Officer a little testily.

"Your Honor, we finally have located the other witness who was present in the Daniel Kearny Oakland office on the day and time in question. Miss Verna Rounds has just arrived from the East Coast to testify. Since it will be familiar ground, I do not believe her testimony will be extensive."

"Very well. Miss Verna Rounds, please take the stand to be sworn. Mr. Kasimir Pivarski is directed to remain."

For the first time, tall, courtly Wayne Hawkley was getting to his feet. But it was not to object to his client being told to remain. He merely bent and squeezed the arm of his nephew, Norbert Franks, and then spoke softly in the younger attorney's ear.

"Norb, danged if I didn't forget a phone call I promised to make before noon. You can hold the fort here for a minute?"

"Sure, Unc." Franks grinned and gave him the thumb-and-forefinger O.K. circle.

Hawkley walked with stately stride from the room. Sure, Unc. That simpering, stupid fool! He didn't even comprehend what the appearance of Verna Rounds on that stand would lead to. Well, the old fox Wayne Hawkley knew. And was getting out while he could. The one good feature of this whole sorry spectacle would be not having to listen to idiot Norbert any more.

Get the car out of the lot with the spare set of keys he always carried. A quick trip to the Oakland safe deposit box for his traveling money, the first flight from the Oakland airport to New York, thence to Montreal and from there to Switzerland. He could decide which of the three passports with the traveling money he would use first once he was airborne. His wife would keep the house, live on the joint bank accounts, and not even miss one of her weekly bridge parties. His daughter Maddy, she would take over the law offices and get rid of that idiot Norbert . . .

So concerned was he with his plans that as he entered the elevator he did not even notice the slouching, bulky man who began to get off and then stepped quickly back in so as to be riding the cage with him down to the McAllister Street exit.

In the hearing room Verna Rounds had been sworn and Tranquillini had started her through her testimony. "I understand that you were operating the switchboard at the Kearny offices in Oakland on the afternoon of Friday, November fifth of last year. Is that correct, Miss Rounds?"

"Yessir, you're right."

"Was a Mr. Pivarski discussed?"

"Oh, yessir! Miss Kathy, she tole me—"

"That is Kathy Onoda, the DKA Office Manager?"

"Yessir. Miss Kathy, she tole me 'bout four o'clock that he was due between five an' to make a payment of two hundred dollars, an' that I was to bring him right in."

"What time did he actually arrive?"

"Mr. Pee-somethin' he come in just 'bout five-thirty."

The Hearing Officer leaned forward to interrupt. "I didn't catch the name you spoke, Miss Rounds."

Verna looked at her hands and then at the floor, embarrassed for the first time during her testimony. Finally she looked over at him. "I'm sorry, sir . . . uh . . . Your Honor. I caint pronounce that man's name nohow."

"You mean Mr. Pivarski?"

"Yessir. I always jus' called him Mr. Pee-somethin'."

The Hearing Officer masked a smile. "I see. Please proceed, Mr. Tranquillini."

Tranquillini waved a hand at the opposing counsel table. "When this gentleman came into the office, what happened?"

Verna shook her head, a stubborn light coming into her eyes. "Was Mr. Pee-somethin' come in, like I tole you. He said he—"

"Mr. Pivarski," agreed Tranquillini. "The gentleman seated at the table over there."

Verna looked at the man calling himself Pivarski. She shook her head. "That ain't him," she said. "Ain't ever laid eyes on that dude in my life before."

For the first time in his life Hector Tranquillini was

stopped dead. His mouth dropped open and he gaped. He turned to gape at the man known as Pivarski. The man known as Pivarski was on his feet and taking a snub-nosed Python .38 revolver adroitly from his left armpit with his right hand.

"I told that goddam Hawkley it wasn't going to work," he said, and started edging his way toward the door.

Bart Heslip hung up the phone, his heart singing. Yeah, *man!* Wasn't any other woman anywhere, ever, like his Corinne. Get this hearing finished up, get Verna over to Oakland for a one-day reunion with her mother and brother, then home to Corinne. Who was right now in the process of taking the rest of the day off.

Tomorrow to get Verna back to Harlem and himself back to Boston to see if he could point a finger at the two hit men who had blown up Johnny Mack Brown and probably messed up Fleur Lisette in New Orleans. Today and tonight was for him and Corinne. Especially tonight.

He turned from the phone, whistling cheerily, and saw Larry Ballard coming through the doors from McAllister Street. Must have parked in the Civic Center Garage, his mind registered, even as he exclaimed, "Larry! What in the hell—" While Ballard was exclaiming, "Bart! Where in the hell . . ."

"Just in from Boston with little Verna, who's upstairs testifying right now."

Ballard began, "Hey, that's terrific!" and then suddenly froze stock still. "Verna? She's here? Holy Christ!"

"Hey, what's the matter? What . . ."

"Greenly has a girlfriend who—"

"And him a married man, too. Tsk, tsk."

"Christ, Bart, she works in the Department of Motor Vehicles." He paused for an instant. "In the Driving License Picture Section!"

With a common impulse, both men raced for the stairwell. At this time of day the stairs would probably be quicker than the elevator at the other end of the hall. Heslip sputtered out their mutual thoughts as they ran down the corridor, ducking slower pedestrians like bikers weaving through freeway traffic.

"They had a pipeline into Benny's investigation into Flip Fazzino's murder... When the call was going to go out for DMV photos of the Teamster local's members..."

Ballard jerked open the stairwell door, sputtering disconnected thoughts as he did. "Greenly was ordered to get someone in the section... to switch the hit man's photo with that of Pivarski... He did..."

"So the Pivarski who's upstairs in that hearing room right now is *not* the Pivarski who was in the Oakland office last year."

They charged up the stairs two at a time.

When Wayne Hawkley emerged from the first floor men's room he found his way blocked by a big, sloppy-looking man who matched his own six-three in height and outweighed him by at least seventy-five pounds. "The hearing room is back that way and upstairs, counselor," said Benny Nicoletti. He had never met Hawkley, but had seen him in surveillance photos often enough. Always fruitlessly until—maybe—right now.

"I am an attorney and I have a very important—"

"Upstairs, pal." Nicoletti flashed his badge with one hand and began steering Hawkley back toward the elevators with the other.

"I'm going to have that shield, you... you..."

"Inspector Benny Nicoletti, Police Intelligence. That last name has two t's, counselor, for when you make your complaint. Meanwhile, we're going back upstairs."

By chance they had an elevator to themselves. Hawkley tried again to object, but Nicoletti cut him short. "Y'see, counselor, I been walking and thinking. And I decided that you knew we were going to give our witness to the Flip Fazzino hit an eyeball of Pivarski. I also decided that you made such a fuss about keeping Pivarski from showing up at this hearing because you really *wanted* him to show up."

"That's ridiculous," sputtered Hawkley.

"Wanted him to show up according to *your* timetable. I don't know why, but . . ."

The elevator doors opened and Nicoletti dragged his reluctant companion into the hall. ". . . course if I'm wrong, I'll apologize and you can go after my badge. But first we'll see what's happening in the hearing—"

A gun went off somewhere down the hall. Nicoletti made a magically quick movement at great variance with his bulk, and a Police Positive with a four-inch barrel appeared in his hand.

"You bastard!" he grated, dragging Hawkley forward, "if someone got shot . . ."

Dan Kearny got shot.

He sat down abruptly on the floor, one shoulder feeling like someone had slammed it in a car door, and stared stupidly at the blood running down off his lax fingers to the floor. How much blood, he wondered hazily, was there in a fifty-year-old fool who had been so stupid as to try and be a hero? He'd made a grab for the gun and it had swung around to look at him from a muzzle as big as a rain barrel, and then the rain barrel had spoken and Kearny had sat down.

The professional killer who had taken out Flip Fazzino and seven others over a ten-year career swirled the fingers of his left hand through Giselle Marc's long blond hair and jerked her to her feet. She yelped with pain and then went white with shock as he rammed the muzzle of the .38 up under her chin. "She gets the next one," grated the pseudo-Pivarski, and kept moving. No one else did. Verna was almost placid in the witness chair, the Hearing Officer had disappeared behind his desk, Hec Tranquilini was frozen half out of his chair, and John Delaney was holding Norbert Franks by the throat so Franks was unable to leave with his confederate.

Kearny finally understood most of it, as he watched the killer sliding out the door with Giselle. He wanted to throw a chair at the gunman, but was just too tired. The blood was puddling under his hand now. Pretty soon it would reach his thigh and ruin his suit pants. Blood was very hard to get out.

Or get back, once it was lost.

Sleepy.

But his brain seemed to work pretty well, even if the rest of him was sliding away.

Hawkley finds out there's an eyewitness to the Fazzino hit who thinks he can I.D. the killer. The killer therefore needs an absolute alibi. Among his not especially bright nephew's clients is somebody who has an alibi. He was in the DKA office making a payment at the time of the Fazzino hit. He looks a little like the hit man. Maybe the fact that his payment was being made to the office of Dan Kearny, who originally blew the whistle on Fazzino, is what triggers the idea of a substitution in Hawkley's mind.

So he gets his nephew to push for a misconduct hearing with the Professional Standards Bureau. Easy, when the auditor is already in your pocket. At the hearings, if it comes to that, he can always try to get the phony Pivarski to testify on a day when none of the witnesses to the real Pivarski's payment are scheduled to testify. The real Pivarski himself? Bought off or dead.

Kearny looked back at the doorway. His mind had been running so fast that he could still see part of Giselle's back as she was dragged into the corridor by the killer. Poor Giselle. Ought to help her but . . . *so tired* . . .

So then Nicoletti turned up the witness. It was getting hot. And then Kathy died of natural causes. Suddenly the whole thing was necessary *and would work*. One witness dead, a second with a bad memory and willing to perjure himself anyway, a third disappeared.

So he tried it. And until the missing witness showed up, unexpectedly, *on the day he brought the phony Pivarski in to testify*, everything was working for Hawkley. Still was, since Hawkley had skipped clean, and the killer had just disappeared into the hall—clean. Enough to make you weep.

Suiting actions to thoughts, Dan Kearny put down his head and wept. Wept with physical weakness while cursing himself inwardly for what he thought was will-power weakness. And there was, at one side, Hec Tranquillini, using a belt as a tourniquet and saying the wound looked more bloody than bad, and on the other, the little black girl—what was her name—Verna Rounds, that was it, comforting him. Because, although Kearny didn't know it, if there was one thing Verna had learned in the past months it was how to care for frightened little fellers who had started crying.

Without any need, because out in the hall the killer had, on coming from the hearing room, happened to look the wrong way first. He looked to his left, up toward the elevators, instead of to his right, over toward the stairwell. He saw a very bulky Benny Nicoletti dragging that goddamned screw-up Hawkley with him, and he saw a Police Positive in Benny Nicoletti's right hand, pointed up the hall right at him.

And at Giselle, but he didn't think of that. Being a killer, *he* would have fired instantly if the roles had been reversed. He didn't know Nicoletti would not shoot as long as Giselle was endangered. There was no way he could comprehend such softness. When *he* pointed a gun at someone who also had a gun pointed at him, *his* gun went off.

So he whirled toward Nicoletti to blow him away, but in so doing jerked his gun away from Giselle's face.

Which meant that Bart Heslip, crossing the hall silently from the stairwell in desperate preparation for an attempt to wrest the gun from his hand, could attack without endangering Giselle.

Bart Heslip hit the gunman in the kidneys with the hardest punch he had ever thrown in his life. He'd won thirty-nine out of forty professional fights, almost all of them by knockouts, and this was the hardest punch he'd ever thrown. Because he knew all about kidney punches. He'd suffered one in the fight he had lost. He'd finished the fight—and lost it by a split decision—and had gone home and urinated blood for a week afterwards.

The killer of eight men, struck in the kidneys as Heslip had been, screamed and fell on the floor. As he did, Larry

Ballard came down on his gun arm with both feet, crushing his wrist and pulverizing his fingers so he wouldn't be shooting any guns with that hand anymore once he got out of prison. If the men he was going to spill his guts about to stay out of the gas chamber would let him live long enough to get out of prison.

Heslip and Ballard said in unison to Giselle, "You okay?"

"He almost tore my hair out by the roots," she said crossly. And then, remembering that Dan Kearny had been shot, fainted. Both men caught her before she could hit the floor.

As Nicoletti, still dragging counselor Hawkley with him, came up with a pleased look on his face. "I don't know what happened in there, but it must have been dynamite."

"A girl happened," said Heslip. "She *is* dynamite."

And he thought of Corinne, and knew there was one who was even more dynamite than Verna, at the same time Ballard thought the same thing about Yana, the gypsy girl.

Nicoletti nodded, still grinning, and slapped the cuffs around the elegant wrists of Wayne Hawkley—until a few moments before, the rich and brilliant counsel for the mob.